"Let me buy this one," said Witherwax firmly. "What I was going to ask was about this selective breeding."

The professor shook himself, blinked twice, leaned back in his chair, and placed one hand on the table. "You wish me to be academic? Very well; but I have witnesses that it was at your own request."

Mrs. Jonas said: "Now look what you've done. You've got him started and he won't run down until he falls asleep."

"What I want to know—" began Witherwax, but Thott beamingly cut across: "I shall present only the briefest and most nontechnical of outlines," he said. "Let us suppose that, of sixteen mice, you took the two largest and bred them together. Their children would in turn be mated with those of the largest pair from another group of sixteen. And so on. Given time and material enough, and making it advantageous to the species to produce larger members, it would be easy to produce mice the size of lions."

"Ugh!" said Mrs. Jonas. "You ought to give up drinking. Your imagination gets gruesome."

"I see," said Witherwax, "like in a book I read once where they had rats so big they ate horses, and wasps the size of dogs."

Tales from the Spaceport Bar

Edited by
George H. Scithers
and
Darrell Schweitzer

NEW ENGLISH LIBRARY
Hodder and Stoughton

First published in the United States of America in 1987 by Avon Books

First published in Great Britain in 1988 by New English Library Paperbacks

British Library C.I.P.

Tales from the spaceport bar.
I. Scithers, George, *1929–*
II. Schweitzer, Darrell, *1952–*
813'.54 [F]

ISBN 0-450-48909-4

Printed and bound in Great Britain for Hodder and Stoughton Paperbacks, a division of Hodder and Stoughton Ltd., Mill Road, Dunton Green, Sevenoaks, Kent TN13 2YA (Editorial Office: 47 Bedford Square, London WC1B 3DP) by Richard Clay Ltd., Bungay, Suffolk.

Dedicated to John B. Gaughan
A Good Man

Acknowledgments

"The Green Marauder" by Larry Niven. Copyright © 1980 by Larry Niven. Reprinted by the kind permission of the author.

"Don't Look Now" by Henry Kuttner. Copyright © 1948 by Better Publications, Inc., renewed 1976 by Henry Kuttner. Reprinted by the kind permission of Don Congdon Associates, Inc.

"Getting Even" by Isaac Asimov. Copyright © 1980 by Montcalm Publishing Corp. Reprinted by the kind permission of the author.

"What Goes Up" by Arthur C. Clarke. Copyright © 1955 by Mercury Publications, Inc. Reprinted by the kind permission of the author and the author's agents, Scott Meredith Literary Agency, Inc., 845 Third Avenue, New York, NY 10022.

"Social Lapses" by Darrell Schweitzer. Copyright © 1985 by TSR, Inc. Reprinted by the kind permission of the author.

"One for the Road" by Gardner Dozois. Copyright © 1982 by HMH Publications, Inc. First published in *Playboy*. Reprinted by the kind permission of the author and the author's agent, Virginia Kidd.

"Elephas Frumenti" by Fletcher Pratt and L. Sprague de Camp. Copyright © 1950 by Fantasy House, Inc. Reprinted by the kind permission of L. Sprague de Camp, on behalf of himself and the literary estate of Fletcher Pratt.

"Unicorn Variation" by Roger Zelazny. Copyright © 1981 by Davis Publications, Inc.; copyright © 1982 by the Amber Corp. Reprinted by the kind permission of the author.

"Strategy at the Billiards Club" by Lord Dunsany. Copyright © 1948 by Lord Dunsany. Reprinted by the kind permission of Curtis Brown, Ltd., on behalf of John Child Villiers and Valentine Lamb, as literary executors for the estate of Lord Dunsany.

"Through Time & Space with Ferdinand Feghoot!" by Grendel

Briarton. Copyright © 1981 by Davis Publications, Inc. Reprinted by the kind permission of the author.

"On the Rocks at Slab's" by John Gregory Betancourt. Copyright © 1985 by TSR, Inc. Reprinted by the kind permission of the author.

"Hands of the Man" by R. A. Lafferty. Copyright © 1970 by R. A. Lafferty. Reprinted by the kind permission of the author and the author's agent, Virginia Kidd.

"Endurance Vile" by Steven Barnes. Copyright © 1980 by Davis Publications, Inc. Reprinted by the kind permission of the author.

"The Centipede's Dilemma" by Spider Robinson. Copyright © 1977 by Spider Robinson. Reprinted by the kind permission of the author.

"The Causes" by Margaret St. Clair. Copyright © 1952 by Fantasy House, Inc.; copyright renewed 1980 by Margaret St. Clair. Reprinted by the kind permission of the author.

"For a Foggy Night" by Larry Niven. Copyright © 1971 by Mercury Press, Inc. Reprinted by the kind permission of the author.

"They Loved Me in Utica" by Avram Davidson. Copyright © 1970 by Avram Davidson. From *New Worlds of Fantasy #2*, edited by Terry Carr. Reprinted by the kind permission of the author.

"A Pestilence of Psychoanalysts" by Janet O. Jeppson. Copyright © 1980 by Davis Publications, Inc. Reprinted by the kind permission of the author.

"The Regulars" by Robert Silverberg. Copyright © 1981 by Davis Publications, Inc. Reprinted by the kind permission of the author.

"The Man Who Always Knew" by Algis Budrys. Copyright © 1956 by Street & Smith, Inc. Reprinted by the kind permission of the author.

"Infinite Resources" by Randall Garrett. Copyright © 1954 by Fantasy House, Inc. Reprinted by the kind permission of the author.

"What's Wrong with This Picture?" by Barry B. Longyear, John M. Ford, and George H. Scithers. Copyright © 1980 by Davis Publications, Inc. Reprinted by the kind permission of the authors.

Contents

PREFACE

by Darrell Schweitzer and
George H. Scithers

Star Wars showed millions upon millions of viewers that magnificent old cliché with chairs, the spaceport bar. Indeed, it's been a long-staggering tradition in science-fiction stories that space pirates, interstellar adventurers, and the Galactic Patrol all stop by the spaceport bar for a quick one before heading out to the untamed reaches of the void, where the hand of man has never set foot, and . . . but you know how it goes. Thus the cantina in Mos Eisley on the planet Tatooine is where Ben and Luke go to find a space pilot with a fast ship . . . and thus have hundreds and hundreds of science-fiction stories started, taken a rest break, or ended—among the old space dogs and strange Things that frequent such places.

But sometimes these characters start reminiscing about curious adventures in far places; sometimes, even, curious adventures happening in the bar itself. It is these, the bar-centered or bar-framed stories, that this book is all about— and not just in spaceports, for strange things happen in bars and clubs back on Earth, where—even in the middle of the twentieth century—the storyteller in the next seat may be from Out There.

The equivalent of the spaceport bar has become a fixture in tales set in fantasy worlds as well, especially heroic fantasy: a place for Conan and Fafhrd and the like to rub

broad shoulders and catch a breath between feats swordly
and sorcerous—but save for a representative sample, we've
left fantasy-world bars for another volume. Here, we focus
on bars, taverns, and clubs set in our own past, present, or
future, and on the odd tales and odder events in them.

Why stories told in bars, rather than—say—railroad
trains or railroad stations? Mostly, it's the ambiance: the
local pub and the London club are places to exchange stories, to get acquainted with strangers while the drinks take
the edge off one's skepticism. If someone told you about
the Martian plot to infiltrate human society in any setting
except a bar, you'd probably be trying too hard to get away
to really listen; in a bar, however, it could be an interesting
evening's entertainment, and—listening—you might even
become *convinced*.

The strange tale told in a bar is a very old and respectable
form of literature, with a pedigree that goes back to the very
beginning of storytelling, as Avram Davidson suggests in
his contribution to this anthology; audiences have always
been interested in how and why and where stories came to
be told—how the storyteller came by his tale, with all the
corroborative detail that gives artistic verisimilitude . . . and
that is why so many nineteenth-century and early-twentieth-
century adventure stories begin with frames: accounts of
finding manuscripts in a bottle, papers in a dispatch case,
long-lost journals, and the like. The contemporary practice
of presenting fiction *as fiction* is quite recent. Consider the
elaborate framework of *The Arabian Nights,* presented, not
as a collection of tales assembled or written by some mere
editor or author, but as the very stories told by Scheherazade
herself.

The framing story, as a literary device, goes back at least
as far as the Romans. The two surviving Latin novels, *The
Satyricon* of Petronius and *The Golden Ass,* or *Metamor-
phoses,* of Lucius Apuleius, are both mixtures of novel and
short story, of framework and foreground narrative. *The
Golden Ass* contains eighteen tales, mostly fantastic, told
by the characters in the framing story to each other; *The*

Satyricon includes a set of ghost stories told around the dinner table at Trimalchio's feast.

This subgenre—sets of stories, surrounded by a framing device—continued through the centuries that followed; the most famous example is Chaucer's *Canterbury Tales* of the late 1300s. Almost as famous is Boccaccio's *The Decameron,* in which the stories are told by refugees from the Black Death to while away the time.

As Arthur Jean Cox recently pointed out to us, the next development was to focus on the *place* where tales were told—a bar with a continuing clientele or a club—as did Charles Dickens in 1837 with *The Posthumous Papers of the Pickwick Club* and again, in 1840, with *The Old Curiosity Shop*. There were also a few deliberate throwbacks, such as Arthur Machen's *The Chronicles of Clemendy* (1888), a pastiche of works like *The Decameron*. John Buchan's *Tales of the Runagates Club* (1928), in which each member tells a story, includes some of the most brilliant horror stories of English literature.

But it was Lord Dunsany who put all the elements of this subgenre together with his tales of Mr. Joseph Jorkens and the Billiards Club: the storyteller, who continues from story to story; the setting, sometimes just a frame for a story and sometimes the scene of the action itself; and the fantastic elements which seem, for the duration of the story at least, to be entirely plausible—certainly to Jorkens's audience at the Billiards Club, some of whom would be delighted to show Jorkens to be a liar but—somehow—can never *prove* any story to be untrue.

Jorkens's antecedents include the Anglers' Rest stories of P. G. Wodehouse, and his name is taken from an offstage character in one of those tales. Dunsany wrote five books of short stories about Jorkens, plus a few stray, uncollected ones; topics include a biplane flight to Mars, a man reincarnated as a snail, and Jorkens's trip to the other side of the Sun.

Lord Dunsany became the inspiration for most science-fictional and fantastic bar stories written since, either directly or through his influence on Arthur C. Clarke and his *Tales from the White Hart* or on Fletcher Pratt and L.

Sprague de Camp and their *Tales from Gavagan's Bar*. Other notable, contemporary series include Larry Niven's Draco Tavern, G. C. Edmondson's Mad Friend, Sterling Lanier's Brigadier Ffellowes, Spider Robinson's tales of Callahan's Place, and Janet Jeppson's Pshrinks Anonymous. The Thieves' World series of heroic-fantasy books, edited by Robert Lynn Asprin and Lynn Abbey, use the Vulgar Unicorn as the leading tavern-of-ill-repute in their series' principal city, Sanctuary; while Isaac Asimov has created— and is actively working on—no less than *three* series of tales told in clubs, though only one has an explicit fantastic content.

In addition to the almost universal use of the spaceport bar as a convenient scene in a larger work—Northwest Smith spent many a night in a sleazy Martian dive; and even the moral and upright Grey Lensman went drinking with the asteroid miners, albeit as part of an undercover assignment—most science-fiction writers have given in to temptation and have written at least one spaceport-bar story; that is, one told in or wholly set in such a bar. We successfully tempted Robert Silverberg, Roger Zelazny, John Gregory Betancourt, and Grendel Briarton; their stories appear in this volume. The Longyear–Ford–Scithers collaboration and the Schweitzer limerick are also the fruits of our editorial coaxing. But then, Tony Boucher, when editor of *The Magazine of Fantasy & Science Fiction*, also encouraged writers to produce strange bar stories; several in this volume were first published by his magazine. Larry Niven challenged Steven Barnes to write one set in a *health-food* bar; Barnes's reply appears in these pages. Finally, both Edmondson and Scithers have each written a tale told in a railway car (Scithers may have cheated; his is told in a railway *bar* car); but there was room for neither in this book.

Whether a bar is located on a side street in Victorian London or at the edge of the purple desert of Rigel IV, the basic ambiance is the same: you go into a dark, friendly place, to meet old friends or just to mix with the crowd.

You sample the local brew, whether a simple Ale or a Pan-Galactic Gargle-Blaster . . . and when you are ready to listen, some being says, "That reminds me of an odd experience I once had, when . . ."

Tales From The
SPACEPORT BAR

THE GREEN MARAUDER

by Larry Niven

The Mount Forel spaceport has a bar, of course...

I was tending bar alone that night. The chirp-sithtra interstellar liner had left Earth four days earlier, taking most of my customers. The Draco Tavern was nearly empty.

The man at the bar was drinking Gin-and-Tonic. Two glig—grey and compact beings, wearing furs in three tones of green—were at a table with a chirp-sithtra guide. They drank Vodka-and-Consommé, no ice, no flavorings. Four farsilshree had their bulky, heavy environment tanks crowded around a bigger table. They smoked smoldering yellow paste through tubes. Every so often I got them another jar of paste.

The man was talkative. I got the idea he was trying to interview the bartender and owner of Earth's foremost multispecies tavern.

"Hey, not me," he protested. "I'm not a reporter. I'm Greg Noyes, with the *Scientific American* television show."

"Didn't I see you trying to interview the glig, earlier tonight?"

"Guilty. We're doing a show on the formation of life on Earth. I thought maybe I could check a few things. The gligstith(click)optok"—he said that slowly, but got it right—"have their own little empire out there, don't they? Earthlike worlds, a couple of hundred. They must know quite a lot about how a world forms an oxygenating atmosphere." He was careful with those polysyllabic words. Not quite sober, then.

"That doesn't mean they want to waste an evening lecturing the natives."

He nodded. "They didn't know anyway. Architects on vacation. They got me talking about my home life. I don't know how they managed that." He pushed his drink away. "I'd better switch to espresso. Why would a thing that shape be interested in my sex life? And they kept asking me about territorial imperatives—" He stopped, then turned to see what I was staring at.

Three chirpsithtra were just coming in. One was in a floating couch with life-support equipment attached.

"I thought they all looked alike," he said.

I said, "I've had chirpsithtra in here for close to thirty years, but I can't tell them apart. They're all perfect physical specimens, after all, by their own standards. I never saw one like *that*."

I gave him his espresso, then put three sparkers on a tray and went to the chirpsithtra table.

Two were exactly like any other chirpsithtra: eleven feet tall, dressed in pouched belts and their own salmon-colored exoskeletons, and very much at their ease. The chirps claim to have settled the entire Galaxy long ago—meaning the useful planets, the tidally locked oxygen worlds that happen to circle close around cool red-dwarf suns—and they act like the reigning queens of wherever they happen to be. But the two seemed to defer to the third. She was a foot shorter than they were. Her exoskeleton

was as clearly artificial as dentures: alloplastic
bone worn on the outside. Tubes ran under the
edges from the equipment in her floating couch.
Her skin between the plates was more gray than
red. Her head turned slowly as I came up. She studied me, bright-eyed with interest.

I asked, "Sparkers?" as if chirpsithtra ever ordered anything else.

One of the others said, "Yes. Serve the ethanol
mix of your choice to yourself and the other native.
Will you join us?"

I waved Noyes over, and he came at the jump. He
pulled up one of the high chairs I keep around to
put a human face on a level with a chirpsithtra's. I
went for another espresso and a Scotch-and-Soda
and (catching a soft imperative *hoot* from the farsilshree) a jar of yellow paste. When I returned they
were deep in conversation.

"Rick Shumann," Noyes cried, "meet Ftaxanthir
and Hrofilliss and Chorrikst. Chorrikst tells me
she's nearly two billion years old!"

I heard the doubt beneath his delight. The chirpsithtra could be the greatest liars in the universe,
and how would we ever know? Earth didn't even
have interstellar probes when the chirps came.

Chorrikst spoke slowly, in a throaty whisper, but
her translator box was standard: voice a little flat,
pronunciation perfect. "I have circled the Galaxy
numberless times, and taped the tales of my travels
for funds to feed my wanderlust. Much of my life
has been spent at the edge of lightspeed, under rela-
tivistic time-compression. So you see, I am not
nearly so old as all that."

I pulled up another high chair. "You must have
seen wonders beyond counting," I said. Thinking:
*My God, a short chirpsithtra! Maybe it's true. She's a
different color, too, and her fingers are shorter.
Maybe the species has actually changed since she
was born!*

She nodded slowly. "Life never bores. Always
there is change. In the time I have been gone, Sa-

turn's ring has been pulled into separate rings, making it even more magnificent. What can have done that? Tides from the moons? And Earth has changed beyond recognition."

Noyes spilled a little of his coffee. "You were here? When?"

"Earth's air was methane and ammonia and oxides of nitrogen and carbon. The natives had sent messages across interstellar space...directing them toward yellow suns, of course, but one of our ships passed through a beam, and so we established contact. We had to wear life support," she rattled on, while Noyes and I sat with our jaws hanging, "and the gear was less comfortable then. Our spaceport was a floating platform, because quakes were frequent and violent. But it was worth it. Their cities—"

Noyes said, "Just a minute. Cities? We've never dug up any trace of nonhuman cities!"

Chorrikst looked at him. "After seven hundred and eighty million years, I should think not. Besides, they lived in the offshore shallows in an ocean that was already mildly salty. If the quakes spared them, their tools and their cities still deteriorated rapidly. Their lives were short too, but their memories were inherited. Death and change were accepted facts for them, more than for most intelligent species. Their works of philosophy gained great currency among my people, and spread to other species too."

Noyes wrestled with his instinct for tact and good manners, and won. "How? How could anything have evolved that far? The Earth didn't even have an oxygen atmosphere! Life was just getting started, there weren't even trilobites!"

"They had evolved for as long as you have," Chorrikst said with composure. "Life began on Earth one and a half billion years ago. There were organic chemicals in abundance, from passage of lightning through the reducing atmosphere. Intelligence evolved, and presently built an impressive civilization. They lived slowly, of course. Their bio-chemistry was less energetic. Communication was difficult. They were not stupid, only slow. I visited Earth three times, and each time they had made more progress."

Almost against his will, Noyes asked, "What did they look like?"

"Small and soft and fragile, much more so than yourselves. I cannot say they were pretty, but I grew to like them. I would toast them according to your customs," she said. "They wrought beauty in their cities and beauty in their philosophies, and their works are in our libraries still. They will not be forgotten."

She touched her sparker, and so did her younger companions. Current flowed between her two claws, through her nervous system. She said, "Sssss..."

I raised my glass, and nudged Noyes with my elbow. We drank to our predecessors. Noyes lowered his cup and asked, "What happened to them?"

"They sensed worldwide disaster coming," Chor-rikst said, "and they prepared; but they thought it would be quakes. They built cities to float on the ocean surface, and lived in the undersides. They never noticed the green scum growing in certain tidal pools. By the time they knew the danger, the green scum was everywhere. It used photosynthesis to turn carbon dioxide into oxygen, and the raw oxygen killed whatever it touched, leaving fertilizer to feed the green scum.

"The world was dying when we learned of the problem. What could we do against a photosynthe-sis-using scum growing beneath a yellow-white star? There was nothing in chirpsithtra libraries that would help. We tried, of course, but we were unable to stop it. The sky had turned an admittedly lovely transparent blue, and the tide pools were green, and the offshore cities were crumbling before we gave up the fight. There was an attempt to transplant some of the natives to a suitable world;

but biorhythm upset ruined their mating habits. I have not been back since, until now."

The depressing silence was broken by Chorrikst herself. "Well, the Earth is greatly changed, and of course your own evolution began with the green plague. I have heard tales of humanity from my companions. Would you tell me something of your lives?"

And we spoke of humankind, but I couldn't seem to find much enthusiasm for it. The anaerobic life that survived the advent of photosynthesis includes gangrene and botulism and not much else. I wondered what Chorrikst would find when next she came, and whether she would have reason to toast our memory.

About the Draco Tavern series, Niven remarks: "I wanted a vehicle for dealing with basic, easily described philosophical questions. I like writing vignettes. And I like multispecies bar stories: the ambiance, the decor, the funny chemicals....

"I found it all in the Draco Tavern. The chirpsithtra in particular claim to own the Galaxy and to have been civilized for billions of years. On that basis they will have solved any general philosophical puzzle long ago.

"With 'The Green Marauder,' I tried to give an intuitive sense of the drastic manner in which photosynthetic life changed the world. I think I succeeded. I'm proud of this story.

"Was there intelligent life on Earth before the green marauder came? The way to bet is that there wasn't, but you can't prove it."

DON'T LOOK NOW

by Henry Kuttner

*"—but he did stop writing science fiction rather
suddenly, didn't he?"*

The man in the brown suit was looking at himself in the mirror behind the bar. The reflection
seemed to interest him even more deeply than the
drink between his hands. He was paying only per-
functory attention to Lyman's attempts at conversation. This had been going on for perhaps fifteen
minutes before he finally lifted his glass and took a
deep swallow.

"Don't look now," Lyman said.

The brown-suited man slid his eyes sidewise toward Lyman, tilted his glass higher, and took another swig. Ice cubes slipped down toward his
mouth. He put the glass back on the red-brown
wood and signaled for a refill. Finally he took a
deep breath and looked at Lyman.

"Don't look at what?" he asked.

"There was one sitting right beside you," Lyman

7

said, blinking rather glazed eyes. "He just went out. You mean you couldn't see him?"

The brown-suited man finished paying for his fresh drink before he answered. "See who?" he asked, with a fine mixture of boredom, distaste, and reluctant interest. "Who went out?"

"What have I been telling you for the last ten minutes? Weren't you listening?"

"Certainly I was listening. That is—certainly. You were talking about—bathtubs. Radios. Orson—"

"Not Orson. H. G. Herbert George. With Orson it was just a gag. H. G. *knew*—or suspected. I wonder if it was simply intuition with him? He couldn't have had any proof—but he did stop writing science fiction rather suddenly, didn't he? I'll bet he knew once, though."

"Knew what?"

"About the Martians. All this won't do us a bit of good if you don't listen. It may not anyway. The trick is to jump the gun—with proof. Convincing evidence. Nobody's ever been allowed to produce the evidence before. You *are* a reporter, aren't you?"

Holding his glass, the man in the brown suit nodded reluctantly.

"Then you ought to be taking it all down on a piece of folded paper. I want everybody to know. The whole world. It's important. Terribly important. It explains everything. My life won't be safe unless I can pass along the information and make people believe it."

"Why won't your life be safe?"

"Because of the Martians, you fool. They own the world."

The man in brown sighed. "Then they own my newspaper, too," he objected, "so I can't print anything they don't like."

"I never thought of that," Lyman said, considering the bottom of his glass, where two ice cubes had fused into a cold, immutable union. "They're not omnipotent, though. I'm sure they're vulnerable, or

why have they always kept under cover? They're
afraid of being found out. If the world had convincing evidence—look, people always believe what
they read in the newspapers. Couldn't you—"

"Ha," said the man in brown with deep significance.

Lyman drummed sadly on the bar and murmured, "There must be some way. Perhaps if I had
another drink. . . ."

The brown-suited man tasted his Collins, which
seemed to stimulate him. "Just what is all this
about Martians?" he asked Lyman. "Suppose you
start at the beginning and tell me again. Or can't
you remember?"

"Of course I can remember. I've got practically
total recall. It's something new. Very new. I never
could do it before. I can even remember my last conversation with the Martians." Lyman favored the
man in brown with a glance of triumph.

"When was that?"

"This morning."

"I can even remember conversations I had last
week," the brown-suited man said mildly. "So
what?"

"You don't understand. They make us forget, you
see. They tell us what to do and we forget about the
conversation—it's post-hypnotic suggestion, I expect—but we follow their orders just the same.
There's the compulsion, though we think we're
making our own decisions. Oh, they own the world,
all right, but nobody knows it except me."

"And how did you find out?"

"Well, I got my brain scrambled, in a way. I've
been fooling around with supersonic detergents,
trying to work out something marketable, you
know. The gadget went wrong—from some stand-
points. High-frequency waves, it was. They went
through and through me. Should have been inaudible, but I could hear them, or rather—well, actually I could *see* them. That's what I mean about my
brain being scrambled. And after that, I could see

and hear the Martians. They've geared themselves
so they work efficiently on ordinary brains, and
mine isn't ordinary anymore. They can't hypnotize
me, either. They can command me, but I needn't
obey—now. I hope they don't suspect. Maybe they
do. Yes, I guess they do."

"How can you tell?"

"The way they look at me."

"How do they look at you?" asked the man in
brown, as he began to reach for a pencil and then
changed his mind. He took a drink instead. "Well?
What are they like?"

"I'm not sure. I can see them, all right, but only
when they're dressed up."

"Okay, okay," the brown-suited man said pa-
tiently. "How do they look, dressed up?"

"Just like anybody, almost. They dress up in—in
human skins. Oh, not real ones, imitations. Like
the Katzenjammer Kids zipped into crocodile suits.
Undressed—I don't know. I've never seen one.
Maybe they're invisible even to me, then, or maybe
they're just camouflaged. Ants or owls or rats or
bats or—"

"Or anything," the man in brown said hastily.

"Thanks. Or anything, of course. But when
they're dressed up like humans—like that one who
was sitting next to you a while ago, when I told you
not to look—"

"That one was invisible, I gather?"

"Most of the time they are, to everybody. But
once in a while, for some reason, they—"

"Wait," the man in brown objected. "Make sense,
will you? They dress up in human skins and then
sit around invisible?"

"Only now and then. The human skins are perfectly good imitations. Nobody can tell the difference. It's that third eye that gives them away. When
they keep it closed, you'd never guess it was there.
When they want to open it, they go invisible—like
that. Fast. When I see somebody with a third eye,
right in the middle of his forehead, I know he's a

Martian and invisible, and I pretend not to notice him."

"Uh-huh," the brown-suited man said. "Then for all you know, I'm one of your visible Martians."

"Oh, I hope not!" Lyman regarded him anxiously. "Drunk as I am, I don't think so. I've been trailing you all day, making sure. It's a risk I have to take, of course. They'll go to any length—any length at all—to make a man give himself away. I realize that. I can't really trust anybody. But I had to find *someone* to talk to, and I—" He paused. There was a brief silence. "I could be wrong," Lyman said presently. "When the third eye's closed, I can't tell if it's there. Would you mind opening your third eye for me?" He fixed a dim gaze on the brown-suited man's forehead.

"Sorry," the reporter said. "Some other time. Besides, I don't know you. So you want me to splash this across the front page, I gather? Why didn't you go to see the managing editor? My stories have to get past the desk and rewrite."

"I want to give my secret to the world," Lyman said stubbornly. "The question is, how far will I get? You'd expect they'd have killed me the minute I opened my mouth to you—except that I didn't say anything while they were here. I don't believe they take us very seriously, you know. This must have been going on since the dawn of history, and by now they've had time to get careless. They let Fort go pretty far before they cracked down on him. But you notice they were careful never to let Fort get hold of genuine proof that would convince people."

The man in brown said something under his breath about a human-interest story in a box. He asked, "What do the Martians do, besides hang around bars all dressed up?"

"I'm still working on that," Lyman said. "It isn't easy to understand. They run the world, of course, but why?" He wrinkled his brow and stared appealingly at the brown-suited man. "Why?"

"If they do run it, they've got a lot to explain."

"That's what I mean. From our viewpoint, there's no sense to it. We do things illogically, but only because they tell us to. Everything we do, almost, is pure illogic. Poe's *Imp of the Perverse*—you could give it another name beginning with M. Martian, I mean. It's all very well for psychologists to explain why a murderer wants to confess, but it's still an illogical reaction. Unless a Martian commands him to."

"You can't be hypnotized into doing anything that violates your moral sense," the man in brown said triumphantly.

Lyman frowned. "Not by another human, but you can by a Martian. I expect they got the upper hand when we didn't have more than ape-brains, and they've kept it ever since. They evolved as we did, and kept a step ahead. Like the sparrow on the eagle's back who hitchhiked till the eagle reached his ceiling, and then took off and broke the altitude record. They conquered the world, but nobody ever knew it. And they've been ruling ever since."

"But—"

"Take houses, for example. Uncomfortable things. Ugly, inconvenient, dirty, everything wrong with them. But when men like Frank Lloyd Wright slip out from under the Martians' thumb long enough to suggest something better, look how the people react. They hate the thought. That's their Martians, giving them orders."

"Look. Why should the Martians care what kind of houses we live in? Tell me that."

Lyman frowned. "I don't like the note of skepticism I detect creeping into this conversation," he announced. "They care, all right. No doubt about it. They *live* in our houses. We don't build for our convenience, we build, under order, for the Martians, the way they want it. They're very much concerned with everything we do. And the more senseless, the more concern.

"Take wars. Wars don't make sense from any human viewpoint. Nobody really wants wars. But we go right on having them. From the Martian viewpoint, they're useful. They give us a spurt in technology, and they reduce the excess population. And there are lots of other results, too. Colonization, for one thing. But mainly technology. In peacetime, if a guy invents jet propulsion, it's too expensive to develop commercially. In wartime, though, it's *got* to be developed. Then the Martians can use it whenever they want. They use us the way they'd use tools or—or limbs. And nobody ever really wins a war—except the Martians."

The man in the brown suit chuckled. "That makes sense," he said. "It must be nice to be a Martian."

"Why not? Up till now, no race ever successfully conquered and ruled another. The underdog could revolt or absorb. If you know you're being ruled, then the ruler's vulnerable. But if the world doesn't know—and it doesn't—

"Take radios," Lyman continued, going off at a tangent. "There's no earthly reason why a sane human should listen to a radio. But the Martians make us do it. They like it. Take bathtubs. Nobody contends bathtubs are comfortable—for us. But they're fine for Martians. All the impractical things we keep on using, even though we know they're impractical—"

"Typewriter ribbons," the man in brown said, struck by the thought. "But not even a Martian could enjoy changing a typewriter ribbon."

Lyman seemed to find that flippant. He said that he knew all about the Martians except for one thing—their psychology.

"I don't know *why* they act as they do. It looks illogical sometimes, but I feel perfectly sure they've got sound motives for every move they make. Until I get that worked out I'm pretty much at a standstill. Until I get evidence—proof—and help. I've got to stay under cover till then. And I've been doing that. I do what they tell me, so they won't

suspect, and I pretend to forget what they tell me to
forget."

"Then you've got nothing much to worry about."

Lyman paid no attention. He was off again on a
list of his grievances.

"When I hear the water running in the tub and a
Martian splashing around, I pretend I don't hear a
thing. My bed's too short and I tried last week to
order a special length, but the Martian that sleeps
there told me not to. He's a runt, like most of them.
That is, I think they're runts. I have to deduce, because you never see them undressed. But it goes on
like that constantly. By the way, how's your Martian?"

The man in the brown suit set down his glass
rather suddenly.

"My Martian?"

"Now listen. I may be just a little bit drunk, but
my logic remains unimpaired. I can still put two
and two together. Either you know about the Martians, or you don't. If you do, there's no point in giving me that 'What, *my* Martian?' routine. I know
you have a Martian. Your Martian knows you have
a Martian. My Martian knows. The point is, do *you*
know? Think hard," Lyman urged solicitously.

"No, I haven't got a Martian," the reporter said,
taking a quick drink. The edge of the glass clicked
against his teeth.

"Nervous, I see," Lyman remarked. "Of course
you *have* got a Martian. I suspect you know it."

"What would I be doing with a Martian?" the
man in brown asked with dogged dogmatism.

"What would you be doing without one? I imagine it's illegal. If they caught you running around
without one they'd probably put you in a pound or
something until claimed. Oh, you've got one, all
right. So have I. So has he, and he, and he—and the
bartender." Lyman enumerated the other barflies
with a wavering forefinger.

"Of course they have," the man in brown said.
"But they'll all go back to Mars tomorrow and then

you can see a good doctor. You'd better have another dri—"

He was turning toward the bartender when Lyman, apparently by accident, leaned close to him and whispered urgently:

"Don't look now!"

The man in brown glanced at Lyman's white face reflected in the mirror before them.

"It's all right," he said. "There aren't any Mar—"

Lyman gave him a fierce, quick kick under the edge of the bar.

"Shut up! One just came in!"

And then he caught the brown-suited man's gaze and with elaborate unconcern said, "—so naturally, there was nothing for me to do but climb out on the roof after it. Took me ten minutes to get it down the ladder, and just as we reached the bottom it gave one bound, climbed up my face, sprang from the top of my head, and there it was again on the roof, screaming for me to get it down."

"What?" the brown-suited man demanded with pardonable curiosity.

"My cat, of course. What did you think? No, never mind, don't answer that." Lyman's face was turned to the brown-suited man's, but from the corners of his eyes he was watching an invisible progress down the length of the bar toward a booth at the very back.

"Now why did he come in?" he murmured. "I don't like this. Is he anyone you know?"

"Is who—?"

"That Martian. Yours, by any chance? No, I suppose not. Yours was probably the one who went out a while ago. I wonder if he went to make a report, and sent this one in? It's possible. It could be. You can talk now, but keep your voice low, and stop squirming. Want him to notice we can see him?"

"I can't see him. Don't drag me into this. You and your Martians can fight it out together. You're making me nervous. I've got to go, anyway." But he didn't move to get off the stool. Across Lyman's

shoulder he was stealing glances toward the back of
the bar, and now and then he looked at Lyman's
face.

"Stop watching me," Lyman said. "Stop watching
him. Anybody'd think you were a cat."

"Why a cat? Why should anybody—do I look like
a cat?"

"We were talking about cats, weren't we? Cats
can see them, quite clearly. Even undressed, I believe. They don't like them."

"Who doesn't like who?"

"Whom. Neither likes the other. Cats can see
Martians—shh!—but they pretend not to, and that
makes the Martians mad. I have a theory that cats
ruled the world before Martians came. Never mind.
Forget about cats. This may be more serious than
you think. I happen to know my Martian's taking
tonight off, and I'm pretty sure that was your Martian who went out some time ago. And have you
noticed that nobody else in here has his Martian
with him? Do you suppose—" His voice sank. "Do
you suppose they could be *waiting for us outside?*"

"Oh, Lord," the brown-suited man said. "In the
alley with the cats, I suppose."

"Why don't you stop this yammer about cats and
be serious for a moment?" Lyman demanded, and
then paused, paled, and reeled slightly on his stool.
He hastily took a drink to cover his confusion.

"What's the matter now?" the man in brown
asked.

"Nothing." Gulp. "Nothing. It was just that—he
looked at me. With—you know."

"Let me get this straight. I take it the Martian is
dressed in—is dressed like a human?"

"Naturally."

"But he's invisible to all eyes but yours?"

"Yes. He doesn't want to be visible, just now. Besides—" Lyman paused cunningly. He gave the
man in brown a furtive glance and then looked
quickly down at his drink. "Besides, you know, I
rather think you *can* see him—a little, anyway."

The man in brown was perfectly silent for about thirty seconds. He sat quite motionless, not even the ice in the drink he held clinking. One might have thought he did not even breathe. Certainly he did not blink.

"What makes you think that?" he asked in a normal voice, after the thirty seconds had run out.

"I—did I say anything? I wasn't listening." Lyman put down his drink abruptly. "I think I'll go now."

"No, you won't," the brown-suited man said, closing his fingers around Lyman's wrist. "Not yet you won't. Come back here. Sit down. Now. What was the idea? Where were you going?"

Lyman nodded dumbly toward the back of the bar, indicating either a jukebox or a door marked MEN.

"I don't feel so good. Maybe I've had too much to drink. I guess I'll—"

"You're all right. I don't trust you back there with that—that invisible man of yours. You'll stay right here until he leaves."

"He's going now," Lyman said brightly. His eyes moved with great briskness along the line of an invisible but rapid progress toward the front door. "See, he's gone. Now let me loose, will you?"

The brown-suited man glanced toward the back booth.

"No," he said, "he isn't gone. Sit right where you are."

It was Lyman's turn to remain quite still, in a stricken sort of way, for a perceptible while. The ice in *his* drink, however, clinked audibly. Presently he spoke. His voice was soft, and rather soberer than before.

"You're right. He's still there. You can see him, can't you?"

The man in brown said, "Has he got his back to us?"

"You *can* see him, then. Better than I can, maybe. Maybe there are more of them here than I

thought. They could be anywhere. They could be
sitting beside you anywhere you go, and you
wouldn't even guess, until—" He shook his head a
little. "They'd want to be *sure*," he said, mostly to
himself. "They can give you orders and make you
forget, but there must be limits to what they can
force you to do. They can't make a man betray himself. They'd have to lead him on—until they were
sure."

He lifted his drink and tipped it steeply above his
face. The ice ran down the slope and bumped coldly
against his lip, but he held it until the last of the
pale, bubbling amber had drained into his mouth.
He set the glass on the bar and faced the man in
brown.

"Well?" he said.

The man in the brown suit looked up and down
the bar.

"It's getting late," he said. "Not many people left.
We'll wait."

"Wait for what?"

The brown-suited man looked toward the back
booth and looked away again quickly.

"I have something to show you. I don't want anyone else to see."

Lyman surveyed the narrow, smoky room. As he
looked the last customer besides themselves at the
bar began groping in his pocket, tossed some
change on the mahogany, and went out slowly.

They sat in silence. The bartender eyed them
with stolid disinterest. Presently a couple in the
front booth got up and departed, quarreling in un-
dertones.

"Is there anyone left?" the brown-suited man
asked in a voice that did not carry down the bar to
the man in the apron.

"Only—" Lyman did not finish, but he nodded
gently toward the back of the room. "He isn't looking. Let's get this over with. What do you want to
show me?"

The reporter took off his wristwatch and pried up

the metal case. Two small, glossy photograph prints slid out. The reporter separated them with a finger.

"I just want to make sure of something," he said. "First—why did you pick me out? Quite a while ago, you said you'd been trailing me all day, making sure. I haven't forgotten that. And you knew I was a reporter. Suppose you tell me the truth, now?"

Squirming on his stool, Lyman scowled. "It was the way you looked at things," he murmured. "On the subway this morning—I'd never seen you before in my life, but I kept noticing the way you looked at things—the wrong things, things that weren't there, the way a cat does—and then you'd always look away—I got the idea you could see the Martians too."

"Go on," the brown-suited man said quietly.

"I followed you. All day. I kept hoping you'd turn out to be—somebody I could talk to. Because if I could *know* that I wasn't the only one who could see them, then I'd know there was still some hope left. It's been worse than solitary confinement. I've been able to see them for three years now. Three years. And I've managed to keep my power a secret even from them. And, somehow, I've managed to keep from killing myself, too."

"Three years?" the man in brown said. He shivered.

"There was always a little hope. I knew nobody would believe—not without proof. And how can you get proof? It was only that I—I kept telling myself that maybe you could see them too, and if you could, maybe there were others—lots of others—enough so we might get together and work out some way of proving to the world—"

The brown-suited man's fingers were moving. In silence he pushed a photograph across the mahogany. Lyman picked it up unsteadily.

"Moonlight?" he asked after a moment. It was a landscape under a deep, dark sky with white clouds in it. Trees stood white and lacy against the darkness. The grass was white as if with moonlight, and the shadows blurry.

"No, not moonlight," the reporter said. "Infrared. I'm strictly an amateur, but lately I've been experimenting with infrared film. And I got some very odd results."

Lyman stared at the film.

"You see, I live near"—the reporter's finger tapped a certain quite common object that appeared in the photograph—"and something funny keeps showing up now and then against it. But only with infrared film. Now I know chlorophyll reflects so much infrared light that grass and leaves photograph white. The sky comes out black, like this. There are tricks to using this kind of film. Photograph a tree against a cloud, and you can't tell them apart in the print. But you can photograph through a haze and pick out distant objects the ordinary film wouldn't catch. And sometimes, when you focus on something like this—" He tapped the image of the very common object again. "You get a very odd image on the film. Like that. A man with three eyes."

Lyman held the print up to the light. In silence he took the other one from the bar and studied it. When he laid them down he was smiling.

"You know," Lyman said in a conversational whisper, "a professor of astrophysics at one of the more important universities had a very interesting little item in the *Times* the other Sunday. Name of Spitzer, I think. He said that if there were life on Mars, and if Martians had ever visited Earth, there'd be no way to prove it. Nobody would believe the few men who saw them. Not, he said, unless the Martians happened to be photographed...."

Lyman looked at the brown-suited man thoughtfully.

"Well," he said, "it's happened. You've photographed them."

The brown-suited man nodded. He took up the prints and returned them to his watchcase. "I thought so, too. Only until tonight I couldn't be sure. I'd never seen one—fully—as you have. It isn't so much a matter of what you call getting your brain scrambled with supersonics as it is of just knowing where to look. But I've been seeing *part* of them all my life, and so has everybody. It's that little suggestion of movement you never catch except just at the edge of your vision, just out of the corner of your eye. Something that's *almost* there—and when you look fully at it, there's nothing. These photographs showed me the way. It's not easy to learn, but it can be done. We're conditioned to look directly at a thing—the particular thing we want to see clearly, whatever it is. Perhaps the Martians gave us that conditioning. When we see a movement at the edge of our range of vision, it's almost irresistible not to look directly at it. So it vanishes."

"Then they can be seen—by anybody?"

"I've learned a lot in a few days," the man in brown said. "Since I took those photographs. You have to train yourself. It's like seeing a trick picture—one that's really a composite, after you study it. Camouflage. You just have to learn how. Otherwise we can look at them all our lives and never see them."

"The camera does, though."

"Yes, the camera does. I've wondered why nobody ever caught them this way before. Once you see them on film, they're unmistakable—that third eye."

"Infrared film's comparatively new, isn't it? And then I'll bet you have to catch them against that one particular background—you know—or they won't show on the film. Like trees against clouds. It's tricky. You must have had just the right lighting that day, and exactly the right focus, and the lens stopped down just right. A kind of minor miracle. It might never happen again exactly that way. But... don't look now."

They were silent. Furtively, they watched the

mirror. Their eyes slid along toward the open door of the tavern.

And then there was a long, breathless silence.

"He looked back at us," Lyman said very quietly. "He looked at us ... that third eye!"

The reporter was motionless again. When he moved, it was to swallow the rest of his drink.

"I don't think that they're suspicious yet," he said. "The trick will be to keep under cover until we can blow this thing wide open. There's got to be some way to do it—some way that will convince people."

"There's proof. The photographs. A competent cameraman ought to be able to figure out just how you caught that Martian on film and duplicate the conditions. It's evidence."

"Evidence can cut both ways," the man in brown said. "What I'm hoping is that the Martians don't really like to kill—unless they have to. I'm hoping they won't kill without proof. But—" He tapped his wristwatch.

"There's two of us now, though," Lyman said. "We've got to stick together. Both of us have broken the big rule—*don't look now*—"

The bartender was at the back, disconnecting the jukebox. The man in brown said, "We'd better not be seen together unnecessarily. But if we both come to this bar tomorrow night at nine for a drink—that wouldn't look suspicious, even to them."

"Suppose—" Lyman hesitated. "May I have one of those photographs?"

"Why?"

"If one of us had—an accident—the other one would still have the proof. Enough, maybe, to convince the right people."

The man in brown hesitated, nodded shortly, and opened his watchcase again. He gave Lyman one of the pictures.

"Hide it," he said. "It's—evidence. I'll see you here tomorrow. Meanwhile, be careful. Remember to play safe."

They shook hands firmly, facing each other in an
endless second of final, decisive silence. Then the
man in the brown suit turned abruptly and walked
out of the bar.

Lyman sat there. Between two wrinkles in his
forehead there was a stir and a flicker of lashes un-
furling. The third eye opened slowly and looked
after the man in brown.

*Henry Kuttner (1914–58) was one of the first
full-time science-fiction writers, a superprolific contributor to the pulps who used so many pseudonyms
(nearly thirty are known) that for many years any
new writer to enter the field was automatically assumed to be a pen name of Henry Kuttner. When this
happened to Jack Vance, he is reputed to have remarked that if he had to be someone's pseudonym,
there were few writers whose pseudonym he'd rather
be than Kuttner's. But to some extent Kuttner's own
reputation was overshadowed by such practices.
Readers often complained that Henry Kuttner wasn't
nearly as good a writer as Lewis Padgett, even
though the two were one and the same. It was as
Padgett that Kuttner took a boozy turn, with a series
about a drunken inventor named Gallagher, who
made brilliant inventions while under the influence
but couldn't remember the details when he sobered
up. The most famous of these is "The Proud Robot,"
which can be found in the perpetually in-print Adventures in Time and Space edited by Healy and
McComas. The series was collected in the now (alas)
quite rare Robots Have No Tails (1952).
On the whole, while Kuttner did produce some
routine work, he distinguished himself from the
usual run of pulpsters by leaving behind a large
body of genuinely superior work, including the novel*

Fury, *the story-cycle* Mutant, *and a host of shorter works, many of which can be found in the collection* The Best of Henry Kuttner. *Most of Kuttner's later efforts were collaborations with his wife, C. L. Moore, to the extent that neither of them could remember who wrote what.*

GETTING EVEN

by Isaac Asimov

*"Two grams, perhaps. One-fourteenth of an
ounce...."*

"I got even," said Griswold grimly, from the
depths of the armchair. He was sipping at his
Scotch-and-Soda.

It was his fourth one, and I suppose he was just a
little bit relaxed, so to speak, or he might not have
been telling us about it. It was raining outside and
the four of us were relaxing in the library of the
Union Club.

I said, "With whom? Why? How?"

That's when he told us the story. Baranov and
Jennings were there, too. They can bear witness to
this.

It's not exactly a unique problem in some ways
[said Griswold] and I suppose it happens all the
time—the little inventor being cheated by the
giant corporation. Still, if it's a giant corporation,

there's at least no human being you can blame and
hate.

What if it *is* a human being?

No use going into all the wearisome details, because that's not really the essence of the story. I had
an ingenious idea and I couldn't put it into action
because I didn't have the capital, so a friend of a
friend of mine recommended a source of capital.

As a result, I got ten thousand dollars to perfect
the notion and build a model for a man named Felix
Hammock. He supplied the money, so he promoted
it and marketed it and apparently made ten million
dollars at least. What I got was the original ten
thousand.

I went to see the fellow. He met me in his office,
all honey-sweet; listened with sympathy; and suggested that first I ought to see a lawyer and then
he'd be glad to talk to me again.

So I did. The lawyer looked at the papers I had
signed and asked me if I had taken legal advice before signing them. I said I hadn't. I needed the
money and it had looked all right to me. He sighed.
He said that Felix Hammock was a well-known promoter and that the papers always looked all right
and they *were*—for Felix Hammock.

"Mr. Griswold," he said, "we could fight this in
court. I figure it might take two years and cost seventy or eighty thousand dollars. And I don't think
you'll get anything out of it except publicity and
sympathy. That might get you a job with some firm
that could use an ingenious tinkerer—or it might
not, if you come to be viewed as a troublemaker. If
you say you'll take it to court, I'll take the case but
only with a heavy retainer. If you say you won't
take it to court, then I'll say good-bye and charge
you fifty dollars for my advice."

I paid the fifty dollars and called up Hammock to
see him again. I had no reason to think he wasn't a
reasonable fellow. He even seemed so, for he invited
me to his home in Fairfield County.

It was a mansion. I'm not much on description, but

it was the kind of house you wouldn't think even millionaires could afford. He was well-protected, too. Electrified fences. Security guards. Like that.

The house itself seemed infinite in size and laden with objets d'art. There were Picassos and Chagalls and other paintings that Hammock assured me were originals and well-insured. There were first editions and Tiffany lamps and I don't know what all. He was a collector and that's how he stored the money he made out of me and others like me—and in an inflation-proof way at that.

We had dinner, just he and I, and two bodyguards in the room.

Over the Brandy I pointed out that he had made thousands for every dollar he had paid me. Should I not have my share?

"No, no, my good Griswold," he said, smiling genially. "Not a penny. Why should I worry about the matter? I am not legally bound to pay you anything."

"I am not speaking from the standpoint of the law," I said, "but from justice."

"Nor in justice, either," he said. "See here. I risk money on many projects and not all succeed. Sometimes I put out ten thousand to a man like you and a hundred thousand additional on promotion—I say nothing about time—and lose it all. Do you suppose that the gentleman to whom I pay ten thousand ever comes to me and says, 'Poor Mr. Hammock, you have lost so much on my stupid idea that I simply must give you back part of the money I have made out of you.'

"No, not once. —But let me be a good judge of values and a clever promoter and quickly each one who has sold his idea to me wants to get his share of the product of my brain and my initiative. No, no, my friend, I have paid you all I will pay you.

"After all, look around you. I live like a prince and I enjoy it, but it costs a vast amount of money. If I began giving out money to each beggarly fellow who whines 'Justice! Justice!' you can imagine that I could not support my way of life."

And he showed me out, still smiling.

Of course, there was something in what he said. Still, if his brain and his initiative could reward him and leave nothing for me, then it was only fair that my brain and my initiative should strip him of what he had gained. —If it could.

Yes, if it could.

The very notion he had bought from me (I couldn't really call it "stolen" after his explanation) could be extended farther, and very boldly, too. I won't tell any of you just how because it is much too dangerous for the world.

It could be extended to tap unusual energies. It required only a slight but very ingenious modification to enable my device to tap supernatural energies.

Oh, don't cry out. Just listen, and think a bit.

There are any number of stories of people who have raised spirits by the proper incantations—and most of them are fiction, of course. But are they all? And if so, what is the significance of the necessary words, gestures, chemical powders?

Even if we grant that so-called magic succeeded in raising spirits and releasing paranormal powers, most of the description must be window dressing. A chandelier may cast a pleasant light, but the essence of the light is in the little filaments through which the current flows. All those glass pendants and curved brass rods and chains are beside the point. They may make the chandelier, but they don't make the light.

So I was looking for something that was not magic, but science. Something that would reach across a gap between our universe and another, and it wasn't easy.

But I didn't mind sweating at it. I was determined to have my revenge on Hammock. I didn't worry about injustice anymore. I could see I had been naïve and stupid and deserved what I had gotten.

It was just that he had talked of his brain and his initiative as though he felt I had none. I wanted to match mine against his, and I was absolutely resolved to do so and win.

Finally, finally, I managed to jar the doorway open just the merest crack, just an infinitesimal amount. There was an odor that was very faint and not quite of brimstone—by which is usually meant sulfur dioxide—but that was faintly irritating. An alien atmosphere. And there was a flash of light, not blinding or frightening in any way, just a spark of an indeterminate color.

And then, on my workbench, there was a figure; not red exactly, or black. Rather lavender, I should say. It was not frightening in any way; no horns, no tails, not really human, in fact—and very small. About two centimeters high. That's less than an inch.

It was as genial as Hammock had been. It had been called in from its world, wherever that was, but it didn't seem annoyed over it. It listened to me with attention. —No, it didn't speak English. I don't know what it spoke. I just understood what it was saying. And it understood me even before I spoke, I think. I imagine it was some kind of telepathy.

It said, "It's a long time since anyone has called on one of us, and I don't recognize your system. It's never been used before."

I tried to explain and it said, "Ingenious. Most ingenious. But very inefficient. So you want to inflict a curse on this Hammock?"

"I don't know if 'curse' is the right word," I said. "I don't want to kill him or hurt him in any way. I just want to get even. He deprived me of a fair share of the profits arising out of my own ingenuity, and I want to deprive him of those profits."

The spirit said, "I understand, but you see I am a small one of my kind. It was all you could get with your inefficient device. There isn't much I can do."

"Can you make his stocks go down? Can you disrupt his business judgment? Can you riddle his house with termites?"

The spirit said, "You have a fanciful notion of the powers of what you think of as magic. In our world, too, we have a law of conservation of energy. I can do only what I have energy for."

"What can you do, then? What *do* you have energy for?"

"I can withdraw anything you wish from this world. All parts of your world are equally accessible to me, and I can obtain the necessary information from your computers. I can reach into his house or somewhere in his business connections to remove something that would represent a loss to him."

"Can you withdraw money from his safe? Documents he has? Some things that are extremely valuable? I don't want them for myself. You can take them to your world if you wish."

The spirit said, "I can't withdraw an unlimited amount. Only so much."

"How much?"

"Two grams, perhaps. One-fourteenth of an ounce."

I said, "But it is impossible to withdraw so little and cause him any significant loss."

"I regret that, but I am as helpless as you are to go against the laws of nature. Please think of something, for I cannot stay with you for long."

I thought! Good heavens, how I thought! I had perhaps ten minutes. I could withdraw something from his house, or his person, or his office, or anyone's office—something that would not harm him physically, but would cause him financial loss. And *enough* financial loss.

A diamond, perhaps; or a rare stamp, if he had a stamp collection. But that would only cost him thousands. He would laugh it off. I wanted to deprive him of at least ten million and I had ten minutes to think of it.

Fortunately, I thought of it!

If you want, you three can have ten minutes too, to see if you can think of what I thought. I would just as soon close my eyes for a moment—

* * *

Eh? Oh, yes, you want the finish of my story. How I got even.

I managed to wangle another invitation to his house. I didn't have to, but I wanted to see with my own eyes that it was missing and I wanted to see his face when he realized it. Of course, he could not imagine I had done it. How could he?

It wasn't easy getting that invitation. He had already had his fun with me. Still, I told him I had a modification of my idea that I wanted to sell for ten thousand more. I told him just enough to make him willing to risk one more invitation. I told him he didn't have to feed me dinner this time.

"Well," he said, "tell me about this modification." The bodyguards were with him, of course.

I wandered in the direction of his paintings and stared at one of them, then at another, then at a third.

"Well," he said impatiently.

I said, "This is a Picasso original, I take it?"

"Absolutely," he said.

"But it doesn't have a signature."

"What?" he cried, rushing to the painting.

"In fact," I said, "not one of them seems—"

My spirit, before leaving, had taken with him less than two grams of paint flakes, and every single picture in his house was without a signature. Every one of them would require expensive and time-consuming authentication to have any value at all, and even then perhaps nothing like their true value. And if he tried to fake a robbery and collect from his insurance company, he would find that his signature, and theirs, was gone from all copies of the policy.

He must easily have lost well over ten million dollars.

———And I was even.

Breathes there a fan with soul so dead as to not have already encountered and enjoyed the works of Isaac Asimov? We doubt it. Among the Good Doctor's over three hundred books is a collection of stories, The Union Club Mysteries, *in which the redoubtable Griswold solves a series of puzzlers, most of which have to do with crime, espionage, and other traditionally mysterious subjects. "Getting Even" wasn't included because, unlike all the others, it is a fantasy. Writes Asimov: "What I did was start a new series about that little demon. I have just written the eleventh in that series, but 'Getting Even' isn't included there, either, because it isn't quite a member of the new series. It falls in between and while it generated both, it fits neither."*

So the editors are especially proud to present this stray piece of Asimoviana, which most readers will not have seen, and which, unquestionably, fits into this *book perfectly.*

WHAT GOES UP

by Arthur C. Clarke

"...editors and science-fiction writers are forgathering..."

One of the reasons why I am never too specific about the exact location of the White Hart is, frankly, because we want to keep it to ourselves. This is not merely a dog-in-the-manger attitude: we have to do it in pure self-protection. As soon as it gets around that scientists, editors, and science-fiction writers are forgathering at some locality, the weirdest collection of visitors is likely to turn up. Peculiar people with new theories of the universe, characters who have been "cleared" by Dianetics (God knows what they were like before), intense ladies who are liable to go all clairvoyant after the fourth gin—these are the less exotic specimens. Worst of all, however, are the Flying Saucerers: no cure short of mayhem has yet been discovered for them.

It was a black day when one of the leading exponents of the Flying Saucer religion discovered our

hideout and fell upon us with shrill cries of delight.
Here, he obviously told himself, was fertile ground
for his missionary activities. People who were already interested in spaceflight, and even wrote
books and stories about its imminent achievement,
would be a pushover. He opened his little black bag
and produced the latest pile of sauceriana.

It was quite a collection. There were some interesting photographs of flying saucers made by an
amateur astronomer who lives right beside Green-
wich Observatory, and whose busy camera has re-
corded such a remarkable variety of spaceships, in
all shapes and sizes, that one wonders what the pro-
fessionals next door are doing for their salaries.
Then there was a long statement from a gentleman
in Texas who had just had a casual chat with the
occupants of a saucer making a wayside halt on
route to Venus. Language, it seemed, had presented
no difficulties: it had taken about ten minutes of
arm-waving to get from "Me—Man. This—Earth"
to highly esoteric information about the use of the
fourth dimension in space travel.

The masterpiece, however, was an excited letter
from a character in South Dakota who had actually
been offered a lift in a flying saucer, and had been
taken for a spin round the Moon. He explained at
some length how the saucer travelled by hauling
itself along magnetic lines of force, rather like a
spider going up its thread.

It was at this point that Harry Purvis rebelled.
He had been listening with a professional pride to
tales which even he would never have dared to spin,
for he was an expert at detecting the yield-point of
his audience's credulity. At the mention of lines of
magnetic force, however, his scientific training
overcame his frank admiration of these latter-day
Munchausens, and he gave a snort of disgust.

"That's a lot of nonsense," he said. "I can prove it
to you—magnetism's my speciality."

"Last week," said Drew sweetly, as he filled two

glasses of Ale at once, "you said that crystal structure was your speciality."

Harry gave him a superior smile.

"I'm a *general* specialist," he said loftily. "To get back to where I was before that interruption, the point I want to make is that there's no such thing as a line of magnetic force. It's a mathematical fiction —exactly on a par with lines of longitude or latitude. Now, if anyone said they'd invented a machine that worked by pulling itself along parallels of latitude, everybody would know that they were talking drivel. But because few people know much about magnetism, and it sounds rather mysterious, crackpots like this guy in South Dakota can get away with the tripe we've just been hearing."

There's one charming characteristic about the White Hart—we may fight among each other, but we show an impressive solidarity in times of crisis. Everyone felt that something had to be done about our unwelcome visitor: for one thing, he was interfering with the serious business of drinking. Fanaticism of any kind casts a gloom over the most festive assembly, and several of the regulars had shown signs of leaving despite the fact that it was still two hours to closing time.

So when Harry Purvis followed up his attack by concocting the most outrageous story that even he had ever presented in the White Hart, no one interrupted him or tried to expose the weak points in his narrative. We knew that Harry was acting for us all—he was fighting fire with fire, as it were. And we knew that he wasn't expecting us to believe him (if indeed he ever did), so we just sat back and enjoyed ourselves.

"If you want to know how to propel spaceships," began Harry, "and mark you, I'm not saying anything one way or the other about the existence of flying saucers—then you must forget magnetism. You must go straight to gravity—that's the basic force of the universe, after all. But it's going to be a tricky force to handle, and if you don't believe me just listen to what happened only last year to a scientist down in Australia. I shouldn't really tell you this, I suppose, because I'm not sure of its security classification, but if there's any trouble I'll swear that I never said a word.

"The Aussies, as you may know, have always been pretty hot on scientific research, and they had one team working on fast reactors—those housebroken atomic bombs which are so much more compact than the old uranium piles. The head of the group was a bright but rather impetuous young nuclear physicist I'll call Dr. Cavor. That, of course, wasn't his real name, but it's a very appropriate one. You'll all recollect, I'm sure, the scientist Cavor in Wells' *First Men in the Moon,* and the wonderful gravity-screening material cavorite he discovered?

"I'm afraid dear old Wells didn't go into the question of cavorite very thoroughly. As he put it, it was opaque to gravity just as a sheet of metal is opaque to light. Anything placed above a horizontal sheet of cavorite, therefore, became weightless and floated up into space.

"Well, it isn't as simple as that. Weight represents energy—an enormous amount of it—which can't just be destroyed without any fuss. You'd have to put a terrific amount of work into even a small object in order to make it weightless. Antigravity screens of the cavorite type, therefore, are quite impossible—they're in the same class as perpetual motion."

"Three of my friends have made perpetual motion machines," began our unwanted visitor rather stuffily. Harry didn't let him get any further: he just steamed on and ignored the interruption.

"Now, our Australian Dr. Cavor wasn't searching for antigravity, or anything like it. In pure science, you can be pretty sure that nothing fundamental is ever discovered by anyone who's actually looking for it—that's half the fun of the game. Dr. Cavor was interested in producing atomic power: what he

found was antigravity. And it was quite some time
before he realised that was what he'd discovered.

"What happened, I gather, was this: The reactor
was of a novel and rather daring design, and there
was quite a possibility that it might blow up when
the last pieces of fissile material were inserted. So it
was assembled by remote control in one of Australia's numerous convenient deserts, all the final
operations being observed through TV sets.

"Well, there was no explosion—which would
have caused a nasty radioactive mess and wasted a
lot of money, but wouldn't have damaged anything
except a lot of reputations. What actually happened
was much more unexpected, and much more difficult to explain.

"When the last piece of enriched uranium was
inserted, the control rods pulled out, and the reactor
brought up to criticality—everything went dead.
The meters in the remote control room, two miles
from the reactor, all dropped back to zero. The TV
screen went blank. Cavor and his colleagues waited
for the bang, but there wasn't one. They looked at
each other for a moment with many wild surmises:
then, without a word, they climbed up out of the
buried control chamber.

"The reactor building was completely unchanged:
it sat out there in the desert, a commonplace cube of
brick holding a million pounds' worth of fissile material and several years of careful design and development. Cavor wasted no time: he grabbed the
Jeep, switched on a portable Geiger counter, and
hurried off to see what had happened.

"He recovered consciousness in hospital a couple
of hours later. There was little wrong with him
apart from a bad headache, which was nothing to
the one his experiment was going to give him during the next few days. It seemed that when he got to
within twenty feet of the reactor, his Jeep had hit
something with a terrific crash. Cavor had got tan-
gled in the steering wheel and had a nice collection
of bruises: the Geiger counter, oddly enough, was

quite undamaged and was still clucking away
quietly to itself, detecting no more than the normal
cosmic-ray background.

"Seen from a distance, it had looked a perfectly
normal sort of accident, that might have been
caused by the Jeep going into a rut. But Cavor
hadn't been driving all that fast, luckily for him;
and anyway there was no rut at the scene of the
crash. What the Jeep had run into was something
quite impossible. It was an invisible wall, apparently the lower rim of a hemispherical dome, which
entirely surrounded the reactor. Stones thrown up
in the air slid back to the ground along the surface
of this dome, and it also extended underground as
far as digging could be carried out. It seemed as if
the reactor was at the exact center of an impenetra-
ble, spherical shell.

"Of course, this was marvellous news and Cavor
was out of bed in no time, scattering nurses in all
directions. He had no idea what had happened, but
it was a lot more exciting than the humdrum piece
of nuclear engineering that had started the whole
business.

"By now you're probably all wondering what the
devil a sphere of force—as you science-fiction
writers would call it—has to do with antigravity.
So I'll jump several days and give you the answers
that Cavor and his team discovered only after much
hard work and the consumption of many gallons of
that potent Australian Beer.

"The reactor, when it had been energised, had
somehow produced an antigravity field. All the
matter inside a twenty-foot-radius sphere had been
made weightless, and the enormous amount of energy needed to do this had been extracted, in some
utterly mysterious manner, from the uranium in
the pile. Calculations showed that the amount of
energy in the reactor was just sufficient to do the
job. Presumably the sphere of force would have
been larger still if there had been more ergs available in the power source.

"I can hear someone just waiting to ask a question, so I'll anticipate them. Why didn't this weightless sphere of earth and air float up into space? Well, the earth was held together by its cohesion, anyway, so there was no reason why it should go wandering off. As for the air, that was forced to stay inside the zone of zero gravity for a most surprising and subtle reason which leads me to the crux of this whole peculiar business.

"Better fasten your seat belts for the next bit: we've got a bumpy passage ahead. Those of you who know something about potential theory won't have any trouble, and I'll do my best to make it as easy as I can for the rest.

"People who talk glibly about antigravity seldom stop to consider its implications, so let's look at a few fundamentals. As I've already said, weight implies energy—lots of it. That energy is entirely due to Earth's gravity field. *If you remove an object's weight,* that's precisely equivalent to taking it clear outside Earth's gravity. And any rocket engineer will tell you how much energy *that* requires."

Harry turned to me and said: "There's an analogy I'd like to borrow from one of your books, Arthur, that puts across the point I'm trying to make. You know—comparing the fight against Earth's gravity to climbing out of a deep pit."

"You're welcome," I said. "I pinched it from Doc Richardson, anyway."

"Oh," replied Harry. "I thought it was too good to be original. Well, here we go. If you hang on to this really very simple idea, you'll be O.K. To take an object clear away from the Earth requires as much work as lifting it *four thousand miles* against the steady drag of normal gravity. Now, the matter inside Cavor's zone of force was still on the Earth's surface, but it was weightless. From the energy point of view, therefore, it was outside the Earth's gravity field. It was inaccessible as if it was on top of a four-thousand-mile-high mountain.

"Cavor could stand outside the antigravity zone

and look into it from a point a few inches away. To cross those few inches, he would have to do as much work as if he climbed Everest seven hundred times. It wasn't surprising that the Jeep stopped in a hurry. No material object had stopped it, but from the point of view of dynamics it had run smack into a cliff four thousand miles high....

"I can see some blank looks that are not entirely due to the lateness of the hour. Never mind: if you don't get all this, just take my word for it. It won't spoil your appreciation of what follows—at least, I hope not.

"Cavor had realised at once that he had made one of the most important discoveries of the age, though it was some time before he worked out just what was going on. The final clue to the antigravitational nature of the field came when they shot a rifle bullet into it and observed the trajectory with a high-speed camera. Ingenious, don't you think?

"The next problem was to experiment with the field's generator and to find just what had happened inside the reactor when it had been switched on. This was a problem indeed. The reactor was there in plain sight, twenty feet away. But to reach it would require slightly more energy than going to the Moon....

"Cavor was not disheartened by this, nor by the inexplicable failure of the reactor to respond to any of its remote controls. He theorised that it had been completely drained of energy, if one can use a rather misleading term, and that little if any power was needed to maintain the antigravity field once it had been set up. This was one of the many things that could only be determined by examination on the spot. So by hook or by crook, Dr. Cavor would have to go there.

"His first idea was to use an electrically driven trolley, supplied with power through cables which it dragged behind it as it advanced into the field. A hundred-horsepower generator, running continuously for seventeen hours, would supply enough energy to take a man of average weight on the perilous twenty-foot journey. A velocity of slightly over a foot an hour did not seem much to boast about, until you remembered that advancing one foot into the antigravity field was equivalent to a two-hundred-mile vertical climb.

"The theory was sound, but in practice the electric trolley wouldn't work. It started to push its way into the field, but began to skid after it had traversed half an inch. The reason was obvious when one started to think about it. Though the power was there, the traction wasn't. No wheeled vehicle could climb a gradient of two hundred miles per foot.

"This minor setback did not discourage Dr. Cavor. The answer, he realised at once, was to produce the traction at a point outside the field. When you wanted to lift a load vertically, you didn't use a cart: you used a jack or an hydraulic ram.

"The result of this argument was one of the oddest vehicles ever built. A small but comfortable cage, containing sufficient provisions to last a man for several days, was mounted at the end of a twenty-foot-long horizontal girder. The whole device was supported off the ground by balloon tires, and the theory was that the cage could be pushed right into the centre of the field by a machine which would remain outside its influence. After some thought, it was decided that the best prime mover would be the common or garden bulldozer.

"A test was made with some rabbits in the passenger compartment—and I can't help thinking that there was an interesting psychological point here. The experimenters were trying to get it both ways: as scientists they'd be pleased if their subjects got back alive, and as Australians they'd be just as happy if they got back dead. But perhaps I'm being a little too fanciful.... (You know, of course, how Australians feel about rabbits.)

"The bulldozer chugged away hour after hour, forcing the weight of the girder and its insignificant payload up the enormous gradient. It was an uncanny sight—all this energy being expended to move a couple of rabbits twenty feet across a perfectly horizontal plain. The subjects of the experiment could be observed throughout the operation: they seemed to be perfectly happy and quite unaware of their historic rôle.

"The passenger compartment reached the centre of the field, was held there for an hour, and then the girder was slowly backed out again. The rabbits were alive, in good health, and to nobody's particular surprise there were now six of them.

"Dr. Cavor, naturally, insisted on being the first human being to venture into a zero-gravity field. He loaded up the compartment with torsion balances, radiation detectors, and periscopes so that he could look into the reactor when he finally got to it. Then he gave the signal, the bulldozer started chugging, and the strange journey began.

"There was, naturally, telephone communication from the passenger compartment to the outside world. Ordinary sound waves couldn't cross the barrier, for reasons which were still a little obscure, but radio and telephone both worked without difficulty. Cavor kept up a running commentary as he was edged forward into the field, describing his own reactions and relaying instrument readings to his colleagues.

"The first thing that happened to him, though he had expected it, was nevertheless rather unsettling. During the first few inches of his advance, as he moved through the fringe of the field, the direction of the vertical seemed to swing around. 'Up' was no longer toward the sky: it was now in the direction of the reactor hut. To Cavor, it felt as if he was being pushed up the face of a vertical cliff, with the reactor twenty feet above him. For the first time, his eyes and his ordinary human senses told him the same story as his scientific training. He could *see* that the centre of the field was, gravitywise, higher than the place from which he had come. However, imagination still boggled at the thought of all the

energy it would need to climb that innocent-looking
twenty feet, and the hundreds of gallons of diesel
fuel that must be burned to get him there.

"There was nothing else of interest to report on
the journey itself, and at last, twenty hours after he
had started, Cavor arrived at his destination. The
wall of the reactor hut was right beside him, though
to him it seemed not a wall but an unsupported
floor sticking out at right angles from the cliff up
which he had risen. The entrance was just above his
head, like a trapdoor through which he would have
to climb. This would present no great difficulty, for
Dr. Cavor was an energetic young man, extremely
eager to find just how he had created this miracle.

"Slightly too eager, in fact. For as he tried to
work his way into the door, he slipped and fell off
the platform that had carried him there.

"That was the last anyone ever saw of him—but
it wasn't the last they heard of him. Oh dear no! He
made a very big noise indeed....

"You'll see why when you consider the situation
in which this unfortunate scientist now found himself. Hundreds of kilowatt-hours of energy had been
pushed into him—enough to lift him to the Moon
and beyond. All that work had been needed to take
him to a point of zero gravitational potential. As
soon as he lost his means of support, that energy
began to reappear. To get back to our earlier and
very picturesque analogy—the poor doctor had
slipped off the edge of the four-thousand-mile-high
mountain he had ascended.

"He fell back the twenty feet that had taken almost a day to climb. 'Ah, what a fall was there, my
countrymen!' It was precisely equivalent, in terms
of energy, to a free drop from the remotest stars
down to the surface of the Earth. And you all know
how much velocity an object acquires in *that* fall.
It's the same velocity that's needed to get it there in
the first place—the famous velocity of escape.
Seven miles a second, or twenty-five thousand miles
an hour.

"That's what Dr. Cavor was doing by the time he got back to his starting point. Or to be more accurate, that's the speed he involuntarily tried to reach. As soon as he passed Mach 1 or 2, however, air resistance began to have its little say. Dr. Cavor's funeral pyre was the finest, and indeed the only, meteor display ever to take place entirely at sea level....

"I'm sorry that this story hasn't got a happy ending. In fact, it hasn't got an ending at all, because that sphere of zero gravitational potential is still sitting there in the Australian desert, apparently doing nothing at all but in fact producing ever-increasing amounts of frustration in scientific and official circles. I don't see *how* the authorities can hope to keep it secret much longer. Sometimes I think how odd it is that the world's tallest mountain is in Australia—and that though it's four thousand miles high the airliners often fly right over it without knowing it's there."

You will hardly be surprised to hear that H. Purvis finished his narration at this point: even he could hardly take it much further, and no one wanted him to. We were all, including his most tenacious critics, lost in admiring awe. I have since detected six fallacies of a fundamental nature in his description of Dr. Cavor's Frankensteinian fate, but at the time they never even occurred to me. (And I don't propose to reveal them now. They will be left, as the mathematics textbooks put it, as an exercise for the reader.) What had earned our undying gratitude, however, was the fact that at some slight sacrifice of truth he had managed to keep flying saucers from invading the White Hart. It was almost closing time, and too late for our visitor to make a counterattack.

That is why the sequel seems a little unfair. A month later, someone brought a very odd publication to one of our meetings. It was nicely printed and laid out with professional skill, the misuse of which was sad to behold. The thing was called *Fly-*

ing Saucer Revelations—and there on the front
page was a full and detailed account of the story
Purvis had told us. It was printed absolutely
straight—and what was much worse than that,
from poor Harry's point of view, was that it was at-
tributed to him by name.

Since then he has had 4,375 letters on the subject, most of them from California: 24 called him a
liar; 4,205 believed him absolutely. (The remaining
ones he couldn't decipher and their contents still remain a matter of speculation.)

I'm afraid he's never quite got over it, and I
sometimes think he's going to spend the rest of his
life trying to stop people believing the one story he
never expected to be taken seriously.

There may be a moral here. For the life of me I
can't find it.

Arthur C. Clarke's famous collection, Tales from
the White Hart, *was apparently inspired in part by
Dunsany's Jorkens series, quite independently of the
Pratt and de Camp series about Gavagan's Bar.*

*Mr. Clarke commented that readers often ask him
if the White Hart actually existed. "Well, it did; I
based the background (and some incidental characters) in the White Horse, which was in Fetter Lane,
just north of Fleet Street in London. In the years immediately after World War II, this was the weekly
rendezvous of the London science-fiction commu-
nity."*

The author also wrote 2001 *and* 2010, *among
other best-selling science-fiction novels. He is chan-
cellor of the University of Sri Lanka (formerly Cey-
lon), where he now lives, and is the inventor of the
stationary-orbit communications satellite, for which
—alas!—he receives no royalties.*

SOCIAL LAPSES

by Darrell Schweitzer

A slime-beast from Fomulhaut Five,
quite drunk in an old spaceport dive,
    proposed to nine men,
    six cats, and a hen,
and bar stools, at least twenty-five.

Clearly there are some forms of the SF bar story shorter than anything possible in prose. Darrell Schweitzer, who has recently "journeymanned" the limerick, as he puts it, has been writing fiction longer than that, and is the author of numerous short stories; a story-cycle, We Are All Legends; *and a novel,* The Shattered Goddess. *He has edited several nonfiction anthologies, most recently* Discovering Stephen King. *He also wrote a Conan novel, then rewrote it as a limerick.*

ONE FOR THE ROAD

by Gardner Dozois

"I believe that it is illegal for a bar not to have a TV set."

I don't go to bars much—I got out of the habit when my generation was "into" sitting around in rooms with posters of Ché on the wall and passing funny little cigarettes back and forth, and even now that we're all middle-class again, with mortgages and potbellies and expense accounts, and my idea of a pleasant evening well-spent no longer consists of listening to the same side of a Grateful Dead album thirty-five times in a row, even now I haven't really gotten back into the swing of being a barfly again.

Still, every now and then, like tonight, I'll want to put down a few drinks on the way back from work, to fortify myself to face life in the haven of domestic tranquility I call home. Last night had been particularly rough, and I'd been getting these blistering, vindictive phone calls from Stacy all day, the kind of call where she starts screaming and

slams the receiver down halfway through...but
you don't want to hear about that. Suffice it to say
that it was one of the few nights of the year when I
wanted to get drunk, wanted that mean, bleak, self-
pitying edge that only lots of quickly ingested alcohol can give you, no more euphoric drug need
apply...and unless you're a back-alley wino, the
only place to do that kind of serious, solitary, and
sorrowful drinking is in a bar.

Trouble is, I don't *like* most bars—either they're
assembly-line pickup joints for horny suburbanities
who are looking for their own Mr. Goodbar, or
they're glitter palaces full of trendy people dancing
to disco music and smiling at their own reflections
in each other's mirror sunglasses, or they're places
with sawdust on the floor where rednecks and
urban cowboys watch football on a blaring TV set
and wait for a good excuse to beat the crap out of
each other. "Not my bag," as we used to say back in
the days when it was obligatory for everybody to
say things like that. I did know one fairly decent
place, though, on a shady side street near the Institute and the Museum, and that's where I ended up.

I'd been in there once or twice while I was working on the film about the metric system with some
of the Museum staffers, and I'd liked it there. It
was a quiet little place, lit dimly enough to avoid
glare but not dimly enough to become Hernando's
Hideaway, drawing a clientele mostly composed of
professional people and technical people, with an
occasional scattering of footsore tourists recuperat-
ing from the Grand Tour of the Museum. There was
no jukebox or Space Invaders game. There was a TV
set, of course—in fact, I believe that it is illegal for
a bar *not* to have one—and it may even have been
tuned to a football game, but its volume control was
kept low enough so that it hardly mattered, except
to those clustered at that end of the bar.

I was all the way at the other end of the bar,
which was somewhat crowded tonight, and had just
gotten outside of my first solitary drink, staring

glumly at myself in the mirror and feeling like Philip Marlowe during one of his whinier paragraphs, when the man came into the bar and sat down beside me on the only unoccupied stool.

He was wearing a well-cut but somewhat rumpled suit, wire-rimmed glasses, and wore his hair just a bit longer than the modish nape-of-the-neck length that is the mark of conformity now that the real avant-gardists are affecting Mohawk hairdos and boot-camp skincuts. He was somewhere in his late forties or early fifties, with one of those smooth, rubbery faces that made it difficult to tell which. I had seen that young-old face somewhere before, although I was having difficulty remembering just where. He flagged down the bartender—who said something to him in the jocular tone that bartenders reserve for regulars—and was served a healthy Double-Knock, which he immediately poured down his throat, all at once, as if it were iced tea. He set the glass down, had it refilled, and tossed it off again. Then—while the bartender was pouring his third drink—he took off his wristwatch and held it up close to his face with both hands. "About five hours to midnight," he announced aloud to no one in particular, "maybe a little more, maybe a little less." He dived into his third drink. The watch he put carefully down on the bar in front of him. It was one of the newest and most expensive of digital watches, with more controls than the cockpit of a 747, and must have cost at least five hundred dollars.

I had been watching all this out of the corner of my eye, mildly intrigued in spite of my better judgment. He felt my eyes on him. He scowled, tossed down the rest of his drink, and then turned his head toward me. "Do you know anything about quantum mechanics?" he asked in a conversational voice. "About the electromagnetic generation of instabilities? About runaway oscillation? About black holes?"

"Not a damn thing," I said cheerfully. My field is computer graphics.

"Good," he said. He fell silent, staring into his glass, and after a few moments I realized that he wasn't going to say anything more.

I sighed. I never could leave well enough alone. "Why did you ask me that?" I said.

"What?" he replied absently. He was staring at his watch in a preoccupied way, occasionally pinging the dial face with a fingernail.

"If I know anything about black holes."

He turned to look at me again, hesitated, and then called for the bartender to give him another drink. I let the bartender hit me again also. When our glasses were full, he raised his to his lips, but took only a small sip this time before setting it down again. "When I was at school," he said ruminatively, glancing at me again, "there was, appropriately enough, a rather sophomoric little game that we used to occasionally play at parties. It consisted of asking everyone there what they would do if they knew—knew without the possibility of a doubt—that the world was going to come to an end that evening. A stupid game, but if enough people answered you began to notice some interesting patterns."

"Such as?" I said. My years as a doper had given me a great deal of tolerance for nonlinear conversations.

He smiled approvingly at me. "After a while, you'd notice that there were really only three basic answers to the question. Some people would say that they'd spend their remaining time screwing, or eating an enormous meal, or getting drunk or stoned, or listening to their favorite music, or walking in the woods... or whatever. This is basically the sensualist's reply, the Dionysian reply. Other people would say that they would try to escape somehow, no matter how hopeless it looked, that they'd spend their last moments searching frantically for some life-sparing loophole in whatever doom was posited—this is either the pragmatist's reply or the wishful thinker's reply, depending on how you look at it. The remaining people would say that they would try to come to terms with the on-coming doom, accept it, settle their own minds and try to find peace within themselves; they'd medi-tate, or pray, or sit quietly at home with their fami-lies and loved ones, cherishing each other as they waited for the end—this is basically the Apollonian reply, the mystic's reply." He smiled. "There was some blurring of categories, of course: sometimes the loophole-seeking response would be to petition God to intervene and stop the catastrophe, and sometimes there would be a sensual edge to the lav-ishness of the orgy of meditation the contemplatives were planning to indulge in...but for the most part, the categories were valid."

He paused to down about half of his drink, swishing it around in his mouth before swallowing, as if he were about to gargle with it. "The next question we'd ask them," he said, "was even more revealing. We'd ask them: If you were the only one who *knew* that the world was about to end, would you tell anyone else? The mystics almost always said that they would tell, to give people time to pre-pare their souls; at the very least, they would tell those people they loved the most. Some of the loop-hole-seekers said that they would tell, give every-one a chance to find their own loopholes; some said that they wouldn't tell, that their own chances for survival would be better if they didn't have to con-tend with a worldwide panic; and some said that they'd just tell a small circle of like-minded friends —depends on just how pragmatic they were, I guess. Almost all of the sensualists said that they would *not* tell, that it was kinder if everyone else— and particularly their loved ones—could enjoy their last hours without knowing the shadow that was hanging over them...although at least one sensua-list said that the only sensual pleasure he would *get* out of the whole thing would be the fun of telling everyone else the bad news..."

Moving with exaggerated care, he polished off his drink and set it carefully back on the water ring it had made on the bar top. He turned to face me again. "Would *you* tell anyone, if you knew?"

I thought about it. "If I did, would there be anything anybody could do to stop it from happening?"

"Nothing at all."

"Any way that anybody could escape from it?"

"Not unless they can figure out a way to get clean off the planet in above five hours' time."

"In that case..." I said, fingering my chin, "in that case, I don't think I would say anything."

"Good," the man said, "then I won't either."

He got up off the stool and strode out of the place, leaving his five-hundred-dollar watch on the bar.

The bartender drifted over to see if he could con me into a refill. "Who was that weirdo?" I said.

"Jeez," the bartender said, "I thought you knew him. That was Dr. Fine, from over at the Institute."

Then I remembered where I'd seen that young-old face: it had been staring at me out of a recent *Time* cover, accompanying an article that hailed Dr. Fine as one of the most brilliant experimental physicists in the world.

It's been about an hour now, and I keep looking at Dr. Fine's watch, toying with it, pushing it around on top of the bar with my finger. It's a damn expensive watch, and I keep thinking that soon he'll notice that it's gone, that he'll certainly come back into the bar for it in a moment or two.

But I'm starting to get worried.

Gardner Dozois reports that he has actually asked many people the question raised in this story, and that the replies tend to fall into the categories he

*has reported, save for the one woman who wanted
to spend her last hours flying out to California to
punch a certain controversial writer in the nose.
What would Dozois do if the world were about to
end? "In reality, go out and find some loophole," he
says.*

*The optimistic Mr. Dozois made a very distin-
guished beginning to his career in the early 1970s,
with so many stories being nominated for awards
(but, alas, never winning) that he founded the still-
flourishing Hugo and Nebula Losers' Club, from
which he was summarily expelled when he won a
Nebula for "The Peacemaker" in 1984. He is the author of the novel* Strangers *and the collection* The
Visible Man, *and has edited many anthologies, including the ongoing series* The World's Best Science
Fiction. *He is now the editor of* Isaac Asimov's
Science Fiction Magazine.

ELEPHAS FRUMENTI

by L. Sprague de Camp and Fletcher Pratt

Gavagan's is an old-fashioned bar, somewhere in the northeastern United States in the 1950s.

The thin, balding man in tweeds almost tipped over his glass as he set it down with a care that showed care had become necessary. "Think of dogs," he said. "Really, my dear, there is no practical limit to what can be accomplished by selective breeding."

"Except that where I come from, we sometimes think of other things," said the brass-blonde, emphasizing the ancient *New Yorker* joke with a torso-wiggle that was pure *Police Gazette*.

Mr. Witherwax lifted his nose from the second Martini. "Do you know them, Mr. Cohan?" he asked.

Mr. Cohan turned in profile to swab a glass. "That would be Professor Thott, and a very educated gentleman, too. I don't rightly know the name of the lady, though I think he has been calling her

Ellie, or something like that. Would you like to be meeting them, now?"

"Sure. I was reading in a book about this selective breeding, but I don't understand it so good, and maybe he could tell me something about it."

Mr. Cohan made his way to the end of the bar and led ponderously toward the table. "Pleased to meet you, Professor Thott," said Witherwax.

"Sir, the pleasure is all mine, all mine. Mrs. Jonas, may I present an old friend of mine, yclept Witherwax? Old in the sense that he is aged in the admirable liquids produced by Gavagan's, while the liquids themselves are aged in wood, ha-ha—a third-premise aging. Sit down, Mr. Witherwax. I call your attention to the remarkable qualities of alcohol, among which *peripeteia* is not the least."

"Yeah, that's right," said Mr. Witherwax, his expression taking on a resemblance to that of the stuffed owl over the bar. "What I was going to ask—"

"Sir, I perceive that I have employed a pedantry more suitable to the classroom, with the result that communication has not been established. *Peripeteia* is the reversal of rôles. While in a state of saintly sobriety, I pursue Mrs. Jonas; I entice her to alcoholic diversions. But after the third Presidente, she pursues me, in accordance with the ancient biological rule that alcohol increases feminine desire while decreasing masculine potency."

From the bar, Mr. Cohan appeared to have caught only a part of this speech. "Rolls we ain't got," he said. "But you can have some pretzel sticks." He reached under the bar for the bowl. "All gone; and I just laid out a new box this morning. That's where Gavagan's profits go. In the old days it was the free lunch, and now it's pretzel sticks."

"What I was going to ask—" said Witherwax.

Professor Thott stood up and bowed, a bow which ended in his sitting down again rather suddenly. "Ah, the mystery of the universe and music of the spheres, as Prospero might have phrased it! Who pursues? Who flies? The wicked. One preserves philosophy by remaining at the Platonian mean, the knife edge between pursuit and flight, wickedness and virtue. Mr. Cohan, a round of Presidentes, please, including one for my aged friend."

"Let me buy this one," said Witherwax firmly. "What I was going to ask was about this selective breeding."

The professor shook himself, blinked twice, leaned back in his chair, and placed one hand on the table. "You wish me to be academic? Very well; but I have witnesses that it was at your own request."

Mrs. Jonas said: "Now look what you've done: You've got him started and he won't run down until he falls asleep."

"What I want to know—" began Witherwax, but Thott beamingly cut across: "I shall present only the briefest and most nontechnical of outlines," he said. "Let us suppose that, of sixteen mice, you took the two largest and bred them together. Their children would in turn be mated with those of the largest pair from another group of sixteen. And so on. Given time and material enough, and making it advantageous to the species to produce larger members, it would be easy to produce mice the size of lions."

"Ugh!" said Mrs. Jonas. "You ought to give up drinking. Your imagination gets gruesome."

"I see," said Witherwax, "like in a book I read once where they had rats so big they ate horses, and wasps the size of dogs."

"I recall the volume," said Thott, sipping his Presidente. "It was *The Food of the Gods,* by H. G. Wells. I fear, however, that the method he describes was not that of genetics and therefore had no scientific validity."

"But could you make things like that by selective breeding?" asked Witherwax.

"Certainly. You could produce houseflies the size of tigers. It is merely a matter of—"

Mrs. Jonas raised a hand. "Alvin, what an awful thought. I hope you don't ever try it."

"There need be no cause for apprehension, my dear. The square-cube law will forever protect us from such a visitation."

"Huh?" said Witherwax.

"The square-cube law. If you double the dimensions, you quadruple the area and octuple the masses. The result is—well, in a practical nontechnical sense, a tiger-sized housefly would have legs too thin and wings too small to support his weight."

Mrs. Jonas said: "Alvin, that's impractical. How could it move?"

The professor essayed another bow, which was even less successful than the first, since it was made from a sitting position. "Madame, the purpose of such an experiment would not be practical but demonstrative. A tiger-sized fly would be a mass of jelly that would have to be fed from a spoon." He raised a hand. "There is no reason why anyone should produce such a monster; and since nature has no advantages to offer insects of large size, it will decline to produce them. I agree that the thought is repulsive; myself, I should prefer the alternative project of producing elephants the size of flies—or swallows."

Witherwax beckoned to Mr. Cohan. "These are good. Do it again. But wouldn't your square-cube law get you in Dutch there, too?"

"By no means, sir. In the case of size reduction, it works in your favor. The mass is divided by eight, but the muscles remain proportionately the same, capable of supporting a vastly greater weight. The legs and wings of a tiny elephant would not only support him, but give him the agility of a hummingbird. Consider the dwarf elephant of Sicily during the Plish—"

"Alvin," said Mrs. Jonas, "you're drunk. Otherwise you'd remember how to pronounce Pleistocene, and you wouldn't be talking about elephants' wings."

"Not at all, my dear. I should confidently expect such a species to develop flight by means of enlarged ears, like the Dumbo of the movies."

Mrs. Jonas giggled. "Still, I wouldn't want one the size of a housefly. It would be too small for a pet and would get into things. Let's make it the size of a kitten, like this." She held out her index fingers about five inches apart.

"Very well, my dear," said the professor. "As soon as I can obtain a grant from the Carnegie Foundation, the project will be undertaken."

"Yes, but," said Witherwax, "how would you feed an elephant like that? And could they be housebroke?"

"If you can housebreak a man, an elephant ought to be easy," said Mrs. Jonas. "And you could feed them oats or hay. Much cleaner than keeping cans of dog food around."

The professor rubbed his chin. "Hmm," he said. "The rate of absorption of nourishment would vary directly as the intestinal area—which would vary as the square of the dimensions—I'm not sure of the results, but I'm afraid we'd have to provide more concentrated and less conventional food. I presume that we could feed our *Elephas micros,* as I propose to call him, on lump sugar. No, not *Elephas micros, Elephas microtatus,* the 'utmost littlest, tiniest elephant.'"

Mr. Cohan, who had been neglecting his only other customer to lean on the bar in their direction, spoke up: "Mr. Considine, that's the salesman, was telling me that the most concentrated food you can get is good Malt Whiskey."

"That's it!" The professor slapped the table. "Not *Elephas microtatus* but *Elephas frumenti,* the Whiskey elephant, from what he lives on. We'll breed them for a diet of alcohol. High energy content."

"Oh, but that won't do," protested Mrs. Jonas. "Nobody would want a house pet that had to be fed on Whiskey all the time. Especially with children around."

Said Witherwax: "Look, if you really want these animals, why don't you keep them some place where children aren't around and Whiskey is—bars, for instance."

"Profound observation," said Professor Thott. "And speaking of rounds, Mr. Cohan, let us have another. We have horses as outdoor pets, cats as house pets, canaries as cage pets. Why not an animal especially designed and developed to be a bar pet? Speaking of which—that stuffed owl you keep for a pet, Mr. Cohan, is getting decidedly mangy."

"They would steal things like that," said Mrs. Jonas dreamily. "They would take things like owls' feathers and pretzel sticks and beer mats to build their nests with, up in the dark corners somewhere near the ceiling. They would come out at night—"

The professor bent a benignant gaze on her as Mr. Cohan set out the drinks. "My dear," he said, "either this discussion of the future *Elephas frumenti* or the actual *spiritus frumenti* is going to your head. When you become poetical—"

The brass-blonde had leaned back and was looking upward. "I'm not poetical. That thing right up there on top of the pillar is the nest of one of your bar elephants."

"What thing up there?" said Thott.

"That thing up there, where it's so dark."

"I don't see nothing," said Mr. Cohan, "and if you don't mind my saying so, this is a clean bar, not a rat in the place."

"They wouldn't be quite tame, ever," said Mrs. Jonas, still looking upward, "and if they didn't feel they were fed enough, they'd come and take for themselves when the bartender wasn't looking."

"That does look funny," said Thott, pushing his chair back and beginning to climb on it.

"Don't, Alvin," said Mrs. Jonas. "You'll break your neck.... Think of it, they'd feed their children—"

"Stand by me, then, and let me put my hand on your shoulder."

"Hey!" said Witherwax suddenly. "Who drank my drink?"

Mrs. Jonas lowered her eyes. "Didn't you?"

"I didn't even touch it. Mr. Cohan just put it down, didn't you?"

"I did that. But that would be a couple of minutes back, and maybe you could—"

"I could not. I definitely, positively did not drink —hey, you people, look at the table!"

"If I had my other glasses..." said Thott, swaying somewhat uncertainly as he peered upward into the shadows.

"Look at the table," repeated Witherwax, pointing.

The glass that had held his drink was empty. Thott's still held about half a cocktail. Mrs. Jonas' glass lay on its side, and from its lip about a thimbleful of Presidente cocktail had flowed pinkly into an irregular patch the size of a child's hand.

As the other two followed Witherwax's finger, they saw that, from this patch, a line of little damp footprints led across the table to the far edge, where they suddenly ceased. They were circular, each about the size of a dime, with a small scalloped front edge, as if made by...

L. Sprague de Camp is the author of numerous science-fiction classics, including Lest Darkness Fall, Rogue Queen, *and* The Hand of Zei. *Fletcher Pratt wrote two distinguished fantasy novels,* The Well of the Unicorn *and* The Blue Star, *along with much science fiction. Together, the two of them formed one of the most successful collaborative teams in the history of the field, producing the clas-*

sic Harold Shea series (The Incomplete Enchanter, etc.) *and* Tales from Gavagan's Bar.

De Camp describes "Elephas Frumenti" as one of his first fictional efforts after World War II, written in late 1948. He recalls further, "The general idea of a series of barroom tales, as well as the basic idea for the present story, were Fletcher Pratt's. When Pratt and I collaborated, we thrashed out the plot together; I wrote a rough draft, and he wrote the final." Over the next five years, they wrote twenty-nine Gavagan's stories; but then Pratt shifted more to nonfiction, and in 1956 suddenly died. De Camp remains reluctant to produce one more story by himself, so the thirtieth, about a vampire with a sweet tooth that only attacked diabetics, must remain unwritten.

UNICORN VARIATION

by Roger Zelazny

A deserted bar in a ghost town in the American
Southwest...

A bizarrerie of fires, cunabulum of light, it
moved with a deft, almost dainty deliberation,
phasing into and out of existence like a storm-shot
piece of evening; or perhaps the darkness between
the flares was more akin to its truest nature—swirl
of black ashes assembled in prancing cadence to the
lowing note of desert wind down the arroyo behind
buildings as empty yet filled as the pages of unread
books or stillnesses between the notes of a song.

Gone again. Back again. Again.

Power, you said? Yes. It takes considerable force
of identity to manifest before or after one's time. Or
both.

As it faded and gained it also advanced, moving
through the warm afternoon, its tracks erased by
the wind. That is, on those occasions when there
were tracks.

A reason. There should always be a reason. Or reasons.

It knew why it was there—but not why it was *there,* in that particular locale.

It anticipated learning this shortly, as it approached the desolation-bound line of the old street. However, it knew that the reason may also come before, or after. Yet again, the pull was there and the force of its being was such that it had to be close to something.

The buildings were worn and decayed and some of them fallen and all of them drafty and dusty and empty. Weeds grew among floorboards. Birds nested upon rafters. The droppings of wild things were everywhere, and it knew them all as they would have known it, were they to meet face to face.

It froze, for there had come the tiniest unanticipated sound from somewhere ahead and to the left. At that moment, it was again phasing into existence and it released its outline which faded as quickly as a rainbow in Hell, that but the naked presence remained beyond subtraction.

Invisible, yet existing, strong, it moved again. The clue. The cue. Ahead. *A gauche.* Beyond the faded word SALOON on weathered board above. Through the swinging doors. (One of them pinned alop.)

Pause and assess.

Bar to the right, dusty. Cracked mirror behind it. Empty bottles. Broken bottles. Brass rail, black, encrusted. Tables to the left and rear. In various states of repair.

Man seated at the best of the lot. His back to the door. Levi's. Hiking boots. Faded blue shirt. Green backpack leaning against the wall to his left.

Before him, on the tabletop, is the faint, painted outline of a chessboard, stained, scratched, almost obliterated.

The drawer in which he had found the chessmen is still partly open.

He could no more have passed up a chess set

without working out a problem or replaying one of his better games than he could have gone without breathing, circulating his blood, or maintaining a relatively stable body temperature.

It moved nearer, and perhaps there were fresh prints in the dust behind it, but none noted them.

It, too, played chess.

It watched as the man replayed what had perhaps been his finest game, from the world preliminaries of seven years past. He had blown up after that—surprised to have gotten even as far as he had—for he never could perform well under pressure. But he had always been proud of that one game, and he relived it as all sensitive beings do certain turning points in their lives. For perhaps twenty minutes, no one could have touched him. He had been shining and pure and hard and clear. He had felt like the best.

It took up a position across the board from him and stared. The man completed the game, smiling. Then he set up the board again, rose, and fetched a can of Beer from his pack. He popped the top.

When he returned, he discovered that white's king's pawn had been advanced to K4. His brow furrowed. He turned his head, searching the bar, meeting his own puzzled gaze in the grimy mirror. He looked under the table. He took a drink of Beer and seated himself.

He reached out and moved his pawn to K4. A moment later, he saw white's king's knight rise slowly into the air and drift forward to settle upon KB3. He stared for a long while into the emptiness across the table before he advanced his own knight to his KB3.

White's knight moved to take his pawn. He dismissed the novelty of the situation and moved his pawn to Q3. He all but forgot the absence of a tangible opponent as the white knight dropped back to its KB3. He paused to take a sip of Beer, but no sooner had he placed the can upon the tabletop than it rose again, passed across the board, and was upended. A gurgling noise followed. Then the can fell to the floor, bouncing, ringing with an empty sound.

"I'm sorry," he said, rising and returning to his pack. "I'd have offered you one if I'd thought you were something that might like it."

He opened two more cans, returned with them, placed one near the far edge of the table, one at his own right hand.

"Thank you," came a soft, precise voice from a point beyond it.

The can was raised, tilted slightly, returned to the tabletop.

"My name is Martin," the man said.

"Call me Tlingel," said the other. "I had thought that perhaps your kind was extinct. I am pleased that you at least have survived to afford me this game."

"Huh?" Martin said. "We were all still around the last time that I looked—a couple of days ago."

"No matter. I can take care of that later," Tlingel replied. "I was misled by the appearance of this place."

"Oh. It's a ghost town. I backpack a lot."

"Not important. I am near the proper point in your career as a species. I can feel that much."

"I am afraid that I do not follow you."

"I am not at all certain that you would wish to. I assume that you intend to capture that pawn?"

"Perhaps. Yes, I do wish to. What are you talking about?"

The Beer can rose. The invisible entity took another drink.

"Well," said Tlingel, "to put it simply, your—successors—grow anxious. Your place in the scheme of things being such an important one, I had sufficient power to come and check things out."

"'Successors'? I do not understand."

"Have you seen any griffins recently?"

Martin chuckled.

"I've heard the stories," he said, "seen the photos of the one supposedly shot in the Rockies. A hoax, of course."

"Of course it must seem so. That is the way with mythical beasts."

"You're trying to say that it was real?"

"Certainly. Your world is in bad shape. When the last grizzly bear died recently, the way was opened for the griffins—just as the death of the last aepyornis brought in the yeti, the dodo, the Loch Ness creature, the passenger pigeon, the sasquatch, the blue whale, the kraken, the American eagle, the cockatrice—"

"You can't prove it by me."

"Have another drink."

Martin began to reach for the can, halted his hand, and stared.

A creature approximately two inches in length, with a human face, a lionlike body, and feathered wings, was crouched next to the Beer can.

"A mini-sphinx," the voice continued. "They came when you killed off the last smallpox virus."

"Are you trying to say that whenever a natural species dies out a mythical one takes its place?" he asked.

"In a word—yes. Now. It was not always so, but you have destroyed the mechanisms of evolution. The balance is now redressed by those others of us, from the morning land—we, who have never truly been endangered. We return, in our time."

"And you—whatever you are, Tlingel—you say that humanity is now endangered?"

"Very much so. But there is nothing that you can do about it, is there? Let us get on with the game."

The sphinx flew off. Martin took a sip of Beer and captured the pawn.

"Who," he asked then, "are to be our successors?"

"Modesty almost forbids," Tlingel replied. "In the case of a species as prominent as your own, it naturally has to be the loveliest, most intelligent, most important of us all."

"And what are you? Is there any way that I can have a look?"

"Well—yes. If I exert myself a trifle."

The Beer can rose, was drained, fell to the floor. There followed a series of rapid rattling sounds retreating from the table. The air began to flicker over a large area opposite Martin, darkening within the growing flamework. The outline continued to brighten, its interior growing jet black. The form moved, prancing about the saloon, multitudes of tiny, cloven hoofprints scoring and cracking the floorboards. With a final, near-blinding flash it came into full view and Martin gasped to behold it.

A black unicorn with mocking yellow eyes sported before him, rising for a moment onto its hind legs to strike a heraldic pose. The fires flared about it a second longer, then vanished.

Martin had drawn back, raising one hand defensively.

"Regard me!" Tlingel announced. "Ancient symbol of wisdom, valor, and beauty, I stand before you!"

"I thought your typical unicorn was white," Martin finally said.

"I am archetypical," Tlingel responded, dropping to all fours, "and possessed of virtues beyond the ordinary."

"Such as?"

"Let us continue our game."

"What about the fate of the human race? You said—"

"...And save the small talk for later."

"I hardly consider the destruction of humanity to be small talk."

"And if you've any more Beer..."

"All right," Martin said, retreating to his pack as the creature advanced, its eyes like a pair of pale suns. "There's some Lager."

* * *

Something had gone out of the game. As Martin sat before the ebon horn on Tlingel's bowed head, like an insect about to be pinned, he realized that his playing was off. He had felt the pressure the moment he had seen the beast—and there was all that talk about an imminent doomsday. Any run-of-the-mill pessimist could say it without troubling him, but coming from a source as peculiar as this . . .

His earlier elation had fled. He was no longer in top form. And Tlingel was good. Very good. Martin found himself wondering whether he could manage a stalemate.

After a time, he saw that he could not and resigned.

The unicorn looked at him and smiled.

"You don't really play badly—for a human," it said.

"I've done a lot better."

"It is no shame to lose to me, mortal. Even among mythical creatures there are very few who can give a unicorn a good game."

"I am pleased that you were not wholly bored," Martin said. "Now will you tell me what you were talking about concerning the destruction of my species?"

"Oh, that," Tlingel replied. "In the morning land where those such as I dwell, I felt the possibility of your passing come like a gentle wind to my nostrils, with the promise of clearing the way for us—"

"How is it supposed to happen?"

Tlingel shrugged, horn writing on the air with a toss of the head.

"I really couldn't say. Premonitions are seldom specific. In fact, that is what I came to discover. I should have been about it already, but you diverted me with Beer and good sport."

"Could you be wrong about this?"

"I doubt it. That is the other reason I am here."

"Please explain."

"Are there any Beers left?"

"Two, I think."

"Please."

Martin rose and fetched them.

"Damn! The tab broke off this one," he said.

"Place it upon the table and hold it firmly."

"All right."

Tlingel's horn dipped forward quickly, piercing the can's top.

"...Useful for all sorts of things," Tlingel observed, withdrawing it.

"The other reason you're here..." Martin prompted.

"It is just that I am special. I can do things that the others cannot."

"Such as?"

"Find your weak spot and influence events to exploit it, to—hasten matters. To turn the possibility into a probability, and then—"

"*You* are going to destroy us? Personally?"

"That is the wrong way to look at it. It is more like a game of chess. It is as much a matter of exploiting your opponent's weaknesses as of exercising your own strengths. If you had not already laid the groundwork I would be powerless. I can only influence that which already exists."

"So what will it be? World War III? An ecological disaster? A mutated disease?"

"I do not really know yet, so I wish you wouldn't ask me in that fashion. I repeat that at the moment I am only observing. I am only an agent—"

"It doesn't sound that way to me."

Tlingel was silent. Martin began gathering up the chessmen.

"Aren't you going to set up the board again?"

"To amuse my destroyer a little more? No, thanks."

"That's hardly the way to look at it—"

"Besides, those are the last Beers."

"Oh." Tlingel stared wistfully at the vanishing

pieces, then remarked, "I would be willing to play you again without additional refreshment..."

"No, thanks."

"You are angry."

"Wouldn't you be, if our situations were reversed?"

"You are anthropomorphizing."

"Well?"

"Oh, I suppose I would."

"You could give us a break, you know—at least, let us make our own mistakes."

"You've hardly done that yourself, though, with all the creatures my fellows have succeeded."

Martin reddened.

"Okay. You just scored one. But I don't have to like it."

"You are a good player. I know that..."

"Tlingel, if I were capable of playing at my best again, I think I could beat you."

The unicorn snorted two tiny wisps of smoke.

"Not *that* good," Tlingel said.

"I guess you'll never know."

"Do I detect a proposal?"

"Possibly. What's another game worth to you?"

Tlingel made a chuckling noise.

"Let me guess: You are going to say that if you beat me you want my promise not to lay my will upon the weakest link in mankind's existence and shatter it."

"Of course."

"And what do I get for winning?"

"The pleasure of the game. That's what you want, isn't it?"

"The terms sound a little lopsided."

"Not if you are going to win anyway. You keep insisting that you will."

"All right. Set up the board."

"There is something else that you have to know about me first."

"Yes?"

"I don't play well under pressure, and this game

is going to be a terrific strain. You want my best game, don't you?"

"Yes, but I'm afraid I've no way of adjusting your own reactions to the play."

"I believe I could do that myself if I had more than the usual amount of time between moves."

"Agreed."

"I mean a lot of time."

"Just what do you have in mind?"

"I'll need time to get my mind off it, to relax, to come back to the positions as if they were only problems..."

"You mean to go away from here between moves?"

"Yes."

"All right. How long?"

"I don't know. A few weeks, maybe."

"Take a month. Consult your experts, put your computers onto it. It may make for a slightly more interesting game."

"I really didn't have that in mind."

"Then it's time that you're trying to buy."

"I can't deny that. On the other hand, I will need it."

"In that case, I have some terms. I'd like this place cleaned up, fixed up, more lively. It's a mess. I also want Beer on tap."

"Okay. I'll see to that."

"Then I agree. Let's see who goes first."

Martin switched a black and a white pawn from hand to hand beneath the table. He raised his fists then and extended them. Tlingel leaned forward and tapped. The black horn's tip touched Martin's left hand.

"Well, it matches my sleek and glossy hide," the unicorn announced.

Martin smiled, setting up the white for himself, the black pieces for his opponent. As soon as he had finished, he pushed his pawn to K4.

Tlingel's delicate, ebon hoof moved to advance the black king's pawn to K4.

"I take it that you want a month now, to consider your next move?"

Martin did not reply but moved his knight to KB3. Tlingel immediately moved a knight to QB3.

Martin took a swallow of Beer and then moved his bishop to N5. The unicorn moved the other knight to B3. Martin immediately castled and Tlingel moved the knight to take his pawn.

"I think we'll make it," Martin said suddenly, "if you'll just let us alone. We do learn from our mistakes, in time."

"Mythical beings do not exactly exist in time. Your world is a special case."

"Don't you people ever make mistakes?"

"Whenever we do they're sort of poetic."

Martin snarled and advanced his pawn to Q4. Tlingel immediately countered by moving the knight to Q3.

"I've got to stop," Martin said, standing. "I'm getting mad, and it will affect my game."

"You will be going, then?"

"Yes."

He moved to fetch his pack.

"I will see you here in one month's time?"

"Yes."

"Very well."

The unicorn rose and stamped upon the floor and lights began to play across its dark coat. Suddenly, they blazed and shot outward in all directions like a silent explosion. A wave of blackness followed.

Martin found himself leaning against the wall, shaking. When he lowered his hand from his eyes, he saw that he was alone, save for the knights, the bishops, the kings, the queens, their castles and both the kings' men.

He went away.

Three days later Martin returned in a small truck, with a generator, lumber, windows, power tools, paint, stain, cleaning compounds, wax. He dusted and vacuumed and replaced rotted wood. He

installed the windows. He polished the old brass
until it shone. He stained and rubbed. He waxed the
floors and buffed them. He plugged holes and
washed glass. He hauled all the trash away.

It took him the better part of a week to turn the
old place from a wreck back into a saloon in appearance. Then he drove off, returned all of the equipment he had rented, and bought a ticket for the
Northwest.

The big, damp forest was another of his favorite
places for hiking, for thinking. And he was seeking
a complete change of scene, a total revision of out-
look. Not that his next move did not seem obvious,
standard even. Yet something nagged.

He knew that it was more than just the game.
Before that he had been ready to get away again, to
walk drowsing among shadows, breathing clean air.

Resting, his back against the bulging root of a
giant tree, he withdrew a small chess set from his
pack, set it up on a rock he'd moved into position
nearby. A fine, mistlike rain was settling, but the
tree sheltered him, so far. He reconstructed the
opening through Tlingel's withdrawal of the knight
to Q3. The simplest thing would be to take the
knight with the bishop. But he did not move to do
it.

He watched the board for a time, felt his eyelids
drooping, closed them, and drowsed. It may only
have been for a few minutes. He was never certain
afterwards.

Something aroused him. He did not know what.
He blinked several times and closed his eyes again.
Then he reopened them hurriedly.

In his nodded position, eyes directed downward,
his gaze was fixed upon an enormous pair of hairy,
unshod feet—the largest pair of feet that he had
ever beheld. They stood unmoving before him,
pointed toward his right.

Slowly—very slowly—he raised his eyes. Not
very far, as it turned out. The creature was only
about four and a half feet in height. As it was look-

ing at the chessboard rather than at him, he took the opportunity to study it.

It was unclothed but very hairy, with a dark brown pelt, obviously masculine, possessed of low brow ridges, deep-set eyes that matched its hair, heavy shoulders, five-fingered hands that sported opposing thumbs.

It turned suddenly and regarded him, flashing a large number of shining teeth.

"White's pawn should take the pawn," it said in a soft, nasal voice.

"Huh? Come on," Martin said. "Bishop takes knight."

"You want to give me black and play it that way? I'll walk all over you."

Martin glanced again at its feet.

"...Or give me white and let me take that pawn. I'll still do it."

"Take white," Martin said, straightening. "Let's see if you know what you're talking about." He reached for his pack. "Have a Beer?"

"What's a Beer?"

"A recreational aid. Wait a minute."

Before they had finished the six-pack, the sasquatch—whose name, he had learned, was Grend—had finished Martin. Grend had quickly entered a ferocious midgame, backed him into a position of dwindling security, and pushed him to the point where he had seen the end and resigned.

"That was one hell of a game," Martin declared, leaning back and considering the apelike countenance before him.

"Yes, we Bigfeet are pretty good, if I do say it. It's our one big recreation, and we're so damned primitive we don't have much in the way of boards and chessmen. Most of the time, we just play it in our heads. There're not many can come close to us."

"How about unicorns?" Martin asked.

Grend nodded slowly.

"They're about the only ones can really give us a good game. A little dainty, but they're subtle. Aw-

fully sure of themselves, though, I must say. Even
when they're wrong. Haven't seen any since we left
the morning land, of course. Too bad. Got any more
of that Beer left?"

"I'm afraid not. But listen, I'll be back this way
in a month. I'll bring some more if you'll meet me
here and play again."

"Martin, you've got a deal. Sorry. Didn't mean to
step on your toes."

He cleaned the saloon again and brought in a keg
of Beer which he installed under the bar and packed
with ice. He moved in some bar stools, chairs, and
tables which he had obtained at a Goodwill store.
He hung red curtains. By then it was evening. He
set up the board, ate a light meal, unrolled his
sleeping bag behind the bar, and camped there that
night.

The following day passed quickly. Since Tlingel
might show up at any time, he did not leave the
vicinity, but took his meals there and sat about
working chess problems. When it began to grow
dark, he lit a number of oil lamps and candles.

He looked at his watch with increasing fre-
quency. He began to pace. He couldn't have made a
mistake. This was the proper day. He—

He heard a chuckle.

Turning about, he saw a black unicorn head
floating in the air above the chessboard. As he
watched, the rest of Tlingel's body materialized.

"Good evening, Martin." Tlingel turned away
from the board. "The place looks a little better.
Could use some music..."

Martin stepped behind the bar and switched on
the transistor radio he had brought along. The
sounds of a string quartet filled the air. Tlingel
winced.

"Hardly in keeping with the atmosphere of the
place."

He changed stations, located a Country-and-
Western show.

"I think not," Tlingel said. "It loses something in transmission."

He turned it off.

"Have we a good supply of beverage?"

Martin drew a gallon stein of Beer—the largest mug that he could locate, from a novelty store—and set it upon the bar. He filled a much smaller one for himself. He was determined to get the beast drunk if it were at all possible.

"Ah! Much better than those little cans," said Tlingel, whose muzzle dipped for but a moment. "Very good."

The mug was empty. Martin refilled it.

"Will you move it to the table for me?"

"Certainly."

"Have an interesting month?"

"I suppose I did."

"You've decided upon your next move?"

"Yes."

"Then let's get on with it."

Martin seated himself and captured the pawn.

"Hm. Interesting."

Tlingel stared at the board for a long while, then raised a cloven hoof which parted in reaching for the piece.

"I'll just take that bishop with this little knight. Now I suppose you'll be wanting another month to make up your mind what to do next."

Tlingel leaned to the side and drained the mug.

"Let me consider it," Martin said, "while I get you a refill."

Martin sat and stared at the board through three more refills. Actually, he was not planning. He was waiting. His response to Grend had been knight takes bishop, and he had Grend's next move ready.

"Well?" Tlingel finally said. "What do you think?"

Martin took a small sip of Beer.

"Almost ready," he said. "You hold your Beer awfully well."

Tlingel laughed.

"A unicorn's horn is a detoxicant. Its possession is a universal remedy. I wait until I reach the warm-glow stage, then I use my horn to burn off any excess and keep me right there."

"Oh," said Martin. "Neat trick, that."

"...If you've had too much, just touch my horn for a moment and I'll put you back in business."

"No, thanks. That's all right. I'll just push this little pawn in front of the queen's rook two steps ahead."

"Really..." said Tlingel. "That's interesting. You know, what this place really needs is a piano— rinky-tink, funky...Think you could manage it?"

"I don't play."

"Too bad."

"I suppose I could hire a piano player."

"No. I do not care to be seen by other humans."

"If he's really good, I suppose he could play blind-folded."

"Never mind."

"I'm sorry."

"You are also ingenious. I am certain that you will figure something out by next time."

Martin nodded.

"Also, didn't these old places used to have saw-dust all over the floors?"

"I believe so."

"That would be nice."

"Check."

Tlingel searched the board frantically for a moment.

"Yes. I meant 'yes.' I said 'check.' It means 'yes' sometimes, too."

"Oh. Rather. Well, while we're here..."

Tlingel advanced the pawn to Q3.

Martin stared. That was not what Grend had done. For a moment, he considered continuing on his own from here. He had tried to think of Grend as a coach up until this point. He had forced away the notion of crudely and crassly pitting one of them against the other. Until P–Q3. Then he recalled the game he had lost to the sasquatch.

"I'll draw the line here," he said, "and take my month."

"All right. Let's have another drink before we say good night. Okay?"

"Sure. Why not?"

They sat for a time and Tlingel told him of the morning land, of primeval forests and rolling plains, of high craggy mountains and purple seas, of magic and mythic beasts.

Martin shook his head.

"I can't quite see why you're so anxious to come here," he said, "with a place like that to call home."

Tlingel sighed.

"I suppose you'd call it keeping up with the griffins. It's the thing to do these days. Well. Till next month..."

Tlingel rose and turned away.

"I've got complete control now. Watch!"

The unicorn form faded, jerked out of shape, grew white, faded again, was gone, like an afterimage.

Martin moved to the bar and drew himself another mug. It was a shame to waste what was left. In the morning, he wished the unicorn were there again. Or at least the horn.

It was a gray day in the forest and he held an umbrella over the chessboard upon the rock. The droplets fell from the leaves and made dull, plopping noises as they struck the fabric. The board was set up again through Tlingel's P–Q3. Martin wondered whether Grend had remembered, had kept proper track of the days...

"Hello," came the nasal voice from somewhere behind him and to the left.

He turned to see Grend moving about the tree, stepping over the massive roots with massive feet.

"You remembered," Grend said. "How good! I trust you also remembered the Beer?"

"I've lugged up a whole case. We can set up the bar right here."

"What's a bar?"

"Well, it's a place where people go to drink—in out of the rain—a bit dark, for atmosphere—and they sit up on stools before a big counter, or else at little tables—and they talk to each other—and sometimes there's music—and they drink."

"We're going to have all that here?"

"No. Just the dark and the drinks. Unless you count the rain as music. I was speaking figuratively."

"Oh. It does sound like a very good place to visit, though."

"Yes. If you will hold this umbrella over the board, I'll set up the best equivalent we can have here."

"All right. Say, this looks like a version of that game we played last time."

"It is. I got to wondering what would happen if it had gone this way rather than the way that it went."

"Hmm. Let me see ..."

Martin removed four six-packs from his pack and opened the first.

"Here you go."

"Thanks."

Grend accepted the Beer, squatted, passed the umbrella back to Martin.

"I'm still white?"

"Yeah."

"Pawn to king six."

"Really?"

"Yep."

"About the best thing for me to do would be to take this pawn with this one."

"I'd say. Then I'll just knock off your knight with this one."

"I guess I'll just pull this knight back to K2."

"...And I'll take this one over to B3. May I have another Beer?"

An hour and a quarter later, Martin resigned. The rain had let up and he had folded the umbrella.

"Another game?" Grend asked.

"Yes."

The afternoon wore on. The pressure was off. This one was just for fun. Martin tried wild combinations, seeing ahead with great clarity, as he had that one day...

"Stalemate," Grend announced much later. "That was a good one, though. You picked up considerably."

"I was more relaxed. Want another?"

"Maybe in a little while. Tell me more about bars now."

So he did. Finally, "How is all that Beer affecting you?" he asked.

"I'm a bit dizzy. But that's all right. I'll still cream you the third game."

And he did.

"Not bad for a human, though. Not bad at all. You coming back next month?"

"Yes."

"Good. You'll bring more Beer?"

"So long as my money holds out."

"Oh. Bring some plaster of paris then. I'll make you some nice footprints and you can take casts of them. I understand they're going for quite a bit."

"I'll remember that."

Martin lurched to his feet and collected the chess set.

"Till then."

"Ciao."

Martin dusted and polished again, moved in the player piano, and scattered sawdust upon the floor. He installed a fresh keg. He hung some reproductions of period posters and some atrocious old paintings he had located in a junk shop. He placed cuspidors in strategic locations. When he was finished, he seated himself at the bar and opened a bottle of mineral water. He listened to the New

Mexico wind moaning as it passed, to grains of sand striking against the windowpanes. He wondered whether the whole world would have that dry, mournful sound to it if Tlingel found a means for doing away with humanity, or—disturbing thought —whether the successors to his own kind might turn things into something resembling the mythical morning land.

This troubled him for a time. Then he went and set up the board through black's P–Q3. When he turned back to clear the bar he saw a line of cloven hoofprints advancing across the sawdust.

"Good evening, Tlingel," he said. "What is your pleasure?"

Suddenly, the unicorn was there, without preliminary pyrotechnics. It moved to the bar and placed one hoof upon the brass rail.

"The usual."

As Martin drew the Beer, Tlingel looked about.

"The place has improved, a bit."

"Glad you think so. Would you care for some music?"

"Yes."

Martin fumbled at the back of the piano, locating the switch for the small, battery-operated computer which controlled the pumping mechanism and substituted its own memory for rolls. The keyboard immediately came to life.

"Very good," Tlingel stated. "Have you found your move?"

"I have."

"Then let us be about it."

He refilled the unicorn's mug and moved it to the table, along with his own.

"Pawn to king six," he said, executing it.

"What?"

"Just that."

"Give me a minute. I want to study this."

"Take your time."

"I'll take the pawn," Tlingel said, after a long pause and another mug.

"Then I'll take this knight."

Later, "Knight to K2," Tlingel said.

"Knight to B3."

An extremely long pause ensued before Tlingel moved the knight to N3.

The hell with asking Grend, Martin suddenly decided. He'd been through this part any number of times already. He moved his knight to N5.

"Change the tune on that thing!" Tlingel snapped.

Martin rose and obliged.

"I don't like that one either. Find a better one or shut it off!"

After three more tries, Martin shut it off.

"And get me another Beer!"

He refilled their mugs.

"All right."

Tlingel moved the bishop to K2.

Keeping the unicorn from castling had to be the most important thing at the moment. So Martin moved his queen to R5. Tlingel made a tiny, strangling noise, and when Martin looked up smoke was curling from the unicorn's nostrils.

"More Beer?"

"If you please."

As he returned with it, he saw Tlingel move the bishop to capture the knight. There seemed no choice for him at that moment, but he studied the position for a long while anyhow.

Finally, "Bishop takes bishop," he said.

"Of course."

"How's the warm glow?"

Tlingel chuckled.

"You'll see."

The wind rose again, began to howl. The building creaked.

"Okay," Tlingel finally said, and moved the queen to Q2.

Martin stared. What was he doing? So far, it had gone all right, but— He listened again to the wind and thought of the risk he was taking.

"That's all, folks," he said, leaning back in his chair. "Continued next month."

Tlingel sighed.

"Don't run off. Fetch me another. Let me tell you of my wanderings in your world this past month."

"Looking for weak links?"

"You're lousy with them. How do you stand it?"

"They're harder to strengthen than you might think. Any advice?"

"Get the Beer."

They talked until the sky paled in the east, and Martin found himself taking surreptitious notes. His admiration for the unicorn's analytical abilities increased as the evening advanced.

When they finally rose, Tlingel staggered.

"You all right?"

"Forgot to detox, that's all. Just a second. Then I'll be fading."

"Wait!"

"Whazzat?"

"I could use one, too."

"Oh. Grab hold, then."

Tlingel's head descended and Martin took the tip of the horn between his fingertips. Immediately, a delicious, warm sensation flowed through him. He closed his eyes to enjoy it. His head cleared. An ache which had been growing within his frontal sinus vanished. The tiredness went out of his muscles. He opened his eyes again.

"Thank—"

Tlingel had vanished. He held but a handful of air.

"—you."

"Rael here is my friend," Grend stated. "He's a griffin."

"I'd noticed."

Martin nodded at the beaked, golden-winged creature.

"Pleased to meet you, Rael."

"The same," cried the other in a high-pitched voice. "Have you got the Beer?"

"Why—uh—yes."

"I've been telling him about Beer," Grend explained, half-apologetically. "He can have some of mine. He won't kibitz or anything like that."

"Sure. All right. Any friend of yours..."

"The Beer!" Rael cried. "Bars!"

"He's not real bright," Grend whispered. "But he's good company. I'd appreciate your humoring him."

Martin opened the first six-pack and passed the griffin and the sasquatch a Beer apiece. Rael immediately punctured the can with his beak, chugged it, belched, and held out his claw.

"Beer!" he shrieked. "More Beer!"

Martin handed him another.

"Say, you're still into that first game, aren't you?" Grend observed, studying the board. "Now, *that* is an interesting position."

Grend drank and studied the board.

"Good thing it's not raining," Martin commented.

"Oh, it will. Just wait awhile."

"More Beer!" Rael screamed.

Martin passed him another without looking.

"I'll move my pawn to N6," Grend said.

"You're kidding."

"Nope. Then you'll take that pawn with your bishop's pawn. Right?"

"Yes..."

Martin reached out and did it.

"Okay. Now I'll just swing this knight to Q5."

Martin took it with the pawn.

Grend moved his rook to K1.

"Check," he announced.

"Yes. That *is* the way to go," Martin observed.

Grend chuckled.

"I'm going to win this game another time," he said.

"I wouldn't put it past you."

"More Beer?" Rael said softly.

"Sure."

As Martin poured him another, he noticed that the griffin was now leaning against the tree trunk.

After several minutes, Martin pushed his king to B1.

"Yeah, that's what I thought you'd do," Grend said. "You know something?"

"What?"

"You play a lot like a unicorn."

"Hm."

Grend moved his rook to R3.

Later, as the rain descended gently about them and Grend beat him again, Martin realized that a prolonged period of silence had prevailed. He glanced over at the griffin. Rael had tucked his head beneath his left wing, balanced upon one leg, leaned heavily against the tree, and gone to sleep.

"I told you he wouldn't be much trouble," Grend remarked.

Two games later, the Beer was gone, the shadows were lengthening, and Rael was stirring.

"See you next month?"

"Yeah."

"You bring any plaster of paris?"

"Yes, I did."

"Come on, then. I know a good place pretty far from here. We don't want people beating about *these* bushes. Let's go make you some money."

"To buy Beer?" Rael said, looking out from under his wing.

"Next month," Grend said.

"You ride?"

"I don't think you could carry both of us," said Grend, "and I'm not sure I'd want to right now if you could."

"Bye-bye then," Rael shrieked, and he leaped into the air, crashing into branches and tree trunks, finally breaking through the overhead cover and vanishing.

"There goes a really decent guy," said Grend. "He sees everything and he never forgets. Knows how everything works—in the woods, in the air—even in the water. Generous, too, whenever he has anything."

"Hm," Martin observed.

"Let's make tracks," Grend said.

"Pawn to N6? Really?" Tlingel said. "All right. The bishop's pawn will just knock off the pawn."

Tlingel's eyes narrowed as Martin moved the knight to Q5.

"At least this is an interesting game," the unicorn remarked. "Pawn takes knight."

Martin moved the rook.

"Check."

"Yes, it is. This next one is going to be a three-flagon move. Kindly bring me the first."

Martin thought back as he watched Tlingel drink and ponder. He almost felt guilty for hitting it with a powerhouse like the sasquatch behind its back. He was convinced now that the unicorn was going to lose. In every variation of this game that he'd played with black against Grend, he'd been beaten. Tlingel was very good, but the sasquatch was a wizard with not much else to do but mental chess. It was unfair. But it was not a matter of personal honor, he kept telling himself. He was playing to protect his species against a supernatural force which might well be able to precipitate World War III by some arcane mind-manipulation or magically induced computer foulup. He didn't dare give the creature a break.

"Flagon number two, please."

He brought it another. He studied it as it studied the board. It was beautiful, he realized for the first time. It was the loveliest living thing he had ever seen. Now that the pressure was on the verge of evaporating and he could regard it without the overlay of fear which had always been there in the past, he could pause to admire it. If something *had* to succeed the human race, he could think of worse choices...

"Number three now."

"Coming up."

Tlingel drained it and moved the king to B1.

Martin leaned forward immediately and pushed the rook to R3.

Tlingel looked up, stared at him.

"Not bad."

Martin wanted to squirm. He was struck by the nobility of the creature. He wanted so badly to play and beat the unicorn on his own, fairly. Not this way.

Tlingel looked back at the board, then almost carelessly moved the knight to K4.

"Go ahead. Or will it take you another month?"

Martin growled softly, advanced the rook, and captured the knight.

"Of course."

Tlingel captured the rook with the pawn. This was not the way that the last variation with Grend had run. Still ...

He moved his rook to KB3. As he did, the wind seemed to commence a peculiar shrieking, above, amid, the ruined buildings.

"Check," he announced.

The hell with it! he decided. I'm good enough to manage my own endgame. Let's play this out.

He watched and waited and finally saw Tlingel move the king to N1.

He moved his bishop to R6. Tlingel moved the queen to K2. The shrieking came again, sounding nearer now. Martin took the pawn with the bishop.

The unicorn's head came up and it seemed to listen for a moment. Then Tlingel lowered it and captured the bishop with the king.

Martin moved his rook to KN3.

"Check."

Tlingel returned the king to B1.

Martin moved the rook to KB3.

"Check."

Tlingel pushed the king to N2.

Martin moved the rook back to KN3.

"Check."

Tlingel returned the king to B1, looked up, and stared at him, showing teeth.

"Looks as if we've got a drawn game," the unicorn stated. "Care for another one?"

"Yes, but not for the fate of humanity."

"Forget it. I'd given up on that a long time ago. I decided that I wouldn't care to live here after all. I'm a little more discriminating than that.

"Except for this bar." Tlingel turned away as another shriek sounded just beyond the door, followed by strange voices. "What is that?"

"I don't know," Martin answered, rising.

The doors opened and a golden griffin entered.

"Martin!" it cried. "Beer! Beer!"

"Uh—Tlingel, this is Rael, and, and—"

Three more griffins followed him in. Then came Grend, and three others of his own kind.

"—and that one's Grend," Martin said lamely. "I don't know the others."

They all halted when they beheld the unicorn.

"Tlingel," one of the sasquatches said. "I thought you were still in the morning land."

"I still am, in a way. Martin, how is it that you are acquainted with my former countrymen?"

"Well—uh—Grend here is my chess coach."

"Aha! I begin to understand."

"I am not sure that you really do. But let me get everyone a drink first."

Martin turned on the piano and set everyone up.

"How did you find this place?" he asked Grend as he was doing it. "And how did you get here?"

"Well..." Grend looked embarrassed. "Rael followed you back."

"Followed a jet?"

"Griffins are supernaturally fast."

"Oh."

"Anyway, he told his relatives and some of my folks about it. When we saw that the griffins were determined to visit you, we decided that we had better come along to keep them out of trouble. They brought us."

"I—see. Interesting..."

"No wonder you played like a unicorn, that one game with all the variations."

"Uh—yes."

Martin turned away, moved to the end of the bar.

"Welcome, all of you," he said. "I have a small announcement. Tlingel, a while back you had a number of observations concerning possible ecological and urban disasters and lesser dangers. Also, some ideas as to possible safeguards against some of them."

"I recall," said the unicorn.

"I passed them along to a friend of mine in Washington who used to be a member of my old chess club. I told him that the work was not entirely my own."

"I should hope so."

"He has since suggested that I turn whatever group was involved into a think tank. He will then see about paying something for its efforts."

"I didn't come here to save the world," Tlingel said.

"No, but you've been very helpful. And Grend tells me that the griffins, even if their vocabulary is a bit limited, know almost all that there is to know about ecology."

"That is probably true."

"Since they have inherited a part of the Earth, it would be to their benefit as well to help preserve the place. Inasmuch as this many of us are already here, I can save myself some travel and suggest right now that we find a meeting place—say here, once a month—and that you let me have your unique viewpoints. You must know more about how species become extinct than anyone else in the business."

"Of course," said Grend, waving his mug, "but we really should ask the yeti, also. I'll do it, if you'd like. Is that stuff coming out of the big box music?"

"Yes."

"I like it. If we do this think-tank thing, you'll make enough to keep this place going?"

"I'll buy the whole town."

Grend conversed in quick gutturals with the griffins, who shrieked back at him.

"You've got a think tank," he said, "and they want more Beer."

Martin turned toward Tlingel.

"They were your observations. What do you think?"

"It may be amusing," said the unicorn, "to stop by occasionally." Then: "So much for saving the world. Did you say you wanted another game?"

"I've nothing to lose."

Grend took over the tending of the bar while Tlingel and Martin returned to the table.

He beat the unicorn in thirty-one moves and touched the extended horn.

The piano keys went up and down. Tiny sphinxes buzzed about the bar, drinking the spillage.

Successful authors are often asked by anthologists if they've ever written a story about rutabagas from outer space or sexy robots or whatever the theme of the editor's anthology might be.

Roger Zelazny's work has been in uncommonly high demand for more than twenty years now, ever since he established himself with such memorable efforts as "A Rose for Ecclesiastes," "The Dream Master," and "The Doors of His Face, the Lamps of His Mouth." When his novel This Immortal *beat Frank Herbert's* Dune *to a tie in the 1965 Hugos, it was clear that Zelazny was a major force to be reckoned with. Since that time he has written many novels, including* Doorways in the Sand, Madwand,*

Eye of Cat, *and the celebrated Amber series (most recently,* Blood of Amber). *His short stories only come once in a great while, but, happily, they come in bunches.*

It was during one of these short-story-fertile periods that Zelazny was approached by one editor looking for stories about unicorns; another looking for fantasy chess stories; and ourselves, seeking stories for the book you are holding in your hands. Now, there have been many unicorn stories, chess stories, and bar stories before (hence the anthologies), but there has never previously been a unicorn/chess/bar story—not like this one, which Zelazny produced in a masterful attempt to please everybody. It worked, too, since "Unicorn Variation" won a Hugo.

STRATEGY AT THE BILLIARDS CLUB

by Lord Dunsany

Mr. Joseph Jorkens is a member of the Billiards Club, London.

Without any intention that is apparent to me we have days in our club, the Billiards Club, when the conversation is entirely sporting, and on another day it will be political, while on another we discuss business. Perhaps somebody starts it; and the rest go on in the same direction, like a stream running down hill, finding it easier to go the way of the rest than to exert themselves by thinking of anything new; and, like the stream by a rock, the conversation will be sometimes turned a little out of its course by a chance remark, or it may not. However these things may be, on one day that I remember our talk was scientific. The presence of Chemsoln, an astronomer, might have accounted for this, and yet Chemsoln hardly ever opened his mouth, and indeed it is for this reason that I have never previously mentioned his name, though he has often been one of those that sat and listened to Jorkens's stories. Well, we were talking of science late one day after lunch, and evening was coming on, but no lights were lighted yet, and I remember a rather eerie glow was coming in from the Moon, that was just outside our window, and as usual Chemsoln was sitting and saying nothing, and we had got on to the atomic bomb, and then Jorkens chimed in.

"I don't know if any of you are interested in spiritualism," he said.

Well, we weren't. And on such occasions we have a rather unmistakable way of saying so at the Billiards Club. And Jorkens, without abandoning his topic entirely, I think dropped a good deal of the detail that he may have been going to give us.

"I wasn't going to tell you anything about spirits," he said, "because there are still laws on the statute-book dealing with that sort of thing; more than you might suppose. I know you wouldn't give anybody away, but when anyone's liberty may depend on one's talk, I think the less one says the better."

And he looked at us in the sort of way that made some of the weaker characters say, "Oh, yes, certainly."

"Very well," said Jorkens; "I will say nothing of who called up that spirit, or how she did it."

"What spirit?" asked Terbut.

"I was going to tell you," said Jorkens.

"Oh, very well," said Terbut.

"In a dim room one summer, a little after sunset, with no lights turned on," said Jorkens, "in a house in London—I will give you no fuller address than that—I was talking to a spirit. That is to say, a spirit that was in the room with us, but invisible, was talking to me; inaudibly to myself, but interpreted by the person whose name I will not divulge, a person to whom the whisperings and whistlings that I could faintly hear were clear and entirely intelligible. She had called it up. I won't tell you how."

Again Jorkens looked up at our faces; and one of

us, a new member, muttered, "I quite understand." And at that Jorkens continued.

"The spirit's story was of a long time ago and a long way off, but strategy is roughly the same in all times and places, and he had had the atomic bomb."

"The atomic bomb!" we exclaimed.

"Yes," said Jorkens, "and used it."

"A long time ago?" we said.

"Certainly," said Jorkens.

"That's interesting," we said rather doubtfully.

"Did he develop it further than we have done?" asked a soldier.

"Much further," said Jorkens.

"It ought to be developed," the soldier said. "The thing is still in its infancy."

"Yes," said Jorkens, "it's in its infancy here. But—"

"You say it's been tried before?" said the soldier, a retired general named Pearkes.

"I'll tell you," said Jorkens. "It happened like this, if the woman interpreted it right; and she was a very reliable woman. Not at all the kind of person to imagine she heard things, or to say what she didn't hear."

"No, no," one or two of us said, some out of mere politeness, and others because we wanted him to get on with his story and to hear what he had to say.

"The spirit," Jorkens went on, "was whispering and squeaking, or it may have been a mouse, or a draught in the wainscot: that I am not prepared to say. I mean that the spirit may have been totally inaudible to me, or only partially so; but at any rate the woman heard him, and this is what she said, speaking slowly as though the spirit spoke slowly, as though it were tired. It was a long time ago. I told you that. And the spirit had wandered a long time. Well, they had the atomic bomb and it was pretty well developed: they had had it for about a hundred years."

"But where was all this?" asked Terbut.

"She didn't say," said Jorkens. "But they had had

the atomic bomb there for about a hundred years. I
gathered that they were a quite pacific people. That
is to say, they preferred peace to war, and took a
good deal of trouble, like us, to make plans to en-
sure peace. Only they had the atomic bomb, and it
seemed a pity not to use it. Well, the war came: I
wasn't quite clear what it was about. The spirit
tried to explain, but it was a little hard to follow, as
other people's causes often are. But they had a *casus
belli* of some sort. I paid more attention to the
spirit's account of the war when it came than to the
cause of it, because I wanted to know what they had
done with their atomic bomb. And, mind you, it
wasn't anything like our atomic bomb, because they
had been improving it for a hundred years."

"Never heard of that," said the general.

"I didn't doubt her," said Jorkens; "and I think
she told me exactly what she heard, and the spirit
gave so many precise details that I, personally, believed every word of it. You, of course, can use your
own judgment."

"Yes, yes," said the general soothingly.

And we all listened to Jorkens, to see what we
could make of it.

"The details were like this," said Jorkens, reaching for a sheet of our large notepaper from a writ-
ing-table behind him. "Can someone lend me a
pencil?"

Somehow he got a pencil, and began to draw
craters roughly. "The armies were like this," he
said. And soon he and the general were bending
over the paper, so that the rest of us could see very
little; and they began to talk in low voices, and
most of us thought it was just a talk about strategy,
and those of us who were not interested in strategy
or spiritualism lost interest and gradually turned
away, but there seemed something a little more
than that in it to me, something a little more than
mere Staff-College shop, however Jorkens got hold
of it, and I listened as well as I could; and I'm glad
that I did, for the thing turned out to be queer. How

Jorkens got in touch with the spirit I did not know, and of course he never told us, but what I did see was that the general was interested in his story, so that I saw that the strategy must be sound, whatever the spiritualism might be. The craters that Jorkens was rapidly drawing were evidently marking out a position held by some army on which the bombs had been dropped. Whether the craters were large or not I could not say; that depended on the scale; but they were large in regard to his sheet of paper, and so probably large in regard to the whole battlefield; which is what you'd expect, if they'd had a hundred years to practise with the atomic bomb, whoever they were.

And Jorkens went on with his chart. He had lost the interest of everyone now, except the general, who appeared fascinated, and me, who was doubtful, and hovering between going and staying, and Chemsoln, who was sitting there silent as usual. Trifles decide such things. What made me doubtful was not being able to see how a spirit with mere words could describe so neat and detailed a chart, however audible he might be. What held me there, leaning forward and looking across the table at crater after crater as Jorkens sketched them in, was when the very point I have mentioned was raised by the general. Jorkens said that the woman he would not name, who had called the spirit up, had a big round crystal lying on dark-blue velvet on the table before her, and she had touched points in the crystal showing exactly the position of the army and the spots where the bombs hit it. It seemed to have been drawn up in a crescent formation in the top left hand of the crystal, that is to say with both flanks a little forward, as the general pointed out, while Chemsoln and I were gazing in silence, trying to make what we could of it.

"Well, they came on like this," Jorkens was saying, "and their bombs came down where I have marked the craters; there were not many of them, because they were too expensive to make, but they were effective, only too effective."

"But which side won?" asked the general. "And who were they? I never heard of anything like that anywhere."

"It was a long time ago," said Jorkens. "Neither side won. It was the end of their history. Only we mustn't suppose that, because they left no record, we are the first to have discovered the rather obvious powers there are in the atom."

"But this is nonsense," the general said. "How can one believe it?"

"Well, come and look," said Jorkens.

"What?" said the general.

"Come to the window," said Jorkens.

Then Chemsoln grabbed the chart that Jorkens had made of the craters.

"You don't mean..." he said.

"I do," said Jorkens.

The three men went to the window, and there was a round Moon shining, a bit past full, with its oddly battered face looking sadly on London.

"They smashed it, you see," said Jorkens.

Jorkens teased and tantalized the other members of the Billiards Club through five volumes and several uncollected short stories, all by Edward John Moreton Drax Plunkett, the eighteenth Baron Dunsany (1878–1957). Dunsany's famous liar was never quite caught lying, but he was never caught telling the irrefutable truth either. The trick was always that no one could be sure.

Lord Dunsany himself led an adventurous life. He was an Anglo-Irish peer, the scion of one of the oldest families in Europe, who saw service in the Boer War and the First World War, and was wounded during the Easter Rebellion in Dublin in 1916. His later life included an unsuccessful run for Parliament and a narrow escape from Athens as the Germans closed in on the city in 1941. Well into his old age he was an enthusiastic world-traveler and big-game hunter. Somehow he found time to write numerous volumes of exquisite fantasy short stories, such as A Dreamer's Tales, The Book of Wonder, *and* The Sword of Welleran, *besides plays, poems, essays, and such classic fantasy novels as* The King of Elfland's Daughter. *It is when we realize that the Jorkens stories represent only one phase of a long and varied career that we understand why, prior to Tolkien, he was widely regarded as the most influential fantasy writer of the twentieth century. Now he is one of two.*

THROUGH TIME &
SPACE WITH FERDINAND
FEGHOOT!

by Grendel Briarton

"...a saloon called the Bilge Pump."

One of Ferdinand Feghoot's favorite haunts, a Time Travellers' Club rendezvous where they told magnificent tales, was a saloon called the Bilge Pump. In the 1980s, however, it became infested by an odd group of science-fictionadoes, writers trying to pilfer story ideas, and addicts scrounging fringe benefits, all arguing bitterly about who did what first.

Old Juniper Widget, author of *Regurgitations from the Glob Galaxy,* boasted that he had once pinched H. G. Wells; even older Veronica Lewdski bragged of being the first woman seduced in a submarine—by a grandnephew of Jules Verne at that; young Pat Squirrell claimed his granddad had organized the first SF convention just before McKinley's election.

103

One evening, Feghoot appeared among them garbed as a Japanese Buddhist priest. "Bah!" he exclaimed. "Newcomers! I have just returned from the century of Japan's civil wars. When I started my wanderings, my friend Norimitsu the swordsmith was worried. 'Feghoot-*sama*,' he said, 'though a priest wears no sword, no man should go unarmed in these evil times. Allow me to forge you an *uchiwa*—a steel war-fan. With it, because of the virtue and strength of my name, you can smite any assailant.' Of course, I accepted." Feghoot produced the heavy steel weapon. "Here it is. See how he signed it? *Bishū jū Norimitsu, Chōroku Third Year.*"

"What's that got to do with SF?" shrilled Ms. Lewdski.

"*Chōroku Third Year,*" said Ferdinand Feghoot, "was A.D. 1460. That is the date of the first Feghoot fan club."

The adventures of Ferdinand Feghoot (through time & space!, of course) have appeared in the pages of The Magazine of Fantasy & Science Fiction, Venture Science Fiction, Isaac Asimov's Science Fiction Magazine, *and* Amazing Science Fiction Stories, *as well as three editions of* The Compleat Feghoot, *each one more compleat than the one before.*

Feghoot first manifested himself during a game of Scrabble, when E F G H O O T *appeared in Mr. Briarton's tray.*

Of the present story, Mr. Briarton remarks: "As to the Bilge Pump, it is a San Francisco waterfront bar which I invented for a story I have not yet written. It derives from a vessel, the H.M.S. *Blighty, commanded by Feghoot's friend, the redoubtable Cap-*

tain Bowen, and which was scuttled by her muti-
nous crew during the gold rush of 1849 and sank at
her moorings. Bowen and seven seamen, including
the second officer and ship's carpenter, made it back
to England in a longboat. The crew perished to a
man in the savage mining country of California. So
there."

ON THE ROCKS AT SLAB'S

by John Gregory Betancourt

*Naturally there are taverns on this fantasy world,
which happens to be flat, with a sun that travels
around it, rising and setting as any proper sun
should....*

*The Oracle rode alone through the gates of Zello-
que: around him crackled an almost-visible aura of
power and authority. The City Guard fell in behind
him as he headed, intent on his mission, straight for
the steps of the palace.*

I was watching two disembodied heads sing
drunken songs when the trouble started. A couple
of City Guards sauntered in, glanced around with
disdain, then headed toward my private table. They
looked splendid in full uniform, with their red capes
flapping boldly behind them.

Quite a few of my tavern's patrons made a hasty
retreat through the back door. The floating heads

vanished in puffs of ethereal gases. I had nothing to hide—nothing much, anyway—so I waited.

"Ulander," the guard on the right said, "I have a message for you." Only then did I recognize him beneath his red-plumed helm—Nim Bisnar, an old City Guard who'd worked off and on for me during the last ten years.

"What is it?" I demanded. "You know you're supposed to use the back entrance—you'll give my place a bad reputation!"

He ignored my protests. "Captain Yoonlag sent us. An Oracle from Ni Treshel—that's right, *the* Ni Treshel, where the bones of Shon Atasha are kept —came to the Great Lord's palace yesterday. He's looking for more splinters of his god's bones. Somewhere he'd heard tales about Slab's Tavern—and he persuaded the Great Lord to let him search your place!"

I jolted to my feet, alarmed. "What? *When?*"

"In an hour, maybe two."

Calling to Lur, my doorman and bodyguard, I dug a handful of silver royals from my pouch and poured them into Nim's hands. "Half are Yoonlag's. Split the other half between you."

"Thank you, sir!" they both said, then turned to go—through the back door, this time.

Lur lumbered over to my side. He was a large man—about seven feet tall, with broad shoulders and muscles enough to make him look twice as large. I'd always found those characteristics ideal for my purposes.

"Master?"

"Throw everybody out," I said, "except the servants."

"Sir?" he said, bewildered.

"You heard me—*do it!*"

The tavern was large and dark, its dim light concealing the crumbling plaster and footworn paving stones. Huge wooden columns—hewn from the hearts of ancient oaks—supported the high ceiling.

Weird shadows stretched everywhere. There were numerous secluded spots, and off at the curtained booths along the edge of the room, illegal transactions were taking place.

I marked the pirates at their tables, with their rich, colorful, jewel-encrusted clothes that mimicked but never equaled nobles' dress, and nodded to the ones I knew—Rigelem Teq, Hilan Lammiat, Kol Fesseda, a few others. (In return for protection for his city's ships, the Great Lord of Zelloque had made his city an open port ten years earlier.) In one dark corner a couple of black-robed slavers threw dice; in another, two dockhands threatened each other with knives. With little patience or gentleness, various barkeeps persuaded them to take their squabble to a nearby alley. But mostly the people drank and talked and sang too loudly, the room ringing with boisterous shouts as they swore, laughed, and argued.

Lur moved among them, bending now and then to whisper something in various ears. Usually the men would turn pale, then tremble, then bolt for the door. Even the pirates left without a fight—Lur's imposing bulk was just too much for them, I guessed. Within minutes the place was deserted.

For a long minute, I just stood there and pondered the Guard's words. An Oracle, coming to search my tavern for a splinter of a god's bone...

More than ghostly, disembodied heads that sang drunken songs, my tavern had quite a reputation for strange, magical happenings...it had helped keep away all but the least bloodthirsty clientele. Slab's was the sort of place anything could happen: rumor said that, late at night, drunks sometimes inexplicably became sober, the furniture rearranged itself (always when nobody was looking), and people sometimes vanished, never to be seen again. Of course, that was only rumor...but I *did* know that against the far wall stood a table where chilled wine tasted like warm blood, and there was a certain spot (which moved every night) where Slab Vethiq himself, the man who'd founded my noble drinking establishment, was known to appear from time to time—or at least, his spirit was. And even if Slab didn't come, chances were someone—or some*thing*—else would...if you stepped too close.

The two drunken, singing heads suddenly appeared, hovering over a table. They both wore the colorful silk scarves and earrings of sailors; only the mistiness of their necks and lack of bodies marked them as other than human. One of the barmaids seized a broom and swatted at them until they disappeared.

If the Oracle saw them—or anything else magical—he'd tear the building down in search of his bone.

I barred the doors and shuttered the windows. At once the barmaids lit tallow candles and set them in various niches. The place filled with a warm, somewhat hazy light. Everyone stared at me, wondering (I was sure) whether I had gone completely mad. It was then that I told them, in short, blunt, angry words, what Nim had told me, and what I planned to do about it.

The Oracle moved through the streets of Zelloque like a hot knife cutting through fat. He wore gold and blue silk pantaloons and a gold silk shirt, slippers of soft, white klindu fur, and he carried a golden wheel in his arms. His wheel glittered brightly, red and blue from rubies and sapphires, gold and silver from the dying sun's light. Behind him, in perfect formation, marched twenty members of the City Guard.

He held his divine purpose firmly in mind: to gather all the bones of Shon Atasha the Creator together into one place, to use their magic to summon His spirit back to Earth.

The noise of tramping feet echoed loudly through the deserted streets.

* * *

Trying to reason with ghosts seldom succeeds. Like with Slab. I stood before him, as I'd stood before him a thousand times when I worked as his servant, and stared into his pale blue eyes. He wore his finest robes—green, embroidered with gold and silver thread—almost as though he was expecting the Oracle and had dressed for the occasion.

"Bones!" he mocked. "Bones!" And then he trailed off in laughter.

I stepped back and he slowly disappeared, disintegrating in wisps of green fog.

"Well," I told him, "at least *I'm* not going to die by trying to swallow fifty blue-backed crabs—alive!" But gloating wouldn't help; *he* didn't have to worry about having his livelihood demolished. He could always go haunt someplace else.

I should have known better than to try to persuade him and all the other ghosts not to appear during the Oracle's visit. Now I had a terrible suspicion they'd be certain to show up, if anyone stepped close to their special spot (which, fortunately, was off in one dark corner tonight).

I stood back and surveyed everyone else's work, then gave the signal for the doors to be unbolted and the shutters thrown open. Afternoon sunlight flooded in.

Most of my dozen or so employees now sat at various tables, with bottles and goblets of wine before them, looking like the tavern's regulars. I'd stationed them in all the places where I knew odd things occurred; they all had orders to prevent anything unusual from happening—at any cost. Only Lur and a couple of the barmaids kept to their regular duties, moving from table to table as usual. For the thousandth time, I thanked my good fortune in having the loyalest servants money could buy. None of them would give my secrets away.

"Master?" Lur said, looming over me. I took a

quick step back and he still loomed over me. "I hear
them coming."

Straining, I heard them, too—the tramp-tramp
of many booted feet somewhere close at hand. Then
they marched outside and halted there. One of the
Guards, silhouetted in the door, stood for a second
and surveyed the place before entering. Then I recognized him: Tayn Lastoq, the Captain of all the
City Guard—one of the few city officials I'd never
been able to bribe. Behind him came another figure:
the Oracle.

Like all the Rashendi, this one wore gaudy, bril-
liantly colored silk clothing. He carried his future-
telling wheel in front of him like a holy relic, which
of course it was.

"This is the place?" he asked, with obvious disdain. He sniffed.

"Yes, Oracle," Tayn said.

"So be it. Find what I seek."

I stepped forward. "Wait a minute—"

"Be quiet, Ulander!" Tayn snapped. I could see
the Oracle had begun to annoy him—and he was
taking it out on me. "I know you better than you
think. You know why we're here! Now let us get on
with our business."

"I have friends in high places!"

He whirled around, his sword suddenly in his
hand. Its point touched my chest just below my
heart. "Narmon Ri himself ordered the search. You
have no choice. Do you understand?"

Lur tensed beside me, growling softly, ready to
attack Tayn. I restrained him with a quick look,
then turned back to the Captain of the Guard. "I
understand," I told him, smiling faintly. "But if
anything's broken, I'm sending Lord Ri the bill."

He laughed, then, and resheathed his sword.
"You have a quick wit, Ulander. I'll tell the men to
keep the damage to a minimum."

He turned and sauntered out, leaving the Oracle
there alone. I heard Tayn instructing his men
through the open door.

"Who are you?" the Rashendi asked me.

"Ulander Rasym, owner of this establishment."

He stared at me a moment, eyes strange and dark.

"Perhaps if you told me more about this god's bone, I'd be able to help. What does it look like? Where would it be?"

"It may take any form," the Rashendi said softly. "A piece of marble, a building stone. They try to remain hidden. For years have I located bones for the shrine in Ni Treshel. Each splinter has been different—and yet the same. They have an odd feel, an uncertain look, as though their shape is untrue. With my wheel I can perceive a splinter's true nature, if it is put before me." He nodded wisely. "So it has always been. I will find one here, I feel." Then he turned and wandered toward the curtained booths.

Off to one side, I saw wisps of fog beginning to gather above a table. I gestured wildly to one of the barmaids. With a gasp, she seized her broom and stepped forward, swinging madly at the two disembodied heads that had begun to appear. They'd started to sing—

> *Vimister Gröll was a merry old soul*
> *Who loved his wine and women—*

but dissipated just before the Oracle turned to look back. The barmaid pretended to chase cobwebs from the ceiling with her broom while two of the barkeeps took turns continuing the song, mimicking the ghosts' high, drunken voices:

> *He picked a brew and drank up to*
> *The point his nose fell brim-in—*

It rapidly became obvious they'd never heard the tune before and were making it up as they went along. Fortunately, they soon became stumped at a rhyme for *sausage* and grew silent.

Tayn Lastoq and his men entered and spread through the tavern. For once, everything seemed to be going well—they found nothing but dust beneath the tables and under the booths. I followed Tayn around, looking over his shoulder, trying my best to bother him.

"You see?" I said again and again. "There's nothing here."

Then I turned around and noticed Slab Vethiq sitting at one of the tables, as solid-looking as he'd ever been in life. He grinned at me, then turned back to his wine. As I stared, other people began appearing at the other tables, gradually filling the place. I recognized one—another—then another. They were all patrons who'd died! Fortunately, they'd brought their own wine.

Nobody else seemed to notice.

The Oracle now stood in the middle of the room as the men searched, ignoring the people seated at tables. He looked mildly annoyed at not having found his bone (though I had repeatedly said it wasn't here in front of him). At last he shouted for Tayn. The Captain of the Guard hurried over.

"Yes, Oracle?"

"Tear out the counter, then have your men start on the booths in the back. I want it found if it takes all night!"

With a sigh, Tayn turned to obey. I threw myself in front of him before he could speak. "There must be another way!" I said. "You can't just tear up my tavern!"

"I'm sorry, Ulander, but—"

Just then, one of his men chose to step too close to that certain spot in the corner. With a roaring sound, a giant mouth appeared, filling the whole ten feet between floor and ceiling. Its lips were thick and bloodless white; its teeth were sharp, jagged spikes; its tongue lolled out like some immense gray carpet. Gazing down its gullet, I saw only blackness.

This seemed to be what Slab was waiting for.

With an insane cry he rose and seemed to *flow*
rather than walk to the Oracle. Seizing the Rashendi by the hair, he dragged him forward and into
the mouth, vanishing down its throat. The other
ghosts of patrons long-dead grabbed all the guards,
Tayn included, and spirited them into it as well.

The mouth closed with a snap, the tongue flickered over the lips, and the whole apparition vanished with a slight sucking sound.

Too stunned to do more than stare at the now-
empty corner, I just stood there. Then one of the
barmaids began to scream. I heard a slapping sound
and she shut up.

I retreated to my booth and sat down heavily. I was
ruined, I knew. The Great Lord would have me executed for killing his favorite Captain and twenty of
his guards. His assassins would track me down wherever I went. Well, I figured, at least I could get drunk,
ease the pain of my death—that was the only advan-
tage left in owning a haunted tavern.

Hearing singing, I looked up. The two disembodied
heads had appeared over my table. Slowly they
drifted away. Sounds from outside told me a number
of pirates had entered. Business went on as usual.

As the day wore on and I got progressively
drunker, I began to hear strange rumors...tales of
how twenty-one of Lord Ri's guards had been plucked
from the harbor by slavers—and Lord Ri had de-
clined to buy them back...tales of how their leader,
Tayn Lastoq, had gone mad and led his men and an
Oracle off to fight sea monsters...tales of how the
Oracle had disappeared, never to be seen again.

That night, Slab's haunted spot moved into my
private booth. I first became aware of it when I
looked up and found Slab sitting in front of me, ca-
sually sipping a bottle of my best Coranian Brandy.
He raised it in salute, gave me a knowing wink,
then slowly faded away.

I shuddered. That wink had always disturbed me
back in the days when Slab still lived and I'd been
his right-hand man, with only as much power as he

let me have. That wink had been a private sign, one last reminder that he owned the place and I never would... or so he'd thought.

But I'd saved my money, made sure I knew all the right people, and finally took over when he died. Yet for all the documents that said I owned the place, something deep inside me called me a fool, and cursed, and somehow I knew the truth.

I drank more Wine and tried not to think. My pains eased; somehow everything no longer seemed quite so grim. Slab, they'd said when he was alive, always takes care of his own.

Secure with that thought, I drifted toward sleep.

Slab's Tavern first appeared in "The Brothers Lammiat" (which has appeared in Amazing Science Fiction Stories, *and is intended as the starting point for a whole cycle of heroic-fantasy adventures). Writes Betancourt: "Slab's was first intended as a throwaway bar where pirates could go to have a drink in peace, in the city of Zelloque. But—things being what they are—the tavern and its—um—eccentric owner and clientele took on a life of their own, and promptly demanded their own story."*

Betancourt's first book is an interactive science fiction adventure, Starskimmer. *His stories have appeared in a number of magazines and anthologies; his first novel,* The Blind Archer, *is forthcoming from Avon, and is also set in Zelloque.*

HANDS OF THE MAN

by R. A. Lafferty

"...a tavern frequented by skymen and traveling
men of all sorts."

His forearms were like a lion's, sinewed and
corded and mountainous. One could hardly help
looking at them, and he was looking at them himself. His hands, no less remarkable than his forearms, lay palm-up on the bar.

The hands of the man were intricately and pow-
erfully fashioned; on one of the lesser fingers of the
left hand there was a heavy gold band three-
quarters of an inch thick, and wide. The rest of him
was a stocky skyman, fair and freckled. He was
blue-eyed and lightly lashed and browed, and he
gazed at his hands like a boy.

It was a tavern frequented by skymen and traveling men of all sorts. A spotter had seen the man;
and now he came and they talked.

"You are very interested in something," said the
spotter Henry Hazelman.

"Not at all," the skyman said. "A man who is deeply interested has the same appearance as one who is completely absentminded, as was my case. I was staring at my hands, and both they and my mind were empty. But before I had left off thinking, I was musing on the contrast between the two of them."

The skyman was named Hodl Oskanian, and the name was the least odd thing about him.

"I was looking at my left hand which I was born with," continued Hodl, "and at my right hand which I made myself. It is the saying of the palmists that we form the lines of our right hand by the tide of our lives.

"You will notice, my friend, that all the lines of my left hand are graven so deeply that a coin could be stood up in any of them when the hand is flat. Get a hold on your emotions, man, and then look at that Head Line! Should it not betoken genius! You would say that a man with a Head Line like that would be capable of anything, and you would be right. Hold on to your eyeballs with both hands when you take a look at that Heart Line! Notice the Generosity Passage where it goes between the Mountains of Integrity and Nobility. Doesn't it shake you a little to stand beside a man with a Heart Line like that?"

"Yes, something does shake me a little," Henry Hazelman said.

"Look at that Humility Bump!" Hodl all but sang, "I'll bet I've got more humility than any man in creation! If I ever met a man with a hand like mine I'd follow him to the end of the universes just to shake it. Steady yourself now, friend. Look at that Life Line! It curves clear around the heel of my hand like the Ocean-River circling the ancient world. I couldn't die at less than a hundred and twenty with a Life Line like that."

"Yes, it is quite a hand," said Henry Hazelman.

"But not the right hand," said Hodl. "Notice that, while it also is one of the most fascinating hands in

the worlds, it is not up to the left which I was born
with. It is the hand of a compromised genius. Is
there any other kind? It is like the hand of a Leo-
nardo or an Aquinas or an Eoin Dinneen or an
Aristotle or a Willy McGilly—the hand of a man
capable of reaching the ultimates, but perhaps not
of surpassing them. This comparative fuzziness of
line is to be found in the right hands of all really
great men. Even *we* fall short of our destiny. Have
you the price of a Beer?"

"Yes, here, give my friend a Beer," Henry cried to
the barman. It was the green Beer recently intro-
duced from Barathron, and it had become a favorite
of the skymen.

And when the left hand of Hodl flicked out to
take the Beer, Henry Hazelman saw what he had
been waiting to see. He went away.

Henry went to David Daumier the diamond fac-
tor.

"It's as big as a hen's egg, David, my word on it,"
Henry was insisting.

"To you all rocks are as big as hens' eggs," David
said. "I wonder I never see such small eggs. It would
take a hundred of them to make a dozen."

"I've never given you a wrong turn, David, and I
never saw the like of this one."

"And probably glass."

"Wouldn't I know the difference?"

"Yes, you would know the difference." And already David Daumier was going along with Henry
the spotter.

"There are little islands in that Head Line." Hodl
still talked to himself and to several who listened in
both amusement and admiration. "In anyone but
myself it would mean that a person with such islands in his Head Line was a little peculiar. Good
afternoon, sir, is my conversation worth a Beer to
you? I have said it myself a hundred times that I'm
the most interesting person I ever listened to."

"Yes, your talk is worth that," said David Daumier. "Barman, fill my friend again. That is a gaudy little ring you have there, skyman. The stone is simulated, of course."

It was the finest diamond that David had ever seen, and he had traded as many diamonds as any man in the universes.

"There's deception in you," Hodl rebuked him. "Let us be open. You are a professional. There's a little blue light that appears behind the eyes of a professional when he sees a stone like this. Did you know that? You sparkle from it. And the stone is not simulated."

"A little too yellow."

"Golden rather. All great diamonds are golden. The small blue ones are for children."

"We will assume it is hot. Fortunately I can handle it, at somewhat of a discount, of course."

"If it were hot and of this size, would you not know about it?"

"It isn't from Earth," said David. "I doubt that it's of any trabant or asteroid. It hasn't the orange cast of those of Ganymede, and I'd know a diamond from Hokey Planet anywhere. Is it from Astrobe? Pudibundia? Bellota?"

"No, it isn't from any of the Hundred Worlds, nor from any licensed planet. I didn't pick it up in any such backyards. It's from a distance."

"Has it a name?"

"A private name only."

"Likely it has a flaw."

"If it had a dozen it would still be peerless. But it has none."

"Not even a built-in curse?"

"I have worn it in health. I believe it is lucky."

"Since we admit it has value, why are you not afraid to wear it openly?"

"I'm a full-sized man, and armed, and in my wits. I would not be easily taken."

"It is too large to market," said David, "and diamonds are down."

"To the buyer, the market is always down."

"If you would set a price—to turn the conversation to the point."

"Oh, if you like it, I'll give it to you," Hodl said.

David ordered a drink to settle his nerves before he answered.

"For a moment I didn't recognize your opening," he told Hodl after he had sipped and swallowed. "Skyman, I would bet that you have haggled prices on Trader Planets."

"Aye, I've dealt with the gentlemen there and found them not too sharp," said Hodl. "I left the Traders, shirtless and barefoot, it's true, but not much worse than I was when I went there. I'm an easy mark."

"I wouldn't like to play poker with you."

"It is not my game. I am too guileless."

"Would five thousand interest you?"

"Not very much," Hodl said, looking at the Bump of Rectitude of his right hand. "I wouldn't stoop to pick it off the floor, but if it were in my pocket I wouldn't trouble to throw it away."

"Yes, you have haggled on Trader Planets. I could double it, but that is my limit."

"That will do nicely, David," said Hodl.

"What? You will go along with me? You will sell?"

"I will sell nothing. Am I a merchant? I will give it to you as I said that I would. But to salve your feelings, I will accept the small sum you have named. Out of respect to you, I would hardly accept a smaller sum with an easy mind. Bring it here and lay it on the bar."

"I will send Henry," said David. He nodded to Henry, and Henry left.

"You have sent Henry, but not for the money." Hodl smiled as he studied the Island of Icarus of his right hand. "He has gone to collect some comic-strip characters to keep me company. One of them, what we call *Homo conventus* or mechanical man, will analyze myself and my gaud. Only after you are satisfied with the reports (and I'm told that they miss nothing nowadays) will you go and get the money. I admire your prudence, for this is the way that gentlemen do business."

And that is the way that the gentlemen did it. Henry Hazelman returned with three-comic strip characters, and one of them was a machine—a descendant of Structo the Mechanical Man from the strip of that name.

It was Structo (his name in Hodl's mind only) who affably and left-handedly shook hands with Hodl and engaged him in conversation.

"It is a fine hand, sir," said Structo, "(I am told you were saying the same thing about it yourself), and a fine ornament on it. No, do not attempt to withdraw your hand, skyman. It is necessary that I retain my grip in order to analyze yourself and your thing. My own filaments make contact with the crystalline complex, as well as with your own reta. I can read you like a book, to coin a phrase."

"Look out for a little double phrase in a middle chapter," said Hodl.

"It's an antibunko machine, skyman," said David Daumier. "It reads you and your stone at the same time. Well, what do you read, Penetrax Nine?"

"Mr. Daumier, the stone is sound and without flaw," said Structo (Penta 9). "It rings like a bell."

"—to coin a phrase," said Hodl. "How do I ring?"

"Yes, that is the question," said David. "My device, skyman, has appraised the stone, as my eye has done. But at the same time it can read what is in your mind regarding that stone. Should there be a flaw in the stone to escape both myself and my device, my machine will find it in your mind."

"Intelligent-looking contrivance, is he not?" said Hodl. "Can he follow a syllogism to the end? Can he recognize a counterman? Can he count the marbles when the game is over?"

"He can't, but I can," said David. "His job is to detect, and he does it well. My contrivance can sniff out every newest trick in the world."

"Aye, but can he snuffle out the oldest?" Hodl asked. "How do you read me, contrivance?"

"Yes, is there any doubt in the mind of this man about the stone, Penta?" David asked.

"Mr. Daumier, I had to travel some distance into his mind to find the stone," said Structo. "But his mind is serene about the stone. It is good, and he knows it is good. Only—oh, no, sir! Do not attempt to match grips with me, Mr. Skyman, even in fun. I have a grip of iron! I *am* basically iron. You will be injured if you persist. Or do I have it wrong? Why, you have crushed my hand as if it were an eggshell, to coin a phrase. No matter, I always carry a spare. Now, if you will release me, Mr. Skyman—thank you."

"Quite a grip, skyman," said David Daumier. "You crushed an iron probe that was built for durability. But my contrivance had already answered my question for me. You have no mental reservation as to the stone. I will go get the money now. My people will keep you company, skyman, and the contrived one will repair himself meanwhile."

David Daumier left on his errand.

"I meant to say something else," chittered Structo (Penta 9) when its master was gone, "but you squeezed the thought out of me. My nexus at the moment was in my hand which you crushed."

"You intended to say, gentle contrivance, that I knew the stone was good, too good," said Hodl, "and that I was laughing in my mind. Of course I was! I'm a merry man, and it gladdens me to give away a thing too good to keep."

The contrivance put on another hand and busied himself hooking it up. The two human c.s. characters, glowering gunmen, studied Hodl with sleepy evil eyes and seemed more mechanical than their mechanical comrade.

After a decent interval, David Daumier returned with a tightly wrapped brown paper package. It was of fair size and was marked with a deformed Greek

M, Daumier's own code for the amount in the packet.

"Now we will make the exchange," David said softly, and he laid the paper-wrapped package openly on the bar. "Lay the ring beside it. Then I open and count."

"The ring won't come off easily," said Hodl. He worked and turned it vigorously. It was quite tight. "There is an amusing story of how the ring came off the finger of the last owner," Hodl told them. "I finally used a bolt cutter."

"The band doesn't show it," said David. "An expert must have rejoined it."

"The band wasn't cut, the finger was," said Hodl. "Say, that man did make a noise about it!"

"I'll send for a jeweler's saw," said David. "I don't mind the band being cut."

"Soap and hot water are quicker," said Hodl. "It'll slip off easily with that."

And soap and hot water were already there. The basin was brought by a counterman in a dirty apron. And who notices a counterman? Especially who notices that he is a pun? So the only one who recognized the man in the dirty apron as Willy McGilly was Hodl.

Hodl soaked his great hand, and the ring came off. Hodl held it dramatically (while the counterman made his counter unseen) in one of his great hands with their deep lines that betokened genius, and the faint islands in the Head Line that in any other man would indicate something a little peculiar about that genius.

"It's a nice ring," said Hodl with regret. "Now we count."

Two of the comic-strip characters- patted their armpits to indicate that the bulge there had a reason for being, Henry Hazelman the spotter lounged in the doorway of the tavern to spot anything that should come, and David opened the package and began to count out the hundreds. Those bills sing a

soft song to themselves when they fall on each
other.

When he had reached the count of thirteen,
David's eyelid flickered and he paused, but for
much less than a second, only long enough to check
and recheck in his rapid mind and to put down a
faint surge of panic.

When David had reached thirty, Hodl reached
out and lightly touched one of the bills. "It is nice-
looking money," he said. He removed his hand, and
David continued to count.

Only one who knew the diamond-factor well, or
who knew all men well, could have known that
David was nervous. Only a very quick eye could
have detected that his hand trembled when he
passed the fifty mark. And only a consummate
genius like Hodl could have known that the throat
of David was dry, or have guessed why it was.

Hodl reached out and touched another bill, the
sixty-third or the sixty-fourth, it does not matter
which.

"It is nice-looking money, David. Possibly too
nice-looking," he said. "Continue to count."

The comic-strip characters made moves towards
their weapons, but David gulped and went on with
the count.

Seventy...eighty...ninety...ninety-nine, one
hundred. There was ripe finality about it. And
David waited.

"It's a nice pile," said Hodl. "I have never seen
such pretty money. Who makes your money,
David?"

The comic-strip characters and Henry Hazelman
started their moves again, but Hodl froze them at
half-reach. There is a proverb that a gun in the
hand is worth three in a shoulder holster, and Hodl
had one in his hand so fast that it sparkled in all
their eyes.

"I'm surprised at you, Mr. Daumier," Hodl said
softly. "I did not know that you dealt in funny

money. To offer a poor price to a poor skyman is one
thing. To pay even that in counterfeit is another.
The deal is off, sir! I will keep my ring, and you may
keep your pile."

"It can't be," David groaned, bedazed. "I never
take a bad bill. I sure never took a hundred of them.
I myself have just got it from my own safe."

"It *does* look good. It is almost the best I have
ever seen," said Hodl. "But, David, you have han-
dled a million bills. You know what it is."

"You switched the package," said David, hoar-
sely.

"I have not. Your men and your machine have
scanned me the whole time. I have nothing on me
but this ring now back on my hand, and this little
thing back on my other hand. And my pockets
which I turn out for me contain nothing but twelve
cents Earth coin, a small luck charm (a coney's
foot), and a Ganymede guilder. Your machine can
read me as to physical things without contact."

"That's right, Mr. Daumier," said Structo (Penta
9). "That's all he's got on him."

"I came with this, and with this I leave," said
Hodl.

They looked at the stocky skyman with the forearms like a lion's and the little gun in one of his
deep-lined hands. And they were afraid to jump
him.

David still didn't know how the switch had been
made. But now he knew when.

That evening in another tavern, and this a secluded one down in Wreckville, Hodl Oskanian and
Willy McGilly and some of their friends sat and
drank together. And from a bundle of bills similar
to David's, Willy McGilly now counted out bills,
ninety-eight, ninety-nine, one hundred; and these
were valid.

"They have multiplied the Earth by billions and
made all things intricate," said Willy. "Men are not

the same as their fathers were, and a man would need three brains to comprehend all the new devices. And yet in quiet places, like a Green Valley, some of the simple and wholesome things endure— old friends, old customs, old cons—sweet frauds that are ever young. We are like ancient handicrafters in an automated universe, but we do fine and careful work.

"They have multiplied it all, but the basic remains the same: the Setting (and the hands of Hodl *do* set the thing off well); the Bait (and the Stone would have to be the finest ever or we'd have worn it to dust using it for bait); the Warning, to give fun to the game; the Counterplay; and then the Innocent Disclaimer."

Hodl once more gazed at his hands, and he spoke.

"It was a nice touch, Willy, to use his own brown paper to wrap your own bundle, and to tape it so similarly with his own 'David Daumier Jeweler' tape. It was nice to find out and reproduce his own peculiar mark for the amount, and to learn all the little details while you were in his establishment, even though you could not get into The Safe Itself. I hope you didn't help yourself to trinkets while you were there. It would be wrong to burglarize his premises, but it is licit to take a taker in honest combat. You were the good switchman, Willy, while I was the strong magnet to hold their eyes.

"But, Willy, the water was too hot, and the soap was too strong. You are inconsiderate in so many ways."

"And you are always perfectly considerate yourself?" Willy McGilly asked, cocking an eyebrow like a soaring hawk.

"Always," said Hodl. And he studied his hands with their deep Heart Lines passing through the Mounds of Rectitude and Magnanimity and Piety and Sympathy and Generosity and Gentleness and all the Virtues.

Mr. Lafferty writes that he has "seen one ghost and one UFO" and imagines this to be "about par for a lifetime." But he adds "I have also met, absolutely and in the flesh, one of the fictional characters I had made up entirely. It was in a bar in Galveston, and he was about fifteen years younger than I had created him, than I had imagined him. But he was himself absolutely, and he looked at me as though he were the one seeing a ghost. 'How old are you anyhow?' I asked him. 'What's your name and what do you do?' 'I'm nineteen,' he said. 'My wrestling name is Richard the Lion-Hearted. I don't give my real name because I still want to go back north and play college football under it next year.' Then he left quite suddenly, saying something to another man as he went out.

"The other man came over to me. 'He said there's something about you that bugs him out totally,' the other man said. 'Richard the Lion-Hearted isn't very good as a wrestler. Oh, he's never been pinned and he's never lost, but he doesn't make a good villain or a good good-guy either. He's too good-natured, not aggressive enough, and lacks menace.'

"I went home the next week and wrote 'The Hands of the Man,' with Richard the Lion-Hearted at his correct age, about thirty-five, as I had created him; but I've always been glad that I got that glimpse of him when he was younger. I felt a menace in the latter-day Lion-Man, but I suspect that he is still too good-natured. He's been in several of the stories about Willy McGilly and his Wreckville Gang, but often he doesn't have a speaking part and you'd hardly know he was there."

Two collections of Mr. Lafferty's stories have recently appeared from Corroboree Press. He is the author of numerous novels, including Past Master, Archipelago, The Flame Is Green, *and* The Devil Is Dead.

ENDURANCE VILE

by Steven Barnes

*A Los Angeles health-food bar can be a place for
strange stories....*

I was the last customer in Owensville Health
Foods, and Albert Owens rang up my order with
one eye on the clock. He was just beginning to get
those "it's time to close shop" yawns he is famous
for, when The Runner walked into the store.
Walked, not ran, which was a surprise in itself.
Owens lifted his shaggy brows to the heavens in
supplication. "So much for going home early," he
growled in my ear. Owens has an impressive growl,
too. In fact, everything about the man is impressive: over fifty years old, and he still has the broad
shoulders and firm arms of the halfback he was in
college.

"What?" I asked in mock surprise. "And miss the
chance to concoct an Owsly Special? Shame, *shame*
that such a thought should cross your mind. Just
look at that poor lost soul..." I pointed surrepti-

tiously at The Runner, as all of Owensville's customers called the little man. This month. Two
months ago he had been The Yogi, and before that,
The Bodybuilder. He was a male secretary named
Owsly Bostic with a penchant for changing obses-
sions every fortnight or so, and the bad judgment to
fill every available ear with his latest health
theories. The last time I had seen him, he wore
dirty sneakers and raveled white jogging-shorts,
and his stringily muscular legs were flecked in
mud. His jersey smelled as if a platoon of Marines
had taken a sponge bath with it.

The Runner was about thirty-five, perennially
going on eighteen. He was always "almost back in
shape," filling his stomach with nostrums purchased by the armload from Albert's shelves and
punishing his body with a series of brutal exercise
regimes. I reflected that this was, after all, America, and everyone had a right to go to Hell in the
handbasket of their choosing. But did Free Speech
guarantee a man the right to yell "Botulism!" in a
crowded cafeteria?

"Carrot Juice Special," he said to Suzie, the USC
coed who tends the health bar at nights. She looked
at him for an instant as if she didn't recognize him,
then began to fix the drink. I could understand her
confusion. It was the first time I had seen Owsly out
of jockstrap, so to speak. He wore slacks and a knit
shirt, and not a trace of a terry-cloth headband or
other athletic paraphernalia. His usual locker-room
aroma could, in Albert's picturesque phrase, "wilt
wheat germ"; but now he seemed to be freshly
cleaned and polished. Amend that: there was a
small white bandage on his forehead.

"Boy, he sure seems quiet tonight." I grinned at
Albert.

Owens returned my grin with a twist of lemon.
"Listen, Steve, you haven't had to sit through as
many of his lectures about isometrics, or vegetari-
anism, or colonic irrigation, or Sufi dancing, as I
have. I'm counting my blessings." He ran a hand

over his thick mop of black hair, and I found myself wondering when he'd start showing age like normal human beings.

"Oh, well," I countered, "at least it's only one new kick at a time."

"Yeah, there's that."

I looked in my bag at the vitamins and kefir that I had dropped by Owensville to pick up, and was about to say good night and good luck, when Owsly looked up from his Special (carrot juice with brewer's yeast and desiccated liver powder. I remember the night when, in a garrulous mood, Bostic had insisted that I try a swig. I remember a stray thought concerning maggot milk shakes running through my mind as I downed it) and said, "I'm giving it up. Swear on my mother's grave."

"Giving what up?" Suzie asked, uninterested. She was a redhead on the pretty side of plain, with a history major's mind in a cheerleader's body. I sometimes thought the combination was awkward, then remembered that that equation could have been reversed, and remained silent.

"The running. I've—gone too far. I know something I should never have found out."

I nudged Owens. "A door Man was never meant to open, and so forth." Owens sighed and looked at the clock again.

"If I let him start, I won't be out of here until midnight."

"Then don't let him start."

Owens's expression was one of whimsical resignation. "Oh, why the hell not?" He walked up to the front door quickly and pulled the shade. Only the four of us were left inside, now.

We gathered around Bostic, who was still gazing into his carrot juice. "Well?" I asked finally. "Why are you giving it up?"

I searched my writer's mind for a proper description of his eyes. Frightened? No, "haunted" was closer.

"It all started two years ago. You all remember

what I looked like then?" Indeed we did. He was a quiet, plump man with thinning brown hair and a petulant mouth who came and went often, saying little to anyone. He read the Slender Age magazines on the rack, and tanked up on lecithin–kelp–B$_6$–cider-vinegar tablets this week, expanding cellulose tablets the next, or anything else that promised fast, fast, *fast* relief from rotundity. But he never lost weight, until...

"Yeah, well, I went from diet to diet, and never seemed to get anywhere. Finally I read somewhere that diets don't work, because the expression 'going on a diet' always implies that one day you will go *off* of the diet, too. What I had to change, it said, was my whole self-image. If I thought like a skinny person, it would be easier to be one." I nodded. Made sense to me, but Owens sat with his lips pursed as if waiting for a punch line.

"So I tried to think: What is a skinny person like? Or better, a *healthy* person? And I kept thinking about that, and I got into analysis, and self-hypnotism, and pretty soon I was finding out things about myself I'd never known before. I was dealing with stress with celery sticks instead of sausage, and the weight was creeping off. But then I wanted more, and I began exercising."

Suzie wiped the counter lazily with her cloth as she reminisced. "Was that the day you came in and bought all of the Jack La Lanne books?" He nodded vigorous agreement.

"Calisthenics. Then weights. Then yoga, and finally running. I had found it at last. Running is a *skinny-people's* sport, no two ways about it. And I got into it. At first I could puff out a half mile. Then a mile. Then two miles, and finally three. I tried everything I could, but couldn't get above three without getting sick to my stomach. I just couldn't. So I started researching, and improving my diet, and by then I had lost thirty pounds, and *was* a skinny person, but it wasn't enough. Well, I finally squeezed my way up to five miles, but it took months to do, and I was just about to my limit. But wow! I could run five miles in forty minutes, and I was *happy*."

He chewed his lower lip miserably, as if musing over the wisdom of continuing. "I'm going to need another Special if I'm going to finish this," he said.

Owsly nodded to Suzie, and, careful to breathe only through her mouth, she whipped it up and held it out to him. He downed half of it in two glugs, and I felt a fish flopping in my stomach.

He licked a brownish-orange mustache off his upper lip and continued. "One day I was browsing through one of the little metaphysical bookshops off Hollywood Boulevard and Wilcox, and I came across an old, yellowed book called *Body Magicks*. I browsed through it, and was stunned. It claimed to be an exercise manual for accomplished sorcerers and warlocks. I laughed at the time, but the book cautioned over and over against the use of these techniques by the uninitiated. I bought it, and the old man at the cash register made some sort of finger sign at me, and when I didn't return it, he almost refused to sell me the book. I talked him into it finally, but he cautioned me against using the knowledge in the book.

"I took it home, fascinated and amused. Of course the warnings were absurd. Of course."

"What did it say?" Owen asked, curious at last.

"It said that all fatigue was caused by the lack of proper breathing habits. That poisons build up in the bloodstream that must be cleansed by the 'air-fire.' If you don't breathe properly, the muscles will clog with poisons and stop moving."

Owens glanced at me in unspoken question. "That's a pretty fair description of the Kreb cycle," I mused aloud.

"Kreb cycle?"

"Sure," I said. "Your muscles are fueled by a chemical called ATP, adenosine triphosphate. Exertion causes one of the phosphate bonds to break, releasing energy."

"What does that have to do with breathing?"
Suzie asked.

"Plenty. If you get oxygen faster than the ATP
chains break down, you have an *aerobic* exercise,
like distance running. If you break down the chains
faster than oxygen gets in to the muscles, you have
an *anaerobic* exercise, like, oh, sprinting or power
lifting. But lactic acid builds up in the muscles due
to oxygen debt during anaerobic exercise, and if
enough of it builds up the muscles don't get the
message to twitch anymore, and activity stops. Oxygen re-forms the ATP bonds, so breathing is very
important." I searched my memory, and came up
close to empty. "Almost every Eastern meditation or
martial art has its own special breathing patterns.
They all work."

"Yeah, you've got it right," Owsly said, glad to
have me pick up the pieces of his explanation.
"They all work, but this one..." He shook his head,
and a chill seemed to go through him as he sat
quietly. Another pull on his drink, and he was ready
to go on. "I can't say if this technique would work
for anyone else. I don't know if I was a fluke or
what. You decide for yourselves. I started using the
meditations suggested. I fasted, I sniffed salt water
up each nostril to clean my air passages, and I
breathed.

"Lord, I never knew what breathing was until I
got into that book. Breathing to the tips of my
lungs. Breaths inhaled for ten beats, held for six,
exhaled for twelve. That was the crucial thing, the
proportion of inhalation to retention to exhalation.
That, and the number of breaths per minute com-
pared to the number of heartbeats. I don't want to
go into it too far right now. You decide for yourselves if you want to.

"I began to feel—different. Lighter. As if I
weren't really breathing, as if my body were part of
a—a cosmic flow that moved the air in and out of
my body all of its own volition. My breathing
slowed and slowed and deepened, and soon I forgot

where I was. I don't know how long I stayed in trance, but it felt as if I could see myself sitting there. As if I were no longer in my body, that its lungs were breathing, its heart beating, and all of its functions taking place without *me* in it to guide. Then I laughed. Of *course* my body could get along perfectly well without my conscious mind. Lord knows I never told my organs how to operate, or my heart how to pump. They operated perfectly well without me, without my conscious meddling.... And then I understood what the book was trying to say. The body needs only to be pointed in the right direction, then get your brain out of gear and let it go. I was ecstatic. I had found the *way!*"

None of us interrupted Owsly as he drained his glass, and there was a terrible secret stirring in the depths of his bloodshot eyes. "What I didn't notice was that I had trouble reentering my body. It was like trying to engage gears that were moving at different speeds, and neither wanting to yield. I was giddy and dizzy when I finally made it, but too exuberant to see the implications....

"The next day was Saturday, and I knew that the track at the local high school would be closed. That would be perfect, since I didn't want to be disturbed. I climbed the fence and walked out to the center of the field, sat down in a half-lotus, and closed my eyes. My breathing slowed, until the proportions were down to...to where they needed to be." He looked at Suzie with a nervous apology on his lips, and a look that said *Can't you see I'm just trying to protect you?* "After a time, I got up and stretched, still maintaining the same breathing pattern. Then I started to run.

"I ran so slowly it was almost a walk, because I had to do all of my inhalations through my nose, and that limited my speed a lot. If I sped up too quickly, I'd go into...oxygen debt, that's it, oxygen debt, and have to slow down again. Slowly, the rhythm caught, and I was able to pick up a little speed and some smoothness in my movement. And I began to sink deeper and deeper into the lure of the breathing. Every quarter-mile lap I got deeper and deeper into it, so that by the fifth lap, I was beginning to pull away from my body. I could 'see' myself running, but I couldn't feel the exertion. There was no hesitation in my movement, and my muscles weren't fighting themselves. I began to pick up speed.

"It was marvelous. Soon I was whipping around the track at close to top speed, only I was doing it for lap after lap after lap, without fatigue! I 'watched' myself, knowing that if I could only surrender to the deeper rhythms, still more wonderful achievements could be mine. So I concentrated, and widened the gap between my body and my mind, so that I was drifting off alone in a black void while my body moved endlessly around the track.

"At last I noticed that the sun was going down. Why, I must have run eight miles! And without a stumble or single painful moment. I figured that it was time to end the experiment."

He looked at Owen with a face whose muscles had gone the way of warm butter. "I don't know if you will believe this, but I *couldn't* stop. I couldn't regain control of my body. The gears just wouldn't mesh. I tried...Lord, how I tried, but it was as if I just didn't belong in there anymore, that my body preferred running, sweaty and glassy-eyed, around the track. And it was speeding up. The heartbeat was the same, and the breathing was the same, but there was no mistaking the fact that I—or it—was beginning to move at an absurd speed. Maybe that speed was believable for a sprint, but over a distance of *miles,* well, I was starting to panic. Again I tried to get back into my body, and it wouldn't let me back.

"And now I knew why the book had cautioned me. All my life my conscious mind had denied my body exercise, had stuffed it with garbage foods, poured dope smoke and alcohol and God knows what else into it, and now it wasn't letting me back in. It considered me a bad influence.

"Well, I may have been dumb, but I'm still all the brains my body has, and it clearly didn't know what to do without me. I mean, it kept running until the perspiration stopped running from my pores, and until I was staggering and my limbs were shaking, and still it didn't stop, and I knew it—I was going to die if I didn't do something quick.

"I tried again to gain control over my legs, but it was hopeless, they just plodded on and on. I tried to move my hands, and they twitched a little, but when I tried to force them to grab on to a drinking fountain or fence, they wouldn't move more than a few inches, and I almost gave up.

"Then I remembered my eyelids. I focused all my willpower on them, and finally they shut. I stumbled on in total darkness for a lap or so, then ran off of the track and smack into a wall.

"When I woke up, it was daylight. I was so tired I couldn't feel anything, and my feet were a swollen mess, but somehow I managed to get home. I swear I must have run all night." He sighed with the drooping shoulders of one whose story is finished, and trickled out his few remaining words. "I missed a day of work, but I was happy just to be alive. Anyway. That's why I'm giving up running."

Owen and I winked at each other as Owsly slid off his stool and plunked down a couple of bucks and change for the drinks. Owen waved him off. "On the house, Owsly. What you've just got to learn is that you get too wrapped up in your activities. You just overdo."

"Yeah," he said wearily, "I guess you're right. That's why I'm giving this"—he pulled a tattered copy of a book out of his pocket and laid it on the counter—"to you. I hope you use it more wisely than I did." And, shaking his head sadly, Owsly walked out of the store. Owens locked the door behind him.

The three of us, Owens, Suzie, and myself, looked

at the book for a long time before Suzie, bless her fearless little heart, turned it over. Sure enough, the cover read *Body Magicks*. I thumbed through it for a moment, and Suzie whistled under her breath.

"Well, Owen..." I said, laying it down gingerly, "are you game?"

He looked at it with dreadful curiosity, then shook his head. "Not me. I'm an old man, dammit." He said this while trying to poke out his gut and relax his arms into flabbiness. "What about you...?"

I started to be brave, but shook a negative. "Naw. I'm too far behind in my reading to check this out. I guess it'll just have to wait...."

But Suzie's hand had already snaked out and snagged it. "I'll give it a read..." she said thoughtfully.

"Whatever for?" Owens said, curious. "You're not into any sport."

"True enough," she said, gathering her sweater and turning off the lights behind the juice bar. "But I've got a heavy date with the captain of the tennis team Friday night, and...well, you never know, do you...?"

Politely, she affected not to notice our lowered jaws as she skipped to the front door and vanished, the tattered copy of *Body Magicks* tucked firmly under her left arm.

Steven Barnes, who has collaborated with Larry Niven on the SF novels Dream Park *and* The Descent of Anansi, *and published one solo novel,* Streetlethal, *comments that this story came out of a dare from Larry Niven, who bet him that he couldn't write a tall tale set in a health-food bar. So he said, "Oh, yeah?" and "Endurance Vile" is the result. As for the inevitable question, as Barnes put it, of whether or not such a technique as described in the story actually exists: "Yes and no. There is a very definite key to unlocking conscious control over the autonomic nervous system, and I could tell it in one line of type. It would be insanely incautious for me to do so—not every experiment ends as humorously as Owsly Bostic's."*

THE CENTIPEDE'S DILEMMA

by Spider Robinson

*Callahan's Place is somewhere in Suffolk County,
Long Island.*

What happened to Fogerty was a classic example
of the centipede's dilemma. Served him right, of
course, and I suppose it was bound to happen sooner
or later. But things could have gone much worse
with him if he hadn't been wearing that silly hat.

It was this way:

Fogerty came shuffling into Callahan's Place for
the first time on the night of the Third Annual
Darts Championship of the Universe, an event by
which we place much store at Callahan's, and I noticed him the moment he walked in. No great feat;
he was a sight to see. He looked like a barrel with
legs, and I mean a big barrel. On its side. On top of
this abundance sat a head like a hastily peeled
potato, and on top of the head sat—or rather
sprawled—the most ridiculous hat I'd ever seen. It
could have passed for a dead zeppelin, floppy and

disheveled, a villainous yellow in color. From the moment I saw it I expected it to slide down his face like a disreputable avalanche, but some mysterious force held it at eyebrow level. I couldn't estimate his age.

Callahan served him without blinking an eye—I sometimes suspect that if a pink gorilla walked into Callahan's, on fire, and ordered a shot, Callahan would ask if it wanted a chaser. The guy inhaled three fingers of Gin in as many seconds, had Callahan build him another, and strolled on over to the crowd by the dart board, where Long-Drink McGonnigle and Doc Webster were locked in mortal combat. I followed along, sensing something zany in the wind.

Some of us at Callahan's are pretty good with a dart, and consequently the throwing distance is thirty feet, a span which favors brute strength but requires accuracy along with it. The board is a three-foot circle with a head-shot of a certain politician (supply your own) on its face, concentric circles of fifty, forty, twenty, ten, and one point each superimposed over his notorious features. When I got to where I could see the board Doc Webster had just planted a dandy high on the right cheek for forty, and Long-Drink was straining to look unconcerned.

"What's the stakes?" the guy with the hat asked me. His voice sounded like a '54 Chevy with bad valves.

"Quarts of Scotch," I told him. "The challenger stakes a bottle against the previous winner's total. Last year the Doc there went home with six cases of Peter Dawson's." He grunted, watched the Doc notch an ex-presidential ear (you supplied the same politician, didn't you?), then asked how he could sign up. I directed him to Fast Eddie, who was taking a night off from the piano to referee, and kept half an eye on him while I watched the match. He took no part in the conversational hilarity around him, but watched the combat with a vacuous stare, rather like a man about to fall asleep before the TV.

It was reasonably apparent that wit was not his long suit. Doc Webster won the match handily, and the stein that Long-Drink disconsolately pegged into the big fireplace joined a mound of broken glass that was mute testimony to the Doc's prowess. One of my glasses was in that pile.

About a pound of glass later, Fast Eddie called out, "Dink Fogerty," and the guy with the hat stood up. The Doc beamed at him like a bear being sociable to a hive, and offered him the darts.

They made quite a pair. If Fogerty was a barrel, the Doc is what they shipped the barrel in, and it probably rattled a lot. Fogerty took the darts, rammed them together point-first into a nearby tabletop, and stood back smiling. The Doc blinked, then smiled back and toed the mark. Plucking a dart from the tabletop with an effort, he grinned over his shoulder at Fogerty and let fly.

The dart missed the board entirely.

A gasp went up from the crowd, and the Doc frowned. Fogerty's expression was unreadable. The champ plucked another dart, wound up, and threw again.

The dart landed in the fireplace fifteen feet to the left with a noise like change rattling in a pocket.

"It curved," the Doc yelped, and some of the crowd guffawed. But from where I stood I could see that there were four men between Doc Webster and the fireplace, and I could also see the beginnings of an unpleasant smile on Fogerty's thick features.

None of the Doc's remaining shots came close to the target, and he left the firing line like a disconsolate blimp, shaking his head and looking at his hand. Fogerty took his place and, without removing that absurd hat, selected a dart.

Watching his throw I thought for a second the match might turn out a draw. His windup was pitiful, his stance ungainly, and he held the dart too near the feathers, his other arm stiff at his side. He threw like a girl, and his follow-through was nonexistent.

The dart landed right between the eyes with a meaty *thunk*.

"Winner and new champeen, Dink Fogerty," Fast Eddie hollered over the roar of the crowd, and Fogerty took a long, triumphant drink from the glass he'd set down on a nearby table. Fast Eddie informed him that he'd just won thirty-five bottles of Scotch, and the new champ smiled, turned to face us.

"Any takers?" he rasped. The '54 Chevy had gotten a valve job.

"Sure," said Noah Gonzalez, next on the list. "Be damned if you'll take us for three dozen bottles with one throw." Fogerty nodded agreeably, retrieved his dart from the target, and toed the mark again. And with the same awkward, off-balance throw as before, he proceeded to place all six darts in the fifty circle.

By the last one the silence in the room was complete, and Noah's strangled "I concede," was plainly audible. Fogerty just looked smug and took another big gulp of his drink, set it down on the same table.

"Ten dollars says you can't do that again," the Doc exploded, and Fogerty smiled. Fast Eddie went to fetch him the darts, but as he reached the target...

"Hold it!" Callahan bellowed, and the room froze. Fogerty turned slowly and stared at the big red-headed barkeep, an innocent look on his pudding face. Callahan glared at him, brows like thunder-clouds.

"Whassamatter, chief?" Fogerty asked.

"Damned if I know," Callahan rumbled, "but I've seen you take at least a dozen long swallows from that drink you got, and it's *still full.*"

Every eye in the place went to Fogerty's glass, and sure enough. Not only was it full, all the glasses near it were emptier than their owners remembered leaving them, and an angry buzzing began.

"Wait a minute," Fogerty protested. "My hands've been in plain sight every minute—all of you saw me. You can't pin nothin' on me."

"I guess you didn't use your hands, then," Callahan said darkly, and a great light seemed to dawn on Doc Webster's face.

"By God," he roared, "a telekinetic! Why you low-down, no-good..."

Fogerty made a break for the door, but Fast Eddie demonstrated the veracity of his name with a snappy flying tackle that cut Fogerty down before he covered five yards. He landed with a crash before Long-Drink McGonnigle, who promptly sat on him.

"Tele-what?" inquired Long-Drink conversationally.

"Telekinesis," the Doc explained. "Mind over matter. I knew a telekinetic in the Army who could roll sevens as long as you cared to watch. It's a rare talent, but it exists. And this bird's got it. Haven't you, Fogerty?"

Fogerty blustered for a while, but finally he broke down and admitted it. A lot of jaws dropped, some bouncing off the floor, and Long-Drink let the guy with the hat back up, backing away from him. The hat still clung gaudily to his skull like a homosexual barnacle.

"You mean you directed dem darts wit' yer mind?" Fast Eddie expostulated.

"Nah. Not ezzackly. I...I make the dart board *want darts*."

"Huh?"

"I can't make the darts move. What I do, I project a...a state of wanting darts onto the center of the target, like some kinda magnet, an' the target attracts 'em for me. I only learned how ta do it about a year ago. The hard part is to hang on to all but one dart."

"Thought so," growled Callahan from behind the bar. "You make your glass want Gin, too—don't ya?"

Fogerty nodded. "I make a pretty good buck as a fisherman—my nets want fish."

It seemed to me that, given his talent, Fogerty was making pretty unimaginative use of it. Imagine a cancer wanting X-rays. Then again, imagine a pocket that wants diamonds. I decided it was just as well that his ambitions were modest.

"Wait a minute," said the Doc, puzzled. "This 'state of wanting darts' you project. What's it like?"

And Fogerty, an unimaginative man, pondered that question for the first time in his life, and the inevitable happened.

There's an old story about the centipede who was asked how he could coordinate so many legs at once, and, considering the mechanics of something that had always been automatic, became so confused that he never managed to walk again. In just this manner, Fogerty focused his attention on the gift that had always been second nature to him, created that zone of yearning for the first time in his head where he could observe it, and...

The whole half-dozen darts ripped free of the target, crossed the room like so many Sidewinder missiles, and smashed into Fogerty's forehead.

If he hadn't been wearing that dumb hat, they might have pulped his skull. Instead they drove him backward, depositing him on his ample fundament, where he blinked up at us blinking down at him. There was a stunned silence (literally so on his part) and then a great wave of laughter that grew and swelled and rang, blowing the cobwebs from the rafters. We laughed till we cried, till our lungs ached and our stomachs hurt, and Fogerty sat under the avalanche of mirth and turned red and finally began to giggle himself.

And like the centipede, like the rajah whose flying carpet would only function if he did *not* think of the word "elephant," Fogerty from that day forth never managed to bring himself to use his bizarre talent again.

Imagine getting a netful of mackerel in the eye!

Spider Robinson, who lives in Nova Scotia between trips to Callahan's Crosstime Saloon, has been writing good, serious (and some not so serious) SF since 1973. In 1974 he shared the John W. Campbell Award for Best New Writer with Lisa Tuttle. His collaboration with Jeanne Robinson, Stardance, won the Hugo Award in 1978.

About "The Centipede's Dilemma" Mr. Robinson writes: "In 1959 a distant relation of mine, Raymond Robinson, was working on one of the last dance-hall gigs of his career. At 12:48 A.M. Ray found himself in a small pickle: He and his band and backup singers had played their entire book—and still had twelve minutes to fill.

"So he began 'noodling,' as he puts it in his autobiography: 'Just a little riff which floated up into my head. It felt good and I kept on going.' The crowd received the result so warmly that he tried it the next few nights, improvising lyrics, until it 'froze into place.' It was fun.

"Later that year he cut it as a single, his twenty-second. It was a breakaway crossover hit, his biggest to date, and Ray—who came up when Sugar Ray was around, and so has always performed under his middle name, Charles—to this day briefly quotes it at the end of every concert.

"It is called (his preferred spelling) 'What I Say.'

"I'm not suggesting for a moment that The Centipede's Dilemma is of that level of quality (it is not the Callahan's story I'd have picked to anthologize, myself, but I was not consulted); I mention the anecdote about Brother Ray only because the story was created in exactly the same way.

"Callahan's Crosstime Saloon, the first Callahan collection, was sold and about to be printed—and the editor called up and said that someone upstairs wanted the book to be longer; did I have any more Callahan stories lying around? No, I did not. Could I write a few at once? I didn't have an idea in my head. Try, he said. (Baby, what I say? ...)

"Well, I thought, a lot of clever, witty, hip people have walked into that bar—isn't it time we had a moron? How about a moron with a secret weapon... that only a moron can use? Just a little riff that floated up in my head, as Brother Ray said. Noodling. It felt good and I kept going.

"It was fun.

"There are two additional volumes of Callahan's Place stories, and there will never be a fourth; nonetheless the series is not, repeat not a trilogy. It merely happens to end with the volume that follows the after-the-first one, that's all. The other books are Time Travelers Strictly Cash and Callahan's Secret, and they can be read in any sequence. Fair warning: They all contain puns. And this story does not, and now I understand why George and Darrell selected it!"

THE CAUSES

by Margaret St. Clair

Another San Francisco bar, this one with music of a kind...

"God rot their stinking souls," the man on the bar stool next to George said passionately. "God bury them in the lowest circle of the pit, under the flaying ashes. May their eyeballs drip blood and their bones bend under them. May they thirst and be given molten glass for liquid. May they eat their own flesh and sicken with it. May they—" He seemed to choke over his rage. After a moment he lifted his glass of Stout and buried his nose in it.

"You Irish?" George asked with interest.

"Irish? No." The man with the Stout seemed surprised. "I'm from New Zealand. Mother was Albanian. I'm a mountain climber. Why?"

"Oh, I just wondered. What are you sore about?"

The man with the moustache patted the newspaper in his pocket. "I've been reading about the H-bomb," he said. "It makes me sick. I'm cursing the

149

scientists. Do they want to kill us all? On both sides, I'm cursing them."

"Yes, but you have to be reasonable," the man on the second bar stool beyond George argued, leaning toward the other two. "None of us like that bomb, but we have to have it. The world's a bad place these days, and those Russians—they're bad cookies. Dangerous." Uneasily he shifted the trombone case he was holding on his lap.

"Oh, sure, they're dangerous." The man with the Stout hesitated, sucking on his moustache. "But basically, the Russians have nothing to do with it," he said. He cleared his throat. "I know what you're going to say, but it's not true. Our real trouble isn't the Russians.... We're in the mess we're in because we've lost our gods."

"Hunh?" said the man on the second bar stool. "Oh, I get it. You mean we've become antireligious, materialistic, worldly. Ought to go back to the old-time religion. Is that what you meant?"

"I did not," the man with the Stout said irritably. "I meant what I said. The gods—our real gods—are gone. That's why everything is so fouled up these days. There's nobody to take care of us. No gods."

"No gods?" asked the man on the second bar stool.

"No gods."

The interchange began to irk George. He finished his drink—Bourbon-and-Soda—and motioned to the bartender for another. When it came, he said to the man with the moustache, "Well, if we haven't got any gods, what's happened to them? Gone away?"

"They're in New Zealand," the man with the moustache said.

He must have sensed the withdrawal of his auditors, for he added hastily, "It's all true dinkum. I'm not making it up. They're living on Ruapehu in Wellington—it's about nine thousand feet—now, instead of Olympus in Thrace."

George took a leisurely pull at his drink. He was

feeling finely credulous. "Well, go on. How did they get there?" he asked.

"It started when Aphrodite lost her girdle—"

"Venus!" said the man on the second bar stool. He rolled his eyes. "This ought to be hot. How'd she lose it?"

"Her motives were above reproach," the man with the Stout said stiffly. "This isn't a smutty story. Aphrodite lent the girdle to a married woman who was getting along badly with her husband for the most usual reason, and the girl was so pleased with the new state of things that she forgot to return it. The couple decided to take a long cruise as a sort of delayed honeymoon, and the woman packed the girdle in her trunk by mistake. When Aphrodite missed it—Olympian society goes all to pieces without the girdle; even the eagles on Father Zeus's throne start fighting and tearing feathers—it was too late. The ship had gone so far she couldn't pick up any emanation from it."

"When did all this happen?" George asked.

"In 1913. You want to remember the date.

"Well, as I was saying, she couldn't pick up any emanation from the girdle. So finally they sent Hermes out to look for it—he's the divine messenger, you know. And he didn't come back."

"Why not?" the man on the second bar stool asked.

"Because, when Hermes located the ship, it had put in at New Zealand. Now, New Zealand's a beautiful country. Like Greece, I guess—I've never been there—but better wooded and more water. Hermes picked up the girdle. But he liked the place so much he decided to stay.

"They got worried then, and they sent others of the Olympians out. Iris was first, and then the Muses and the Moirae. None of them came back to Olympus. Those left got more and more alarmed, and one big shot after another went out hunting the girdle. Finally by 1914 there wasn't anybody left on Olympus except Ares. He said he didn't much care

for the girdle. Things looked interesting where he
was. He guessed he'd stay.

"So that's the situation at present. All the gods
except Ares, and once in a while Athena, are on
Ruapehu. They've been there since 1914. The Maori
are a handsome people anyhow, and you ought to
see some of the children growing up in the villages
around there. Young godlings, that's what they are.

"Athena doesn't like it there as well as the
others. She's a maiden goddess, and I suppose there
isn't so much to attract her. She keeps going back to
Europe and trying to help us. But somehow, everything she does, no matter how well she means it,
always turns out to help that hulking big half
brother of hers."

"Interesting symbolism," George said approvingly. "All the gods we've got left are Ares, the brutal war god, and Athena, the divine patroness of
science. Athena wants to help us, but whatever she
does helps the war god. Neat. Very neat."

The man with the moustache ordered another
bottle of Stout. When it came, he stared at George
stonily. "It is not symbolism," he said, measuring
his words. "It's the honest truth. I told you I was a
mountain climber, didn't I? I climbed Ruapehu last
summer. I *saw* them there."

"What did they look like?" George asked lazily.

"Well, I really only saw Hermes. He's the messenger, you know, and it's easier for people to look
at him without being blinded. He's a young man,
very handsome, very jolly-looking. He looks like
he'd play all kinds of tricks on you, but you
wouldn't mind it. They'd be good tricks. He—you
could see him shining, even in the sun."

"What about the others?"

The man with the Stout shook his head. "I don't
want to talk about it. You wouldn't understand me.
They're too bright. They have to put on other
shapes when they go among men.

"But I think they miss us. I think they're lone-
some, really. The Maori are a fine people, very in-

telligent, but they're not quite what the gods are used to. You know what I think?" The man with the moustache lowered his voice solemnly. "I think we ought to send an embassy to them. Send people with petitions and offerings. If we asked them right, asked them often enough, they'd be sorry for us. They'd come back."

There was a stirring four or five stools down, toward the middle of the bar. A sailor stood up and came toward the man with the moustache. "So you don't like the government?" he said menacingly. There was a Beer bottle in his hand.

"Government?" the man with the moustache answered. George noticed that he was slightly popeyed. "What's that got to do with it? I'm trying to help."

"Haaaaaa! I heard you talking against it," said the sailor. He swayed on his feet for a moment. Then he aimed a heavy blow with the Beer bottle at the center of the moustache.

The man with the moustache ducked. He got off the bar stool, still doubled up. He drew back. He rammed the sailor hard in the pit of the stomach with his head.

As the sailor collapsed, the man from New Zealand stepped neatly over him. He walked to the front of the bar and handed a bill to the bartender who was standing, amazed, near the cash register. He closed the door of the bar behind him.

After a moment he opened it again and stuck his head back in. "God damn everybody!" he yelled.

After the sailor had been revived by his friends and pushed back on a bar stool, the man with the trombone case, who had been on the far side of the Stout drinker, moved nearer to George.

"Interesting story he told, wasn't it?" he said cheerily. "Of course, there wasn't anything to it."

"Oh, I don't know," George answered perversely. "There might have been."

"Oh, no," the man with the trombone case said positively. He shook his head so vigorously that the folds of his pious, starchy, dewlapped face trembled. "Nothing like that."

"How can you be sure?"

"Because..." He hesitated. "Because I know what the real reasons for our difficulties are."

"Well, what's your explanation?"

"I—I don't know whether I ought to say this," the starchy man said coyly. He put his head on one side and looked at George bright-eyed. Then, as if fearing George's patience might be on the edge of exhaustion, he said, quite quickly, "It's the last trump."

"Who's the last trump?" the man on the bar stool around the corner from George asked, leaning forward to listen. George knew him by sight; his name was Atkinson.

"Nobody," the starchy man answered. "I meant that the last trump ought to have been blown ages ago. The world is long overdue for judgment."

"H. G. Wells story," George murmured.

"I beg your pardon?" said the starchy man.

"Nothing." George motioned to the bartender and ordered a round of drinks. Atkinson took Gin-and-Ginger-Ale, and the starchy man Kirschwasser.

"Why hasn't the trump been blown?" Atkinson asked, with the air of one tolerating noisy children.

"Because it's lost," the starchy man replied promptly. "When the time came to blow it, it wasn't in heaven. This wicked, wicked world! Ages ago it should have been summoned to meet its master." He drooped his eyelids.

George felt his tongue aching with the repression of his wish to say, "Plagiarist!" Atkinson said, "Oh, fooey. How do you know the trump's been lost?"

"Because I have it here," the starchy gentleman answered. "Right here." He patted his trombone case.

George and Atkinson exchanged a look. George said, "Let's see it."

"I don't think I'd better..."

"Oh, go on!"

"Well ... No, I'd better not."

Atkinson leaned his elbows on the bar and rested his chin on his interlaced fingers. "I expect there's nothing in the trombone case actually," he said indifferently. "I expect it's only a gambit of his."

The soft, wrinkled skin of the man who was drinking Kirschwasser flushed red around the eyes. He put the trombone case down on the bar in front of George with a thump, and snapped open the lid. Atkinson and George bent over it eagerly.

The trombone case was lined with glossy white silk, like a coffin. Against the white fabric, gleaming with an incredible velvety luster, lay a trumpet of deepest midnight blue. It might have been black, but it wasn't; it was the color of deep space where it lies softly, like a caress, for trillions of miles around some regal, blazing star. The bell of the trumpet was fluted and curved like the flower of a morning glory.

Atkinson whistled. After a moment he paid the trumpet the ultimate tribute. "Gosh," he said.

The man with the trumpet said nothing, but his little mouth pursed in a small, tight, nasty smile.

"Where'd you get it?" George queried.

"I'm not saying."

"How do you know it's the last trump?" Atkinson asked.

The starchy man shrugged his shoulders. "What else could it be?" he asked.

The door at the front of the bar opened and three men came in. George watched them absently as they walked the length of the bar counter and went into the rear. "But ... you mean if this thing were blown, the world would come to an end? There'd be the last judgment?"

"I imagine."

"I don't believe it," Atkinson said after a minute. "I just don't believe it. It's an extraordinary-looking trumpet, I admit, but it can't be ... that."

"Ohhhhh?"

"Yes. If it's what you say, why don't you blow it?"

The starchy man seemed disconcerted. He licked his lips. Then he said, in rather a hostile tone, "You mean you want me to blow? You mean you're ready to meet your Maker—you and all the rest of the world—right now? Right this minute? With all your sins, with all your errors of commission and omission, unforgiven and unshriven on your head?"

"Sure. That's right. Why not? The longer the world goes on existing, the worse it'll get. As to sins and all that, I'll take my chances. They couldn't be much worse than what"—Atkinson made a small gesture that seemed to enclose in itself the whole miserable, explosive terrestrial globe—"than what we have now."

Under his breath, George quoted, "'We doctors know a hopeless case—'"

The starchy man turned to him. "Do you agree with him, young man?" he demanded.

"Yep."

The man with the trombone turned bright red. He reached into the case and picked up the trombone. As he lifted it through the air, George noticed what a peculiarly eye-catching quality the celestial object had. Its color and gloss had the effect on the eye that a blare of horns has on the ear. Heads began to turn toward it. In no time at all, everyone in the bar was watching the starchy man.

He seemed to pause a little, as if to make sure that he had the attention of his audience. Then he drew a deep, deep breath. He set the trumpet to his lips.

From the rear of the bar there burst out a jangling, skirling, shrieking, droning uproar. It was an amazing noise; a noise, George thought, to freeze the blood and make the hair stand upright. There must have been ultrasonics in it. It sounded like a thousand pigs being slaughtered with electric carving knives.

Everyone in the bar had jumped at the sudden clamor, but the effect on the starchy man was remarkable. He jumped convulsively, as if he had sat on a damp tarantula. His eyes moved wildly; George thought he had turned pale.

He shouted, "They're after me!" He shouted it so loudly that it was perfectly audible even above the demoniac noise of the bagpipes. Then he grabbed up the trombone case, slammed the trombone in it, and ran out of the bar on his neat little patent-leather feet.

The two bagpipers came out from the rear of the bar, still playing, and began to march toward the front. Apparently they had noticed nothing at all of the episode of the dark blue trumpet. The third man followed in the rear, beating on a small drum. From time to time he would put the drumsticks to his upper lip and seem to smell at them.

"Remarkable, isn't it?" Atkinson said to George over the racket. "Only bar I ever was in where they kept bagpipes in the rear to amuse the customers. The owner's Scottish, you know."

The instrumentalists reached the front of the bar. They stood there a moment skirling. Then they executed an about-face and marched slowly to the rear. They stood there while they finished their number. It was long, with lots of tootling. At last they laid their instruments aside, advanced to the bar, and sat down on three bar stools near the center. They ordered Irish Whiskey.

"Wonder where he got that trumpet," Atkinson said thoughtfully, reverting to the man with the trombone case. "Stole it somewhere, I shouldn't be surprised.'

"Too bad he didn't get to blow it," George answered. He ordered Atkinson and himself another drink.

"Oh, that!" Atkinson laughed shortly. "Nothing would have happened. It was just a fancy horn. You surely don't believe that wild yarn he told us? Why, I know what the real reason for all our troubles is!"

George sighed. He drew a design on the bar counter with his finger. "Another one," he said.

"Eh? What? Oh, you were talking to yourself. As I was saying, I know the real reason. Are you familiar with Tantrist magic and its principles?"

"Un-hunh. No."

Atkinson frowned. "You almost sound as if you didn't want to hear about this," he observed. "But I was talking about Tantrist magic. One of its cardinal tenets, you know, is the magic power of certain syllables. For instance, if you persistently repeat Avalokiteshvara's name, you'll be assured of a happy rebirth in heaven. Other sounds have a malign and destructive power. And so on."

George looked about him. It was growing late; the bar was emptying. Except for himself and Atkinson, the pipers and the drummer, and a man around the corner of the bar from George, who had been sitting there silently against the wall all evening, the stools were empty. He looked at Atkinson again.

"About 1920," Atkinson was saying, "a lama in a remote little valley in Tibet"—George noticed that he pronounced the word in the austere fashion that makes it rhyme with gibbet—"got a terrific yen for one of the native girls. She was a very attractive girl by native standards, round and brown and plump and tight, like a little bird. The lama couldn't keep his eyes off her, and he didn't want to keep his hands off either. Unfortunately, he belonged to a lamistic order that was very strict about its rule of chastity. And besides that, he was really a religious man.

"He knew there was one circumstance, and one only, under which he could enjoy the girl without committing any sin. He decided to wait for it.

"A few months later, when the girl was out pasturing the buffalo, or feeding the silkworms, or something, she saw the lama coming running down the side of the hill toward her. He was in a terrific froth. When he got up to her, he made a certain request. 'No,' the girl answered, 'my mother told me I mustn't.' You see, she was a well-brought-up girl."

George was looking at Atkinson and frowning hard. "Go on," he said.

"I *am* going on," Atkinson answered. "The lama told her to go home and ask her mother if it wasn't all right to do what the holy man told her. He said to hurry. So she did.

"When she came back the lama was sitting on the field in a disconsolate position. She told him it was all right, her mother had said to mind him. He shook his head. He said, 'The Dalai Lama has just died. I thought you and I could cooperate to reincarnate him. Under the circumstances, it wouldn't have been a sin. But now it's too late. Heaven has willed otherwise. The job has already been attended to.' And he pointed over to a corner of the field where two donkeys were copulating.

"The girl began to laugh. As I said, she was a well-brought-up girl, but she couldn't help it. She laughed and laughed. She almost split her sides laughing. And the poor lama had to sit there listening while she laughed.

"You can't excuse him, but you can understand it. He'd wanted her so much, he'd thought he was going to get her, and then those donkeys— Well, he began to curse. He began to curse those terrible, malign Tantrist curses. He's been cursing ever since.

"Ever since 1920, he's been cursing. Once in a while he pauses for breath, and we think things are going to get better, but he always starts in again. He says those dreadful Tantrist syllables over and over, and they go bonging around the world like the notes of enormous brass bells ringing disaster. War and famine and destruction and revolution and death—all in the Tantrist syllables. He knows, of course, that he'll be punished by years and years of rebirths, the worst possible kind of karma, but he can't help it. He just goes on saying those terrible syllables."

George looked at him coldly. *"Two Kinds of Time,"* he said.

"Hunh?"

"I said, you read that story in a book about China called *Two Kinds of Time.* I read it myself. The donkeys, the lama, the girl—they're all in there. The only original part was what you said about the Tantrist curses, and you probably stole that from someplace else." George halted. After a moment he said passionately, "What's the *matter* with everybody tonight?"

"Oh, foozle," Atkinson replied lightly. *"Om mani padme hum."* He picked up his hat and left the bar.

After a minute or so, the two pipers followed him. That left George, the silent man in the corner, and the instrumentalist who had played on the drum. George decided to have one more drink. Then he'd go home.

The silent man who was leaning against the wall began to speak.

"They were all wrong," he said.

George regarded him with nausea. He thought of leaving, but the bartender was already bringing his drink. He tried to call up enough force to say, "Shut up," but heart failed him. He drooped his head passively.

"Did you ever notice the stars scattered over the sky?" the man in the corner asked. He had a deep, rumbling voice.

"Milky Way?" George mumbled. Better hurry and get this over with.

"The Milky Way is one example," the stranger conceded. "Only one. There are millions of worlds within the millions of galaxies."

"Yeah."

"All those millions of burning worlds." He was silent for so long that George's hopes rose. Then he said, "They look pretty hot, don't they? But they're good to eat."

"Hunh?"

"The stars, like clams..."

"Beg your pardon," George enunciated. He finished his drink. "Misjudged you. You're original."

The man in the corner did not seem to have listened. "The worlds are like clams," he said rapidly, "and the skies at night present us with the glorious spectacle of a celestial clambake. They put them on the fire, and when they've been on the fire long enough they open. They're getting this world of yours ready. When it's been on the fire a little longer, it'll open. Explode."

George realized that that last drink had been one too many. He didn't believe what the man in the corner was saying. He wouldn't. But he couldn't help finding a dreadful sort of logic in it. "How'ju know this?" he asked feebly at last.

The man in the corner seemed to rise and billow. Before George's horrified and popping eyes, he grew larger and larger, like a balloon inflating. George drew back on the bar stool; he was afraid his face would be buried in the vast unnatural bulk.

"Because," said the inflating man in a high, twanging voice, "because I'm one of the clam-eaters!"

This horrid statement proved too much for George's wavering sobriety. He blinked. Then he slid backward off the bar stool and collapsed softly on the floor. His eyes closed.

The billowing form of the clam-eater tightened and condensed into that of a singularly handsome young man. He was dressed in winged sandals and a winged hat; from his naked body there came a soft golden light.

For a moment he stood over George, chuckling at the success of his joke. His handsome, jolly face was convulsed with mirth. Then, giving George a light,

revivifying tap on the shoulder with the herald's
wand he carried, the divine messenger left the bar.

This story had its genesis when the late editor of
The Magazine of Fantasy & Science Fiction, *Tony
Boucher (pseudonym of William Anthony Parker
White), took the charming author, Idris Seabright
(pseudonym of Margaret St. Clair), to a bar and
stood her a drink. Boucher described the bar as an
unobtrusive neighborhood tavern whose peculiarities
were accurately portrayed in this story, along with a
few other oddities that only Miss Seabright could invent.*

*"It's basically a religious story," Margaret St.
Clair tells us. Her first story appeared in* Fantastic
Adventures *in 1946; her most recent work appeared
in* Isaac Asimov's Science Fiction Magazine *in the
1970s. She is best remembered for the polished fantasies she published in Boucher's magazine as Idris
Seabright. The present story is one of them.*

FOR A FOGGY NIGHT

by Larry Niven

"...they know that they might return home to find a Romish camp, or a Druidic dancing ground, or :.."

The bar was selling a lot of Irish Coffee that night. I'd bought two myself. It was warm inside, almost too warm, except when someone pushed through the door. Then a puff of chill, damp fog would roll in.

Beyond the window was grey chaos. The fog picked up all the various city lights: yellow light leaking from inside the bar, passing automobile headlights, white light from frosted street globes, and the rainbow colors of neon signs. The fog stirred all the lights together into a cold grey-white paste and leaked it back through the windows.

Bright spots drifted past at a pedestrian's pace. Cars. I felt sorry for the drivers. Rolling through a grey formless limbo, running from street globe to invisible street globe, alert for the abrupt, dangerous red dot of a traffic light: an intersection; you couldn't tell otherwise. . . . I had friends in San Francisco; there were other places I could be. But it wasn't my city, and I was damned if I'd drive tonight.

A lost night. I'd finished my drink. One more, and I'd cross the street to my hotel.

"You'd best wait until the fog thins out," said the man next to me.

He was a stranger, medium all over; medium height and weight, regular features, manicured nails, feathery brown hair, no scars. The invisible man. I'd never have looked his way if he hadn't spoken. But he was smiling as if he knew me.

I said, "Sorry?"

"The point is, your hotel might not be there when you've crossed the street. Don't be surprised," he added. "I can read minds. We've learned the knack, where I come from."

There are easy ways to interrupt a conversation with a stranger. A blank stare will do it. But I was bored and alone, and a wacky conversation might be just what I needed.

I said, "Why shouldn't my hotel be exactly where I left it?"

He frowned into his Scotch-and-Soda, then took a swallow. "Do you know the theory of multiple world lines? It seems that whenever a decision is made, it's made both ways. The world becomes two or more worlds, one for each way the decision can go. Ah, I see you know of it. Well, sometimes the world lines merge again."

"But—"

"That's exactly right. The world must split on the order of a trillion times a second. What's so unbelievable about that? If you want a real laugh, ask a physicist about fur-coated particles."

"But you're saying it's *real*. Every time I get a haircut—"

"One of you waits until tomorrow," said the brown-haired man. "One of you keeps the sideburns. One gets a manicure, one cuts his own nails.

The size of the tip varies too. Each of you is as real as the next, and each belongs to a different world line. It wouldn't matter if the world lines didn't merge every so often."

"Uh-huh." I grinned at him. "What about my hotel?"

"I'll show you. Look through that window. See the street lamp?"

"Vaguely."

"You bet, vaguely. San Francisco is a town with an active history. The world lines are constantly merging. What you're looking at is the probability of a street lamp being in a particular place. Looks like a big fuzzy ball, doesn't it? That's the locus of points where a bulb might be—or a gas flame. Greatest probability density is in the center, where it shows brightest."

"I don't get it."

"When the world lines merge, everything blurs. The further away something is, the more blurred it looks. I shouldn't say *looks,* because the blurring is real; it's no illusion. Can you see your hotel from here?"

I looked out the appropriate window, and I couldn't. Two hours ago I'd nearly lost my way just crossing the street. Tonight a man could lose himself in any city street, and wander blindly in circles in hopes of finding a curb....

"You see? Your hotel's too far away. In the chaos out there, the probability of your hotel being anywhere specific is too small to see. Vanishingly small. You'd never make it."

Something about the way he talked...

"I wondered when you'd notice that." He smiled, as if we shared a secret.

"All this time," I said, "I've been thinking that you talk just like everyone else. But you don't. It's not just the trace of accent. Other people don't say *probability density* or *theorem of multiple world lines* or *on the order of.*"

"No, they don't."

"Then we must both be mathematicians!" I smiled back at him.

"No," he said.

"But then—" But I backed away from the problem, or from the answer. "My glass is empty. Could you use a refill?"

"Thanks, I could."

I fixed it with the bartender. "Funny thing," I told the brown-haired man. "I always thought the blurring effect of fog came from water droplets in the air."

"Bosh," he said. "Bosh and tish. The water's there, all right, whenever the fog rolls in. I can't explain it. The condensation must be a side effect from the blurring of the world lines. But that's not interfering with your vision. Water's transparent."

"Of course. How could I have forgotten that?"

"I forgot it myself, a long time ago." The Scotch was beginning to reach him, I think. He had an accent, and it was growing stronger. "That's why I'm here. That's why I stopped you. Because you'd remember."

The bartender brought us our drinks. His big shoulders were hunched inward against the damp grey light that seeped in the windows.

I sipped at the burning hot glass. Irish Whiskey and strong black coffee poured warmth through me, to counteract the cold beyond the walls. A customer departed, and the fog swirled and swallowed him.

"I walked into the fog one afternoon," said the brown-haired man. "The fog was thick, like tonight. A cubic mile of cotton, as we say. I was just going out for a pouch of snuff. When I reached the tobacconist's, he tried to sell me a bundle of brown paper sticks with a Spanish trademark."

"Uh-huh. What did you do?"

"Tried to get home, of course. Things changed oddly while I wandered in the fog. When it cleared and left me stranded, even my money was no good. The worst of it was that I couldn't even tell my story. Nobody could read my mind to see that I was sane. It was find another fog bank or try to make a life for myself."

"With no money?"

"Oh, I sold my ring and found a poker game."

"Oh. *Oh!*"

"That was a year ago. It's worked out well enough. I thought I might invent something, like the zipper, but that fell through. You're far ahead of us in the physical sciences. But money's no problem. Sometimes there's a fixed horse race. Sometimes I find a poker game, or a crooked crap game where they'll let me bet the right way."

"Sounds great." But not very honest, I thought.

"You disapprove?" My companion's voice had suddenly gone thin and cold.

"I didn't say that."

"I compensate for what I take," the brown-haired man said angrily. "I know how to untwist a sick man's mind. If a player sits down with emotional problems, I can help him. If he really needs the money, I can see that it comes to him."

"Why don't you become a psychiatrist?"

He shook his head. "It would take years, and then I'd never be able to hold a patient long enough to do myself any good. He'd get well too fast. Besides that, I *hate* certain people: I'd want to harm them instead of helping them.

"Anyway, I don't go out in the fog anymore. I like it here. I stopped you because you're one of those who remember."

"You said that before. What exactly—?"

"After all, people are constantly walking into fogs. Why is it that we don't hear more about people wandering in from alternate world lines? It's because their memories adjust."

"Ah."

"I caught it happening once. A girl from somewhere else . . . I didn't catch the details; they faded too fast. I got her a job as a go-go dancer. I think she was a prize concubine in someone's harem before she ran into the fog.

"Their memories adjust. They forget their friends, their relatives, their husbands and wives in the old world line. They remember what man is king or president or chairman in the new. But not us. You and I are different. I can recognize the rare ones."

"Because you can read minds." Sarcastically. Part of me still disbelieved; yet...it fit too well. The brown-haired man talked like a mathematics professor because he was talking to me, and I was a mathematics professor, and he was reading my mind.

He looked thoughtfully into his glass. "It's funny, how many sense the truth. They won't walk or drive in the fog if they can help it. At the bottom of their minds, they know that they might return home to find a Romish camp, or a Druidic dancing ground, or the center of a city, or a sand dune. You knew it yourself. The top of your mind thinks I'm an entertaining liar. The deepest part of you knew it all before I spoke."

"I just don't like fog," I said. I looked out the window, toward my hotel, which was just across the street. I saw only wet chaos and a swirling motion.

"Wait until it clears."

"Maybe I will. Refill?"

"Thanks."

Somehow I found myself doing most of the talking. The brown-haired man listened, nodded occasionally, asked occasional questions.

We did not mention fog.

"I need an ordered universe," I said at one point. "Why else would I have studied math? There's never an ambiguity in mathematics."

"Whereas in interpersonal relationships..."

"Yes! Exactly!"

"But mathematics is a game. Abstract mathematics doesn't connect with the real universe except by coincidence or convenience. Like the imaginary number system: it's used in circuit design, but it certainly wasn't intended for that."

"No, of course not."

"So that's why you never got married?"

"Right," I said sadly. "Ordered universe. Hey, I never knew that. Did I?"

"No."

The fog cleared about one o'clock. My brown-haired friend accompanied me out.

"Mathematics doesn't fit reality," he was saying. "No more than a game of bridge. The real universe is chaotic."

"Like in-ter-personal re-lation-ships."

"Maybe you'll find them easier now."

"Like fog. Well, maybe I will. I know some new things about myself... where's my hotel?"

There was no hotel across the street.

Suddenly I was cold sober, and cold scared.

"So," said my drinking partner. "You must have lost it earlier. Was it foggy when you crossed the street?"

"Thick as paste. Oh, brother. Now what do I do?"

"I think the fog's starting to roll in again. Why not wait? The bar won't close until four."

"They close at two in my world." *In my world.* When I admitted that, I made it real.

"Then maybe you should stay in this one. At least the bartender took your money. Which reminds me. Here." He handed me my wallet.

He must have picked my pocket earlier. "For services rendered," he said. "But it looks like you'll need the money."

I was too worried to be angry. "My money passes, but my checks won't. I've got half a term of teaching to finish at Berkeley... and tenure, dammit! I've got to get back."

"I'm going to run for it," said the brown-haired man. "Try the fog if you like. You might find your way home." And off he went, running to beat the fog. It was drifting in in grey tendrils as I went back into the bar.

An hour later the fog was a cubic mile of cotton, as they say. I walked into it.

I intended to circle the block where I had left my hotel. But there was no way to get my bearings, and the outlines of the block would not hold still. Sight was gone, sound was strangely altered and muffled. I walked blind and half deaf, with my arms outstretched to protect my face, treading lightly for fear of being tripped.

One thing, at least, the brown-haired man had failed to warn me about. I walked up to a pedestrian-sized grey blur to ask directions, and when I reached it, it wasn't human. It watched me dispassionately as I sidled off.

I might have drifted away from the area. The hotel varied from an ancient barrow to a hot springs (I smelled warm, pungent steam) to a glass-sided skyscraper to a vertical slab of black basalt to an enormous pit with red-glowing rock at the bottom. It never became a hotel.

The mist was turning white with dawn. I heard something coming near: the putt-putt-putt of a motor scooter, but distorted. Distorted to the clop-clop-clop of a horse's hooves ... and still approaching. It became a pad-pad-pad-pad, the sound of something heavy and catlike. I stood frozen. ...

The fog blew clear, and the sound was two sets of footsteps, two oddly dressed men walking toward me. It was dawn, and the fog was gone, and I was stranded.

In eerie silence the men took me by the elbows turned me about, and walked me into the building which had been my hotel. It had become a kind of hospital.

At first it was very bad. The attendants spoke an artificial language, very simple and unambiguous, like deaf-mute sign language. Until I learned it, I thought I had been booked into a mental hospital.

It was a retraining center for people who can't read minds.

I was inside for a month, and then an outpatient for another six. Quick progress, they say; but then, I hadn't suffered organic brain damage. Most patients are there because of damage to the right parietal lobe.

It was no trouble to pay the hospital fees. I hold patents on the pressure spray can and the butane lighter. Now I'm trying to design a stapler.

And when the fog is a cubic mile of cotton, as we say, I stay put until it goes away.

Larry Niven cryptically says about "For a Foggy Night" that "it's the story Jerry Pournelle quotes when he's telling people why he collaborates with me. Jerry isn't crazy enough to write certain stories. I am."

Crazily or otherwise, Mr. Niven has written The Integral Trees *solo, and collaborated with Dr. Pournelle on* Footfall.

THEY LOVED ME IN UTICA

by Avram Davidson

It could have happened this way; it really could....

The room was dirty and badly lit and it smelled strongly of cheap, greasy food and of something else, which the girl noticed as soon as she came in.

"You're at the Wine again, huh? You can't wait till after the performance?"

"And what the hell is the idea, may I ask, of telling everybody you're my daughter? My daughter, for crying out loud! Who do you think is going to believe that?" he wanted to know.

They were at it again.

Nobody was sup*posed* to believe it, she said. It was just a convention. As a matter of fact, it would stand a better chance of being believed if the story was that she was his *grand*daughter, but she wanted to save his face.

If this meant that he was supposed to look on with fatherly approval while some young punk made a play for her, he said, in that case, he didn't

173

want his face saved, and she could forget the whole idea. Convention! That was a hot one! Since when was she getting so conventional? As if anyone in this burg gave a damn if they were married or not.

"I went over great in Utica," he said. "Capacity house. They loved me in Utica." He drank some more of the Sneaky Pete. The girl, who had opened her mouth, closed it again. She cocked her head and shook it, half-annoyed, half-pitying. He was apt to go off on tangents like that, more and more every day. The guy was going to pieces fast. But she still thought she'd be able to pull him together again. All he needed was a little success—although, of course, a big one wouldn't hurt, either. Not in a one-night stand like this, of course. But if he went over good here, if he just got his self-confidence back, if he'd stay away from the Wine, if—

He was still a good-looking guy, with lots of stuff none of these young studs had. His voice was still good, even if he couldn't take the high notes. She noted that he'd cut himself shaving again, and this, for some reason, annoyed her.

You mean *you* don't care if we're married or not!" she snapped. "All I am to you is a traveling shack-up job." But her heart wasn't in it, and he could tell it wasn't.

"Now, honey," he said. "Don't pick at me, sweetie. I'm a sick man. There's nothing the matter with a little light Wine. It's like medicine, it's good for you. Have some."

But she said, No, thank you. "How about going over your material some more?" she suggested.

He shrugged. "I don't need to go over it. Once I learn a thing I never forget it. The rhapsodies—"

"Will you for heaven's *sake* please for*get* the rhapsodies?"

"—and the hymns—"

"Forget the hymns *too!* 'All new material' is what you're giving them here, remember?" Yes, he remembered. But he still had his doubts. The ballads were okay; though, boy! what a lie to call them "new"! Maybe they were new here, but, golly, he was singing them before the war—not the last war, the one before it. But he gave them up when the rhapsodies started going over so good.

Then, seeing her frown, he hastily said, "But they're good stuff, the ballads. I had good material, nobody had better. They don't write material like that anymore."

He brooded over his cup. The girl could hear the crowd (if you could call that handful of yokels a crowd!), and this reminded her that the guy's act was supposed to open. "Okay, so you know the stuff. So let's hear it. The strings in tune?" He ran his fingers over them, nodded. He was still in the dumps. "Hey, you never told me where you picked up the ballads." Not that she really cared.

The guy shrugged. "Who the hell knows. Here, there. One of them—this one—" He sang the opening line. His voice was a little husky, but it was warm and sweet. "I was knocking it off with this hoofer, see...But you don't want to hear about that....In those days I used to figure, once you're in big time, you're always in. What did I know? Never figured I'd be singing for cakes in the boondocks again. But that's the way it is. You're only as good as your last season, kid. Gee, this past winter was the toughest I ever remember. I used to go down to the islands every winter. Haven't been able to afford it for years."

He warmed up to his troubles. "...and then the sky-pilots started in on me. 'What's with this guy?' they complain. 'Who needs *his* hymns?' I tell you, sweetie, once you're down, they all jump on you. It's a great life if you don't weaken." An idea rippled its way across his face. He threw a swift, sly glance in her direction.

How would it be, he said; how would it be if he just threw in one, maybe two, of the rhapsodies? After all, they'd be expecting it. That was what made his rep.

She looked at him and shook her head with a

bitter little smile. "Some people never *learn,*" she said. "Can't you face up to it that the old material is strictly from Oldsville? Just give the ballads everything you've got. And, oh, say, listen. The MC says to throw in a little narration. Some story connecting the songs together."

"Yeah, but doll. I mean, these ballads. Like there *isn't* any story connecting them together. *You* know. There's *war* bits, *love* bits, *tragedies* ... but, uh, no *story.*"

Then he'd have to vamp one, she said; make it up as he went along. Why, for crying out loud! she complained—he, of all people, shouldn't have any trouble thinking up stories.

"Boy!" she said. "When I remember the stories you told *me!* Hey. What's with the tears bit all of a sudden?"

It took a minute, but he got control of himself. Then he said, "My lamps are giving out on me, babe. I can't even shave myself anymore. I can hardly make you out, over there. Don't leave me, kid. What would I do?" She didn't say a word. "Anything you want. A story to hold the songs together? All right. Sure. I can do that. But don't run out on me. Don't—"

The MC knocked, and came in without waiting for an answer. There were Wine stains on his clothes, and his sandals were badly scuffed, but he had a measure of coarse handsomeness; a long look passed between him and the girl which the older man didn't see.

"You ready to go on, Grandpa?" he asked.

"Who the hell are you calling 'Grandpa'?" the singer snapped, forgetting his troubles.

The MC bowed, exaggeratedly. "Oh, pardon *me,*" he said. "Are you ready to go on now, O sweet singer, whose songs deserve the laurels for all times to come?"

"That's better. That's the way to talk to the servant of the Muses...that's what somebody once called me in Utica, you know. They loved me in

Utica. Hand me my strings, hon. Sure I'm ready.
And, say—listen, pal: Give me a big buildup, will
you, huh?"

"Yeah, yeah...sure— Oh, say, listen: Y'got a
new name for your new act, so I can announce it?"

The old man gaped and blinked and moved his
mouth, started to give his head a shake, No.

But swiftly the girl interposed. "A lot of these
songs are about Troy, aren't they? Or what's the
other name they used to call it? Ilium? Okay, then:
so call your set the *Troiad*. Or the *Iliad*. What the
hell's the difference? —Here's your lyre, Homer,
honey...."

*We will let the inimitable Avram Davidson write
his own inimitable biographical note:*

*"Unlike Frank Harris, of whom it has been said,
'Frank Harris was born in two different countries on
three different dates, and his name was not Frank
Harris,' it is generally agreed that Avram Davidson
was born in Yonkers, New York, on April 23, 1923;
although the practice of the Yonkers Chamber of
Commerce in asking, 'Avram who?' and then hanging up its phone is, admittedly, rather unhelpful. Mr.
Davidson attended four colleges without getting any
degrees higher than 98.6, served in the U.S. Navy
and with the U.S. Marines, was for a few years editor of The Magazine of Fantasy and Science Fiction,
has been a college professor and fish-liver inspector,
was once the husband of Grania Davis, and is still
the father of their conjoint son Ethan Davidson.
Rumors that he once tried to strangle Harlan Ellison
with a thuggee knot he dismisses as lies, spread by
his political enemies. The story which you have just
read had its genesis in a conversation with Randall
Garrett; otherwise he doesn't remember anything*

about it. Avram Davidson lives at the State Veterans Home in Retsil, Washington, where he sometimes re-fights the Battle of Trafalgar with the other old snuff-dippers."

The editors find they can add nothing to that, ex-cept to recommend to those unfortunates who have not previously encountered them such vintage vol-umes of Davidsoniana as the novel The Phoenix and the Mirror *and the collections* Collected Fantasies, The Best of Avram Davidson, The Redward Edward Papers, *and* The Inquiries of Dr. Eszterhazy.

A PESTILENCE OF PSYCHOANALYSTS

by Janet O. Jeppson

Tales are told in luncheon clubs too....

As usual, an undertone of argument permeated the sacred precincts of the Psychoanalytic Alliance, an exclusive luncheon club known to its intimates and its enemies as Pshrinks Anonymous. The Oldest Member was holding forth. This also was not unusual.

"I tell you again that these newfangled analysts use peculiar words that no one understands. If I hear any more about the parameters of the paradigmatic processes I'll eat my hat."

"You've got it wrong," said one of his younger Freudian colleagues who liked to keep up to date, "and you haven't got a hat anyhow."

"Furthermore," continued the Oldest Member, "I object to the pollution to which all of you have subjected the name of our club, adding a silent *p* to shrinks...."

179

"Perhaps it was inevitable," said one of the Interpersonals. "And even ominous," she added.

For once the Oldest Member looked pleased to be interrupted by a female and an Interpersonal (in order of annoyance).

"Ominous?" he asked.

Simultaneously, the rest of the membership groaned and bent closely over their desserts, Bananas Castrata Flambé. The Oldest Member nodded encouragingly at the Interpersonal, who grinned.

The experience I am about to reveal [said the Interpersonal] happened only recently and has been much on my mind. This vignette, while obviously clinical, is not a case, since the person who brought the problem to my attention was not a patient but a colleague I hadn't seen for years, a Pshrink that I used to know when we both carried large iron keys to the locked wards of a well-known psychiatric hospital.

This colleague had always been a rather pedantic, phlegmatic man who yawned his way through analytic school some years after finishing his psychiatric residency when the rest of us were already analysts, struggling to stay afloat on the ever-increasing ocean of jargon. I recalled that this down-to-earth type had a limited vocabulary and what some of us referred to as poverty of imagination. He had, naturally, left Manhattan for some Other Place when he started his analytic practice.

I was shocked, then, to get a frantic phone call from him, begging me for a private lunch because he needed to discuss a confidential problem affecting his work. I told him my noon hour was free and he said he would bring lunch in his briefcase.

As we munched corned beef on pumpernickel in my office, I discovered that he was in town for one of the psychoanalytic conventions. Being allergic to cigar smoke, I had not yet been to the meetings; and

I wondered what psychologically traumatic paper had affected my old friend.

"Listen, I remember that you're a sci-fi buff," he began.

"SF!"

"Whatever. Do you believe in that stuff about ESP and dreams that come true and mysterious extraterrestrial beings and whatnot?"

"I'm still waiting for the hard evidence."

"Well, I don't have any, but after attending this convention it seems to me that I detect—something."

"Alien influence?" I asked facetiously through my corned beef.

"How did you know! Are you part of the conspiracy?"

I began to wonder whether or not I was doing a regular psychiatric consultation after all. I swallowed the last of my sandwich and studied my colleague. While plumper and greyer than he had been, the striking change was the faint twitching of his shoulders, possibly due to muscle strain caused by his new habit of looking nervously over them.

"No," I said. "Tell me what on Earth you are talking about."

He sighed. "I never was much good with words, you know. I barely made it through analytic school because I had so much trouble mastering the vocabulary. Since then I've tried—oh, how I've tried, and then my wife..."

"She's in the field, as I recall," I said.

"Yes, a ———" (he named one of the more verbally agile allied fields). "She tried to help me; and so did some sympathetic colleagues, because at meetings I was a total loss. My papers were so easy to understand that nobody paid any attention to them, and I couldn't understand what anyone else was saying. Finally, after years of study and trying to catch up, I began to use and even understand some of the important words."

"The jargon."

"A pejorative word if I ever heard one," he said with a shrill laugh. "You see—I did it! I'm always doing it!"

"Using a big obscure word?"

"No! I mean, yes—a word with a *p* in it!"

"I am puzzled..."

"There, now you're doing it! I'm convinced that it's a disease, catching and deadly dangerous."

"Unfortunately our field is riddled with *p*'s—psychiatry, psychology, psychoanalysis..."

He moaned. "That's just it. That's why we're the conduits for the malevolent influence from outer space."

"The what?"

"You heard me." He bit into the untouched second half of his sandwich, eyeing me suspiciously over a fringe of buttered lettuce that was sticking out. My colleague was a WASP who always ate butter and lettuce with his corned beef sandwiches, which may be another reason why he had to emigrate from New York.

I decided to humor him. "Supposing there is a mysterious alien influence—how do you know it's malevolent?"

"You haven't been to a psychoanalytic convention lately, have you?"

"No."

"Then don't ask. Or maybe I should tell you. No, I'll just describe my own symptoms. It began with dreams, and don't try to analyze them the way Siggy would have."

"You know perfectly well that I'm non-Freudian. Tell me about your dreams."

"You sound just like me when I'm humoring a psychotic patient."

"Yep."

"What the hell. The dreams come every night. And they're full of words, most of which begin with *p*, that come to life in my head and chase each other around and threaten me. When the dreams began, I became aware of how everyone in my local psychoanalytic society talks like that. I used to feel I didn't belong, but suddenly I began to be part of the group."

"Comrades in jargon?"

"That's it. You don't know how I've been fighting it since I entered your office for lunch. Trying not to use many words beginning with *p*. I can feel them straining at the leash inside my skull, trying to get out, to join an invisible network throughout the terrestrial electromagnetic sphere...."

"Whoa!" I shouted, since his face was beginning to turn purple. "It does seem to be true that our fellow Pshrinks speak in a lot of *p*'s. Does it matter whether they are silent or vocalized—the *p*'s, I mean?"

"I don't think so, but the vocalized seem worse. Proclivities instead of tendencies, parsimonious instead of stingy, paranoid instead of suspicious, and of course the multitude of words beginning with the unvocalized *p* in psycho."

"You'll have to blame most of the problem on the ancient Greeks."

He frowned. "Maybe they were subject to alien influence first. Come to think of it, maybe you're one of the ringleaders. You've got several *p*'s in your name. The world is full of pee—"

As his voice rose in a wail, I interrupted. "You can always go to a Freudian and have your urethral complex analyzed."

["*P*—U!" murmured one of the club's pundits.]

My highly disturbed colleague gulped and began again, in a whisper. "It's much worse out where I live and work."

"Cheer up," I said. "Around here they're into illusory others and imaging and identifications that are introjective..."

"But where you have introjective you also have projective!"

["At least that gets us off the excretory system and onto more interesting anatomical analogies," said one of the Eclectics.]

"Now let's not get carried away," I admonished him. "The world is full of people who don't use words beginning with *p*."

"Is it? My son came home from college asking me to define the parameters of a meaningful marital pairing. My daughter at medical school heard a lecture on probability factors in the success of paternal participation in parturition. When I complained to my wife that the passion was going out of our partnership, she said I was predictably puerile. Then I started having repetitive dreams of being surrounded by a posse of parameters with pink faces and pallid tongues, or possibly the other way around."

"Well, I agree with you that all these *p*'s do get to be pretentious, pompous, ponderous, and pedantic," I said.

"Pshaw! You've got it too."

"How can any of us help it?" I said, hoping that if I got into the spirit of the thing he might start analyzing me and stop being so crazy himself. "Sometimes I think that the patients have it much worse than the Pshrinks. Why just the other day..."

"You're right. Nobody says anything simply, anymore. Even patients postulate prohibitive propositions like trying to persuade me to cure their passive-aggressive personality with psychodrama or their psychosomatic punishment with positioning patterns. They say they want profound sex and peak experiences..."

["I think I may be having one now," snarled a Freudian.]

"...and I ask you, isn't it likely that we Pshrinks are the most likely to be affected by all these *p*'s? Day after day we listen to the voices of the people, talking and talking and talking..."

"Which accounts for why we tend to get verbal diarrhea when let loose from our offices," I said, proud that I had managed a sentence with no *p* in it.

He was not amused. "Just last week one of my patients complained about the propinquity of the couch to my chair."

"Perish forbid," I said without thinking.

"Where did you get that expression?"

"My father used to say it when he wasn't actually swearing."

"Aha! You see! Unto the fourth generation!"

"If you go back that far they weren't speaking English."

"I was speaking metaphorically, implying that the alien influence began a long time ago," he said, picking crumbs off his pants. "My theory is that if you think and speak often enough and hard enough in words containing prominent p's, your mind jells up and gets petrified."

"Paralyzed by p's?" It was impossible to resist.

He glared at me. "You are then locked into an alien mind somewhere in the universe—maybe in outer space, maybe hiding somewhere in our solar system. I don't like what could be developing in the middle layers of Jupiter, or under the ice cover of Europa."

Since his voice was rising again, I said, "So what?"

"Idiot! Don't you understand that after the aliens have gotten enough human minds locked to their system, they'll take control—take over Earth civilization!"

"I think you are—you should excuse the expression—projecting. Haven't you been worried about how the lunatic elements are trying to take over our field? I seem to remember now that you wrote a scathing paper on fringe groups."

"A paper that psychoanalysts and psychiatrists and psychologists perused without perceiving the profundity of the principles!"

"Hey! You have it bad, don't you!"

He burst into tears and threw himself prone on my couch.

The afternoon sun streaming into the window made the room warm, and I was too bemused by the problem to turn on the air conditioner. My next hour, I tardily recalled, was also free, since the patient was a young psychoanalyst in training who was at that moment delivering a paper at the same convention from which my friend was playing hooky. Soon my colleague was snoring and I was drowsy enough to have a hypnagogic hallucination...

["You mean you fell asleep," said another Interpersonal.

["I did not," she said.]

I had a momentary impression of strange lines of force from far away, converging on my snoring colleague and then transferring to me. It was rather eerie, and I was glad when he woke up and bounded off the couch.

"You're marvelous! I'm cured!" He bent down, hugged me, grabbed his briefcase, and made for the door, where he paused. "It's all clear to me. I just had to tell someone about it in order to feel OK. I guess I was only a carrier."

"You perfidious proselytizer!" I exclaimed.

"Sorry about that. I'm going home. Maybe I'll see you at next year's convention." He held up two fingers. "Live long."

"And prosper peacefully," I said as he left.

A pregnant silence ensued around the luncheon table when the Interpersonal finished speaking.

Suddenly and simultaneously some of the more argumentative members of the club began to talk.

"The parameters of the problem are..."

"The physiological principles in pronouncing the p..."

"You Interpersonals and your parataxic distortions..."

"And your participant observation..."

"Prostituting the precepts of psychoanalytical..."

"Perseverating in the problem of the *p*..."

"Perhaps it's only a problem of psychic phenomena..."

"Probably poisoned by polypramasy..."

"The proposition is positively polymorphously perverse..."

And just as suddenly they all shut up. There was an uncomfortable shuffling of feet under the table. Then the youngest member, a first-year psychiatric resident allowed in to learn from his superiors, spoke timidly.

"Perhaps it's the fault of philosophers. I almost majored in philosophy in college, and it seems to me that they promote a plethora of phrases..." He stopped abruptly, eyes wide.

"Piffle," said the Oldest Member. "None of the jargon is absolutely necessary, although I'm partial to 'id' myself."

"Would you willingly give up 'penis envy'?" asked the Interpersonal.

"I think you should keep it in your prefrontal cortex," said the Oldest Member with frosty dignity as he stroked the erect waxed tips of his silver moustache, "that *I* do not need to have penis envy. Nor did the Master..."

"Who was primarily a physicalistic psychobiologist," said one of the more militant non-Freudians.

"But the Master had no *p*'s in his name," said the Interpersonal, favoring the Oldest Member's moustache with a glance of unalloyed admiration.

"Thank you," said the Oldest Member, patting the Interpersonal on the patella. "You do think that hypothesis about aliens is a lot of stuff and nonsense, don't you?"

The Interpersonal shrugged. "I haven't the slightest idea. I wish, however, that I didn't have this insatiable desire to go home and read *Pickwick Papers*—or possibly promulgate a parody."

Janet Jeppson, M.D., is a psychiatrist, psychoanalyst, and writer; "the order," she tells us, "subject to astonishing variation." She lives in Manhattan and is married to another contributor to this anthology, Dr. Asimov. As for the genesis of this story, she remarks, "I was in a pique about the polysyllabic puzzlements of psychoanalytic jargon and I happily vented my spleen." The Pshrinks stories ran for several years in Isaac Asimov's Science Fiction Magazine *and* Amazing Science Fiction Stories, *and Doubleday recently published them in a collection,* The Mysterious Cure.

THE REGULARS

by Robert Silverberg

"Charley never needs to ask. Of course, he knows us all very well."

It was the proverbial night not fit for man nor beast, black and grim and howling, with the rain coming on in sidewise sheets. But in Charley Sullivan's place everything was as cozy as an old boot, the lights dim, the heat turned up, the neon Beer signs sputtering pleasantly, Charley behind the bar filling them beyond the Plimsoll line, and all the regulars in their regular places. What a comfort a tavern like Charley Sullivan's can be on a night that's black and grim and howling!

"It was a night like this," said The Pope to Karl Marx, "that you changed your mind about blowing up the stock exchange, as I recall. Eh?"

Karl Marx nodded moodily. "It was the beginning of the end for me as a true revolutionary, it was." He isn't Irish, but in Charley Sullivan's everybody picks up the rhythm of it soon enough. "When you

get too fond of your comforts to be willing to go out
into a foul gale to attack the enemies of the prole-
tariat, it's the end of your vocation, sure enough."
He sighed and peered into his glass. It held nothing
but suds, and he sighed again.

"Can I buy you another?" asked The Pope. "In
memory of your vocation."

"You may indeed," said Karl Marx.

The Pope looked around. "And who else is needy?
My turn to set them up!"

The Leading Man tapped the rim of his glass. So
did Ms. Bewley and Mors Longa. I did the same.
The Ingenue passed, but Toulouse-Lautrec, down at
the end of the bar, looked away from the television
set long enough to give the signal. Charley efficiently handed out the refills—Beer for the apostle
of the class struggle, Jack Daniels for Mors Longa,
Valpolicella for The Pope, Scotch-and-Water for The
Leading Man, White Wine for Ms. Bewley, Perrier
with slice of lemon for Toulouse-Lautrec, since he
had had the Cognac the last time and claimed to be
tapering off. And for me, Myers-on-the-Rocks.
Charley never needs to ask. Of course, he knows us
all very well.

"Cheers," said The Leading Man, and we drank
up, and then an angel passed by, and the long silence ended only when a nasty rumble of thunder
went through the place at about 6.3 on the Richter
scale.

"Nasty night," The Ingenue said. "Imagine trying to elope in a downpour like this! I can see it now,
Harry and myself at the boathouse, and the car—"

"Harry and *I*," said Mors Longa. "'Myself' is re-
flexive. As you well know, sweet."

The Ingenue blinked sweetly. "I always forget.
Anyway, there was Harry and I at the boathouse,
and the car was waiting, my cousin's old Pierce-
Arrow with the—"

—*bar in the backseat that was always stocked
with the best imported Liqueurs,* I went on silently
just a fraction of a second ahead of her clear high

voice, *and all we had to do was drive ninety miles
across the state line to the place where the justice of
the peace was waiting—*

I worked on my Rum. The Leading Man, moving
a little closer to The Ingenue, tenderly took her
hand as the nasty parts of the story began to unfold.
The Pope wheezed sympathetically into his Wine,
and Karl Marx scowled and pounded one fist
against the other, and even Ms. Bewley, who had
very little tolerance for The Ingenue's silliness,
managed a bright smile in the name of sisterhood.

"—the rain, you see, had done something awful
to the car's wiring, and there we were, Harry on his
knees in the mud trying to fix it, and me half crazy
with excitement and impatience, and the night getting worse and worse, when we heard dogs barking
and—"

*—my guardian and two of his men appeared out
of the night—*

We had heard it all fifty times before. She tells it
every horrid rainy night. From no one else do we
tolerate any such repetition—we have our sensibilities, and it would be cruel and unusual to be forced
to listen to the same fol-de-rol over and over and
over—but The Ingenue is a dear sweet young
thing, and her special foible it is to repeat herself,
and she and she alone gets away with it among the
regulars at Charley Sullivan's. We followed along,
nodding and sighing and shaking our heads at all
the appropriate places, the way you do when you're
hearing Beethoven's *Fifth* or Schubert's *Unfinished,*
and she was just getting around to the tempestuous
climax, her fiancé and her guardian in a fight to the
death illuminated by baleful flashes of lightning,
when there was a crack of real lightning outside,
followed almost instantly by a blast of thunder that
made the last one seem like the sniffle of a mos-
quito. The vibrations shook three glasses off the bar
and stood Charley Sullivan's framed photos of President Kennedy and Pope John XXIII on their
corners.

The next thing that happened was the door opened and a new customer walked in. And you can imagine that we all sat to attention at that, because you would expect only the regulars to be populating Charley's place in such weather, and it was a genuine novelty to have a stranger materialize. Well timed, too, because without him we'd have had fifteen minutes more of the tale of The Ingenue's bungled elopement.

He was maybe thirty-two or a little less, roughly dressed in heavy-duty Levi's, a thick black cardigan, and a ragged pea jacket. His dark unruly hair was soaked and matted. On no particular evidence I decided he was a merchant sailor who had just jumped ship. For a moment he stood a little way within the door, eyeing us all with that cautious look a bar-going man has when he comes to a new place where everyone else is obviously a longtime regular; and then he smiled, a little shyly at first, more warmly as he saw some of us smiling back. He took off his jacket, hung it on the rack above the jukebox, shook himself like a drenched dog, and seated himself at the bar between The Pope and Mors Longa. "Jesus," he said, "what a stinking night! I can't tell you how glad I was to see a light burning at the end of the block."

"You'll like it here, brother," said The Pope. "Charley, let me buy this young man his first."

"You took the last round," Mors Longa pointed out. "May I, Your Holiness?"

The Pope shrugged. "Why not?"

"My pleasure," said Mors Longa to the newcomer. "What will it be?"

"Do they have Old Bushmill here?"

"They have everything here," said Mors Longa. "*Charley* has everything. Our host. Bushmill for the lad, Charley, and a double, I think. And is anyone else ready?"

"A sweetener here," said The Leading Man. Toulouse-Lautrec opted for his next Cognac. The Ingenue, who seemed to have forgotten that she hadn't finished telling her story, waved for her customary Rye-and-Ginger. The rest of us stood pat.

"What's your ship?" I asked.

The stranger gave me a startled look. *"Pequod Maru,* Liberian flag. How'd you know?"

"Good guesser. Where bound? D'ye mind?"

He took a long pull of his Whiskey. "Maracaibo, they said. Not a tanker. Coffee and cacao. But I'm not going. I—ah—resigned my commission. This afternoon, very suddenly. Jesus, this tastes good. What a fine warm place this is!"

"And glad we are to see you," said Charley Sullivan. "We'll call you Ishmael, eh?"

"Ishmael?"

"We all need names here," said Mors Longa. "This gentleman we call Karl Marx, for example. He's socially conscious. That's Toulouse-Lautrec down there by the tube. And you can think of me as Mors Longa."

Ishmael frowned. "Is that an Italian name?"

"Latin, actually. Not a name, a sort of a phrase. *Mors longa, vita brevis.* My motto. And that's The Ingenue, who needs a lot of love and protection, and this is Ms. Bewley, who can look after herself, and—"

He went all around the room. Ishmael appeared to be working hard at remembering the names. He repeated them until he had them straight, but he still looked a little puzzled. "Bars I've been in," he said, "it isn't the custom to make introductions like this. Makes it seem more like a private party than a bar."

"A family gathering, more like," said Ms. Bewley.

Karl Marx said, "We constitute a society here. It is not the consciousness of men that determines their existence, but on the contrary their social existence determines their consciousness. We look after one another in this place."

"You'll like it here," said The Pope.

"I do. I'm amazed how much I like it." The sailor

grinned. "This may be the bar I've been looking for all my life."

"No doubt but that it is," said Charley Sullivan. "And a Bushmill's on me, lad?"

Shyly Ishmael pushed his glass forward, and Charley topped it off.

"So friendly here," Ishmael said. "Almost like—home."

"Like one's club, perhaps," said The Leading Man.

"A club, a home, yes," said Mors Longa, signaling Charley for another Bourbon. "Karl Marx tells it truly: we care for each other here. We are friends, and we strive constantly to amuse one another and protect one another, which are the two chief duties of friends. We buy each other drinks, we talk, we tell stories to while away the darkness."

"Do you come here every night?"

"We never miss a one," Mors Longa said.

"You must know each other very well by this time."

"Very well. Very, very well."

"The kind of place I've always dreamed of," Ishmael said wonderingly. "The kind of place I'd never want to leave." He let his eyes pan in a slow arc around the whole room, past the jukebox, the pool table, the dart board, the television screen, the tattered 1934 calendar that had never been changed, the fireplace, the piano. He was glowing, and not just from the Whiskey. "Why would anyone ever want to leave a place like this?"

"It is a very good place," said Karl Marx.

Mors Longa said, "And when you find a very good place, it's the place where you want to remain. Of course. It becomes your club, as our friend says. Your home away from home. But that reminds me of a story, young man. Have you ever heard about the bar that nobody actually ever does leave? The bar where everyone stays forever, because they couldn't leave even if they wanted to? Do you know that one?"

"Never heard it," said Ishmael.

But the rest of us had. In Charley Sullivan's place we try never to tell the same story twice, in order to spare each other's sensibilities, for boredom is the deadliest of afflictions here. Only The Ingenue is exempt from that rule, because it is her nature to tell her stories again and again, and we love her all the same. Nevertheless it sometimes happens that one of us must tell an old and familiar story to a newcomer; but though at other times we give each other full attention, it is not required at a time such as that. So The Leading Man and The Ingenue wandered off for a tête-à-tête by the fireplace, and Karl Marx challenged The Pope to a round of darts, and the others drifted off to this corner or that, until only Mors Longa and the sailor and I were still at the bar, I drowsing over my Rum and Mors Longa getting that faraway look and Ishmael, leaning intently forward, saying, "A bar where nobody can ever leave? What a strange sort of place!"

"Yes," said Mors Longa.

"Where is there such a place?"

"In no particular part of the universe. By which I mean it lies somewhere outside of space and time as we understand those concepts, everywhere and nowhere at once, although it looks not at all alien or strange apart from its timelessness and its spacelessness. In fact, it looks, I'm told, like every bar you've ever been in in your life, only more so. The proprietor's a big man with black Irish in him, a lot like Charley Sullivan here, and he doesn't mind setting one up for the regulars now and then on the house, and he always gives good measure and keeps the heat turned up nicely. And the wood is dark and mellow and well polished, and the railing is the familiar brass, and there are the usual two hanging ferns and the usual aspidistra in the corner next to the spittoon, and there's a dart board and a pool table and all those other things that you find in bars of the kind that this one is. You understand me? This is *a perfectly standard sort of bar,* but it doesn't happen to be in New York City or San Francisco or Hamburg or Rangoon, or in any other city you're likely to have visited, though the moment you walk into this place you feel right at home in it."

"Just like here."

"Very much like here," said Mors Longa.

"But people never leave?" Ishmael's brows furrowed. "Never?"

"Well, actually, some of them do," Mors Longa said. "But let me talk about the other ones first, all right? The regulars, the ones who are there *all the time.* You know, there are certain people who absolutely never go into bars, the ones who prefer to do their drinking at home, or in restaurants before dinner, or not at all. But then there are the bar-going sorts. Some of them are folks who just like to drink, you know, and find a bar a convenient place to get their whistles wetted when they're en route from somewhere to somewhere else. And there are some who think drinking's a social act, eh? But you also find people in bars, a lot of them, who go to the place because there's an emptiness in them that needs to be filled, a dark cold hollow space, to be filled not just with good warm Bourbon, you understand, but a mystic and invisible substance that emanates from others who are in the same way, people who somehow have had a bit of their souls leak away from them by accident, and need the comfort of being among their own kind. Say, a priest who's lost his calling, or a writer who's forgotten the joy of putting stories down on paper, or a painter to whom all colors have become shades of gray, or a surgeon whose scalpel hand has picked up a bit of a tremor, or a photographer whose eyes don't quite focus right anymore. You know the sort, don't you? You find a lot of that sort in bars. Something in their eyes tells you what they are. But in this particular bar that I'm talking about, you find *only* that sort, good people, decent people, but people with that empty zone inside them. Which makes it even more like all the other bars there are, in fact the Platonic ideal of a bar, if you follow me, a kind of three-dimensional stereotype populated by flesh-and-blood clichés, a sort of perpetual stage set, do you see? Hearing about a place like that where everybody's a little tragic, everybody's a bit on the broken side, everyone is a perfect bar type, you'd laugh, you'd say it's unreal, it's too much like everybody's idea of what such a place ought to be like to be convincing. Eh? But all stereotypes are rooted firmly in reality, you know. That's what makes them stereotypes, because they're exactly like reality, only more so. And to the people who do their drinking in the bar I'm talking about, it isn't any stereotype and they aren't clichés. It's the only reality they have, the realest reality there is, for them; and it's no good sneering at it, because it's their own little world, the world of the archetypical saloon, the world of the bar regulars."

"Who never leave the place," said Ishmael.

"How can they? Where would they go? What would they do on a day off? They have no identity except inside the bar. The bar is their life. The bar is their universe. They have no business going elsewhere. They simply stay where they are. They tell each other stories and they work hard to keep each other happy, *and for them there is no world outside.* That's what it means to be a regular, to be a Platonic ideal. Every night the bar and everything in it vanishes into a kind of inchoate gray mist at closing time, and every morning when it's legal to open, the bar comes back, and meanwhile the regulars don't go anywhere except into the mist, because that's all there is, mist and then bar, bar and then mist. Platonic ideals don't have daytime jobs and they don't go to Atlantic City on the weekend and they don't decide to go bowling one night instead of to their bar. Do you follow me? They stay there the way the dummies in a store window stay in the store window. Only they can walk and talk and feel and

drink and do everything else that window dummies
can't do. And that's their whole life, night after
night, month after month, year after year, century
after century—maybe till the end of time."

"Spooky place," said Ishmael with a little shud-
der.

"The people who are in that bar are happier than
they could possibly be anywhere else."

"But they never leave it. Except you said some of
them do, and you'd be telling me about those people
later."

Mors Longa finished his Bourbon and, unbidden,
Charley Sullivan gave him one more, and set another Rum in front of me, and an Irish for the sailor.
For a long while Mors Longa studied his drink.
Then he said, "I can't really tell you much about the
ones who leave, because I don't know much about
them. I intuit their existence logically, is all. You
see, from time to time there's a newcomer in this
bar that's outside of space and time. Somebody
comes wandering in out of the night the way you
did here tonight, and sits down and joins the regular crowd, and bit by bit fits right in. Now, obviously, if every once in a while somebody new
drops in, and nobody ever leaves, then it wouldn't
take more than a little for the whole place to get
terribly crowded, like Grand Central at commuter
time, and what kind of a happy scene would that
make? So I conclude that sooner or later each of the
regulars very quietly must disappear, must just
vanish without anybody's knowing it, maybe go into
the john and never come out, something like that.
And not only does no one ever notice that someone's
missing, but *no one remembers that that person was
ever there*. Do you follow? That way the place never
gets too full."

"But where do they go, once they disappear from
the bar that nobody ever leaves, the bar that's outside of space and time?"

"I don't know," said Mors Longa quietly. "I don't
have the foggiest idea." After a moment he added,

"There's a theory, though. Mind you, only a theory. It's that the people in the bar are really doing time in a kind of halfway house, a sort of purgatory, you understand, between one world and another. And they stay there a long, long time, however long a time it is until their time is up, and then they leave, but they can only leave when their replacement arrives. And immediately they're forgotten. The fabric of the place closes around them, and nobody among the regulars remembers that once there used to be a doctor with the D.T.'s here, say, or a politician who got caught on the take, or a little guy who sat in front of the piano for hours and never played a note. But everybody has a hunch that that's how the system works. And so it's a big thing when somebody new comes in. Every regular starts secretly wondering, Is it I who's going to go? And wondering too, Where am I going to go, if I'm the one?"

Ishmael worked on his drink in a meditative way. "Are they afraid to go, or afraid that they won't?"

"What do you think?"

"I'm not sure. But I guess most of them would be afraid to go. The bar's such a warm and cozy and comforting place. It's their whole world and has been for a million years. And now maybe they're going to go somewhere horrible—who knows?—but for certain they're going to go somewhere *different*. I'd be afraid of that. Of course, maybe if I'd been stuck in the same place for a million years, no matter how cozy, I'd be ready to move along when the chance came. Which would you want?"

"I don't have the foggiest," said Mors Longa. "But that's the story of the bar where nobody leaves."

"Spooky," said Ishmael.

He finished his drink, pushed the glass away, shook his head to Charley Sullivan, and sat in silence. We all sat in silence. The rain drummed miserably against the side of the building. I looked over at The Leading Man and The Ingenue. He was holding her hand and staring meaningfully into her eyes. The Pope, hefting a dart, was toeing the line and licking his lips to sharpen his aim. Ms. Bewley and Toulouse-Lautrec were playing chess. It was the quiet part of the evening, suddenly.

Slowly the sailor rose and took his jacket from the hook. He turned, smiled uncertainly, and said, "Getting late. I better be going." He nodded to the three of us at the bar and said, "Thanks for the drinks. I needed those. And thanks for the story, Mr. Longa. That was one strange story, you know?"

We said nothing. The sailor opened the door, wincing as cold sheets of rain lashed at him. He pulled his jacket tight around him and, shivering a little, stepped out in the darkness. But he was gone only a moment. Hardly had the door closed behind him but it opened again and he stumbled back in, drenched.

"Jesus," he said, "it's raining worse than ever. What a stinking night! I'm not going out into that!"

"No," I said. "Not fit for man nor beast."

"You don't mind if I stay here until it slackens off some, then?"

"Mind? Mind?" I laughed. "This is a public house, my friend. You've got as much right as anyone. Here. Sit down. Make yourself to home."

"Plenty of Bushmill's left in the bottle, lad," said Charley Sullivan.

"I'm a little low on cash," Ishmael muttered.

Mors Longa said, "That's all right. Money's not the only coin of the realm around here. We can use some stories we haven't heard before. Let's hear the strangest story you can tell us, for openers, and I'll undertake to keep you in Irish while you talk. Eh?"

"Fair enough," said Ishmael. He thought a moment. "All right. I have a good one for you. I have a really good one, if you don't mind them weird. It's about my uncle Timothy and his tiny twin brother, that he carried around under his arm all his life. Does that interest you?"

"Most assuredly it does," I said.

"Seconded," said Mors Longa. He grinned with a

warmth I had not seen on his face for a long time. "Set them up," he said to Charley Sullivan. "On me. For the house."

Robert Silverberg has been publishing science fiction for more than thirty years now. Among his best-known books are Nightwings, Dying Inside, *and* Lord Valentine's Castle. *He has written nearly as much in the field as anyone ever has, and nearly as many kinds of stories as are possible. Consequently, when the editors of this anthology couldn't think of a Silverberg-written spaceport-bar story, we naturally assumed that there was one somewhere, and we asked Silverberg about it. Only there wasn't one— not then; but there is now, for Silverberg promptly rose to the challenge.*

THE MAN
WHO ALWAYS KNEW

by Algis Budrys

...that was his only talent: knowing when and where...

The small, thin, stoop-shouldered man sat down on the stool nearest the wall, took a dollar bill out of his wallet, and laid it on the bar. Behind their rimless glasses, his watery blue eyes fastened vacantly on a space somewhere between the end of his nose and the bottles standing on the back-bar tiers. An old porkpie hat was squashed down over the few sandy hairs that covered his bony skull. His head was buried deep in the collar of his old, baggy tweed overcoat, and a yellow muffler trailed down from around his neck. His knobby-knuckled hands played with the dollar bill.

Harry, the barkeep, was busy mixing three Martinis for a table in the dining room, but as soon as the small man came in he looked up and smiled. And as soon as he had the three filled glasses lined up on a tray for the waiter to pick up, he hurried up to the end of the bar.

"Afternoon, Mr. McMahon! And what'll it be for you today?"

The small man looked up with a wan sigh. "Nothing yet, Harry. Mind if I just sit and wait a minute?"

"Not at all, Mr. McMahon, not at all." He looked around at the empty stools. "Quiet as the grave in here this afternoon. Same thing over at the lab?"

The small man nodded slowly, looking down at his fingers creasing the dollar bill. "Just a quiet afternoon, I guess," he said in a tired voice. "Nothing's due to come to a head over there until sometime next week."

Harry nodded to show he understood. It was that kind of a day. "Haven't seen you for a while, Mr. McMahon—been away again?"

The small man pleated the dollar bill, held one end between thumb and forefinger, and spread the bill like a fan. "That's right. I went down to Baltimore for a few days." He smoothed out the bill and touched the top of the bar. "You know, Harry, it wouldn't surprise me if next year we could give you a bar varnish you could let absolute alcohol stand on overnight."

Harry shook his head slowly. "Beats me, Mr. McMahon. I never know what's coming out of your lab next. One week it's steam engines, the next it's bar varnish. What gets me is where you find the time. Doing all that traveling and still being the biggest inventor in the world—bigger than Edison, even. Why, just the other day the wife and I went out and bought two of those pocket transceiver sets of yours, and Emma said she didn't see how I could know you. 'A man as busy as Mr. McMahon must be,' she said, 'wouldn't be coming into the bar all the time like you say he does.' Well, that's a wife for you. But she's right. Beats me, too, like I said."

The small man shrugged uncomfortably and didn't say anything. Then he got a suddenly determined look on his face and started to say something, but just then the waiter stepped up to the bar.

"Two Gibson, one Whiskey Sour, Harry."

"Coming up. Excuse me, Mr. McMahon. Mix you something while I'm down there?"

The small man shook his head. "Not just yet, Harry."

"Right, Mr. McMahon."

Harry shook up the cocktails briskly. From the sound of it, Mr. McMahon had been about to say something important, and anything Mr. McMahon thought was important would be something you shouldn't miss.

He bumped the shaker, dropped the strainer in, and poured the Gibsons. He just hoped Mr. McMahon hadn't decided it wasn't worth talking about. Let's see what Emma would have to say if he came home and told her what Mr. McMahon had told him, and a year or two later something new— maybe a new kind of home permanent or something—came out. She'd use it. She'd have to use it, because it would just naturally be the best thing on the market. And every time she did, she'd have to remember that Harry had told her first. Let's see her say Mr. McMahon wasn't a steady customer of his then! Bar varnish wasn't in the same league.

The small man was looking into space again, with a sad little smile, when Harry got back to him. He was pushing the dollar bill back and forth with his index fingers. A bunch of people came in the door and Harry muttered under his breath, but they didn't stop at the bar. They went straight from the coatrack to the dining room, and Harry breathed easier. Maybe he'd have time to hear what Mr. McMahon had to say.

"Well, here I am again, Mr. McMahon."

The small man looked up with a sharp gleam in his eyes. "Think I'm pretty hot stuff, eh, Harry?"

"Yes, sir," Harry said, not knowing what to make of it.

"Think I'm the Edison of the age, huh?"

"Well—gosh, Mr. McMahon, you are *better* than Edison!"

The small man's fingers crumpled up the dollar bill and rolled it into a tight ball.

"The Perfect Combustion Engine, the Condensing Steam Jet, the Voice-Operated Typewriter, the Discontinuous Airfoil—things like that, eh?" the small man asked sharply.

"Yes, sir. And the Arc House, and the Minute Meal, and the Lintless Dustcloth—well, gosh, Mr. McMahon, I could go on all day, I guess."

"Didn't invent a one of them," the small man snapped. His shoulders seemed to straighten out from under a heavy load. He looked Harry in the eye. "I never invented anything in my life."

"Two Gibson and another Whiskey Sour, Harry," the waiter interrupted.

"Yeah—sure." Harry moved uneasily down the bar. He tilted the Gin bottle slowly, busy turning things over in his mind. He sneaked a look at Mr. McMahon. The small man was looking down at his hands, curling them up into fists, and smiling. He looked happy. That wasn't like him at all.

Harry set the drinks up on the waiter's tray and got back up to the end of the bar.

"Mr. McMahon?"

The small man looked up again. "Yes, Harry?" He *did* look happy—happy all the way through, like a man with insomnia who suddenly feels himself drifting off to sleep.

"You were just saying about that varnish—"

"Fellow in Baltimore. Paints signs for a living. Not very good ones; they weather too fast. I noticed him working the last time I was down that way."

"I don't follow you, Mr. McMahon."

The small man bounced the balled-up dollar bill on the bar and watched it roll around. "Well, I knew he was a conscientious young fellow, even if he didn't know much about paint. So, yesterday I went back down there, and, sure enough, he'd been fooling around—just taking a little of this and a little of that, stirring it up by guess and by gosh—and he had something he could paint over a sign that would stand up to a blowtorch."

"Golly, Mr. McMahon. I thought you said he didn't know much about paint."

The small man scooped up the bill and smoothed it out. "He didn't. He was just fooling around. Anybody else would have just come up with a gallon of useless goo. But he *looked* like the kind of man who'd happen to hit it right. And he looked like the kind of man who'd hit it sometime about yesterday. So I went down there, made him an offer, and came back with a gallon of what's going to be the best varnish anybody ever put on the market."

Harry twisted his hands uncomfortably in his pockets. "Gee, Mr. McMahon—you mean you do the same thing with everything else?"

"That's right, Harry." The small man pinched the two ends of the dollar bill, brought them together, and then snapped the bill flat with a satisfied *pop!* "Exactly the same thing. I was on a train passing an open field once, and saw a boy flying model airplanes. Two years later, I went back and, sure enough, he'd just finished his first drawings on the discontinuous airfoil. I offered him a licensing fee and a good cash advance, and came home with the airfoil." The small man looked down sadly and reminiscently. "He used the money to finance himself through aeronautical engineering school. Never turned out anything new again."

"Gosh, Mr. McMahon. I don't know what to say. You mean you travel around the country just looking for people that are working on something new?"

The small man shook his head. "No. I travel around the country, and I stumble across people who're going to accidentally stumble across something good. I've got secondhand luck." The small man rolled the bill up between his fingers, and smiled with a hurt twist in his sensitive mouth. "It's even better than that. I know more or less *what* they're going to stumble across, and *when* they're going to." He bent the tube he'd made out of the bill. "But I can't develop it myself. I just have to wait. I've only got one talent."

"Well, gee, Mr. McMahon, that's a fine thing to have."

The small man crushed the dollar bill. "Is it, Harry? How do you use it directly? How do you define it? Do you set up shop as McMahon and Company—Secondhand Luck Bought and Sold? Do you get a Nobel Prize for Outstanding Achievement in Luck?"

"You've got a Nobel Prize, Mr. McMahon."

"For a cold cure discovered by a pharmacist who mislabeled a couple of prescriptions."

"Well, look, Mr. McMahon—that's better than no Nobel Prize at all."

The small man's sensitive mouth twisted again. "Yes, it is, Harry. A little bit." He almost tore the dollar bill. "Just a little bit." He stared into space.

"Mr. McMahon. I wouldn't feel so bad about it if I was you. There's no sense to taking it out on yourself," Harry said worriedly.

The small man shrugged.

Harry shuffled his feet. "I wish there was something I could do for you." It felt funny, being sorry for the luckiest man in the world.

The small man smoothed the dollar out again.

"Two Whiskey Sour, and another Gibson," the waiter said. Harry moved unhappily down the bar and began to mix, thinking about Mr. McMahon. Then he heard Mr. McMahon get off his stool and come down the bar.

He looked up. The small man was standing opposite him, and looking down at the bar. Harry looked down too, and realized he'd been trying to make a Whiskey Sour with Gibson liquor. It looked like nothing he'd ever seen before.

Mr. McMahon pushed the dollar bill across the

bar. He reached out and took the funny-looking drink. There was a sad-happy smile on his face.

"That's the one I wanted, Harry," he said.

Algis Budrys tells us that he wrote this for fun and money, and that it's not his usual kind of thing. It's also notable for having appeared in Astounding Science Fiction Stories, *one of the very few bar stories to do so.*

The author has also written Rogue Moon, Michaelmas, *and* Who? *He has edited books, magazines, and trade journals, worked in public relations, and even written a screenplay (*Dinosarus! 1957). *Since the 1960s, he has been one of the most respected critics in science fiction. His most recent book,* Benchmarks: Galaxy Bookshelf by Algis Budrys, *is a collection of his columns from* Galaxy Science Fiction.

INFINITE RESOURCES

by Randall Garrett

*The ultimate reduction of all parallel-universe
stories...*

At the bar of the Green Lizard Lounge, Dr. Rumfort was saying: "In my forthcoming monograph to
the *Journal,* I show that it is mathematically possible to describe a six-dimensional continuum in
which—" His voice trailed off as he noticed that
Latimer was no longer listening.

Irritated, he swiveled his head to follow Latimer's gaze.

The oddly dressed gentleman was wearing a long
blue cutaway coat, a pair of white shorts that half
covered his thighs, long crimson hose that came up
to his knees, and a soft white shirt that had no collar. His head was completely shaved.

On his back, he carried something that looked
like a walkie-talkie radio with a peculiar antenna.

"What is it?" whispered Latimer.

Rumfort frowned. "A nut," he said, turning back to his drink.

The man peered around in the dimness of the bar and then headed directly towards Latimer. "Oh, I do say," he said worriedly, "could you very possibly be Dr. Oswald Latimer?"

Latimer nodded, grinning. "I am."

"*The* Dr. Latimer? The expert on the mathematics of infinity?"

"That's me." Latimer was still grinning.

"Thank heavens I've found you!" he breathed. "I have the honor to be Professor George Featherby, of Columbia."

Rumfort swiveled his head around again. "Ridiculous! There's no such person at Columbia!" He had never approved of the manner in which Latimer took up with strangers so easily.

"Oh, no, of course not," Featherby said. "Not in this continuum. Dr. Latimer, do you mind if I ask a few questions?"

Rumfort butted in before Latimer had a chance to answer.

"What do you mean, 'in this continuum'?"

Featherby beamed broadly. "Well, you see, I'm not actually from this space-time continuum. This apparatus"—he jerked a thumb over his shoulder to indicate the pack on his back—"this apparatus is capable of shifting its wearer from one of an infinite series of universes to another."

Dr. Rumfort snorted again.

Latimer, who was enjoying the screwy little man immensely, nodded his understanding. "Yes. Dr. Rumfort, here, was just saying that he has proved mathematically that there are such things as parallel continua."

Rumfort almost choked on his drink. "That, sir, was only an exercise in mathematics! It does not necessarily pertain to the real universe!"

"Ah, there, old chap," smiled Featherby, "but it does, you know!"

"Ridiculous!" Rumfort snapped. He turned back

to his drink, thus dismissing the subject entirely. Then he pulled a notebook and pencil out of his pocket and began to scribble furiously.

"That's very interesting," said Latimer to Featherby. "I suppose each continuum is different from the others, eh?"

"Oh, no! Rather not! Infinite number of universes, you know, so there's an infinite number of 'em all exactly alike. Of course, there's an infinite number of 'em that are different, too, so you're right, in a way. But, then, that's why I've come to you, you know."

Latimer didn't know, but he nodded and lit a cigarette. "Go on."

"Well, sir, you see, I'm lost. Lost! I hadn't learned how to control this blasted thing at first, and I got myself too far away from my own continuum." Featherby looked desolate. "Ours is rather different from this, you see. But I finally heard of you in another continuum. Unfortunately, you'd been killed in an—uh—is it automobile?—yes, automobile accident in 1952. So I had to come looking for you in one where you'd survived."

Latimer blinked. He still had a deep scar on his chest from that accident. Then he grinned again; the little guy had read the papers, of course. "I'm glad you found me. How can I help you?"

"Well, sir, I understand you know a great deal about the mathematics of infinity; I thought perhaps you might tell me, if you could, how to get home."

Latimer looked at the ceiling, chuckling inwardly.

"Well, you say there are an infinite number of universes. That would, as you say, imply an infinite number of *different* universes, each of which is infinitely duplicated, identically.

"I should say that it would be a first-order, or aleph-null, infinity. For instance, a line has an infinite number of points on it, a plane contains an infinite number of lines, and a solid contains an infinite number of planes. That should, it would seem, indicate that a solid had infinity-cubed points in it. But infinity cubed is still infinity, so a line has the same number of points as a solid."

"Yes, yes," said Featherby impatiently. "I know all that! You're talking to a professor of physics! — Pardon me, but I *am* impatient, you know." He looked contrite.

"The point I'm getting at," said Latimer, unruffled, "is that you really don't have to get back to the same universe you left. If the one you go back to is identical, you wouldn't know the difference. Hmmmmm—still— By George!" His face broke into a grin.

"What is it? What?" Featherby asked.

"Why, don't you see? That implies that *there are an infinite number of Featherbys galloping all over the metauniverse!* Also, there are an infinite number of Featherbys who stayed home. If you got into one of those continua, there'd be two of you. And if—"

"Oh, my God!" said Featherby, turning white. "How horrible!"

"Oh, come now," said Latimer, "it's not as bad as all that. Really, if—"

"Just a minute!" bellowed Dr. Rumfort, who had finished his writing in the notebook. He looked straight at Featherby. "You're a liar, and I can prove it!"

"A liar?" Featherby exploded. "A *liar,* sir? I demand satisfaction, sir! My dueller will meet yours at any time you stipulate! I— Oh, dear!"

"What's the matter?" asked Latimer.

"Dear me! This *is* awkward! I forgot I hadn't brought my private dueller along. And I can't fight one *myself,* you know!"

"That's all right. Duelling's illegal here, you know," said Latimer comfortingly.

"I said," repeated Dr. Rumfort, "that I could prove it!"

Featherby faced him, scowling. "All right, if

you're so sanguinarily smart, go ahead and prove it!"

Rumfort spread a sheaf of papers arrogantly. "There; take a look. I have shown that moving from one space-time continuum to another would require instantaneous acceleration to the velocity of light!"

"All right, all right," snapped Featherby. "I admit all that. It's self-evident. So what?"

"So what? Why, my dear man, that would require an infinite amount of energy applied in an infinitesimally short time!"

"Yes, yes. Go on. Where's your proof that I'm a liar?"

Rumfort looked baffled. "Well, dammit, you couldn't possibly carry that much power on your back!"

"Hah! Who said I carried it on my back? Who, I ask?"

"Why, *you* did! You said—"

"I said no such thing! This mechanism draws power from the Universal ether!"

Rumfort pounced on that statement as though it were the entire keystone of his argument. "Ahh-HAH! It has already been shown that the Universal ether does not exist! And if it did, you wouldn't be able to draw enough energy from it!

"It requires infinite energy! Infinite! That means that if you left some other continuum, you used every bit of energy in it! All the energy and all the matter in that universe would have to be used instantaneously as energy for your machine! If you had done as you said, the universe you left would be nonexistent now! And that's impossible! You, sir, are a confounded liar!"

Latimer turned to Rumfort. "For heaven's sake, Rumfort! The poor guy's a little off his rocker! That's no reason to tease the unfortunate chap."

Featherby's face grew purple. "You! You—*argh! Liar! Off my rocker!* If only my dueller were here! Well, by gad, I haven't got to stay about and listen to your foul insults!"

He reached up and pressed a button on the control panel on his chest.

Neither Latimer nor Rumfort felt anything, of course. One can't feel anything when one is instantaneously converted into energy along with the rest of one's universe.

At the bar of the Green Lizard Lounge, Dr. Rumfort was saying: "In my forthcoming monograph to the *Journal,* I show that it is mathematically possible to describe a six-dimensional continuum in which an infinite number of points could exist, each of these points being, in reality, three-dimensional."

Latimer nodded, sipping his Beer. He had been watching the door, hoping somebody interesting would come in. Anybody would be better than old Rumfort.

Nobody had come in yet, but he thought they might. After all, in an infinite number of universes, there might be somebody who...

Randall Garrett, a mainstay of the science-fiction field for the last thirty years or so, is best known from his Lord Darcy series, about an alternate Earth in which magic rather than science is the basis of civilization. There is one Darcy novel, Too Many Magicians, *and one collection,* Lord Darcy Investigates. *A collection of Garrett's humorous pieces,* Takeoff!, *has been published by Donning, and* The Best of Randall Garrett *has appeared from Pocket Books. He has recently collaborated on a series of SF adventure novels with Vicki Ann Heydron.*

WHAT'S WRONG WITH THIS PICTURE?

By Barry B. Longyear, John M. Ford, and George H. Scithers

"...stories within stories, frames within frames..."

He was rolled into the hearing room, a drip bottle attached to the back of his wheelchair. The nurse following the attendant pushing the wheelchair carried a portable cardiac unit. The trace on the screen was jagged and irregular, and hanging ominously at its side by insulated coils were the white handles of two large electrodes. As the attendant stopped the chair before the long, polished mahogany table, the seven board members filed into the room from a door behind the table. Each one glanced at the man in the wheelchair, then shook his head before taking his chair at the table. The man in the wheelchair stared with vacant eyes at the wall above and behind the board members. His tongue hung from the left corner of his mouth, and the attendant would lean forward every few moments to wipe the drool from the man's chin. A doctor entered the room, studied the cardiac readings, frowned, then turned and *walked to the man seated in the center of the seven at the table. The one seated sadly nodded his head, and the doctor returned to the man in the wheelchair. He removed a case from his pocket, took a syringe from it, and inserted the needle into an entry port connected to the drip bottle line. After another moment, the doctor stood and nodded at the man seated at the table, then he walked around the chair and stood next to the nurse.*

The man in the wheelchair jerked, then retracted his tongue. His eyes became less vacant, his glance darting about the room until it finally came to rest on the men seated behind the table. He jerked again. The man seated in the center smiled at him and nodded.

This is . . . it. This is it. The hearing, isn't it? Yes, I can see that. I'm not crazy, you know. Very dreadfully nervous, but why do you call me crazy?—a little upset—not crazy. Not at all. I'm still John . . . John . . . Well, you know me! Yes, of course you do. Best one you ever had. Best damned one . . .

You want to know what happened? . . . It's getting clearer. The wig-picker and I, we've been working on it. Working on it a lot! At least we have when this quack here doesn't have me junked up to my eyeballs. A shrink can't work with a piece of meat; I have to be awake. . . . What happened? Give it a moment. It's coming back. Aaaahh! No! This jerk business is just nerves. Anybody would have a case of nerves after what I've been through. Anybody . . .

Well, I remember waking up in that alley. All that garbage, the cans, the cartons. It was dark. Night. Yes, it was night, and I woke up in that alley. My head was fuzzy, but my mind was . . . blank. How I got to the alley, who I was . . . all of it was gone! That would upset anyone, wouldn't it? No, don't give me any more of that knockout juice. I'm all right.

All right. I was in the alley waking up. My mouth tasted funny. Maybe drugs or something else. Someone had dumped me in that alley, and that same someone must have slipped something into me, I guess.

I stood up and weaved about, trying to get my bearings, in the fog and the maze of rickety wooden buildings. My chest felt like the drummer for Steppenwolf had used it to practice on. More turns, more twists, more fog. I didn't know where I was; this place looked like a waterfront, but I couldn't smell the sea, just a scent like something burning. San Francisco maybe. Where little cable cars climb halfway to the stars, above the blue and windy sea. Or maybe somewhere in Maine. It was tough to say.

And I didn't know who I was. My head felt like Enrico Fermi was running a reactor test inside it. I was wearing a brown trench coat. I shoved my hands in my coat pockets, searching for ID of some kind. In the left pocket was a pack of cigarettes, Gauloises, the French ones that smell like grass, and a bit of Normandie butter in foil. I wished I hadn't put my hands in so hard, and licked my thumb. The butter was salted. I was no gourmet, either.

In the right pocket was a gun. I took it out and turned it over in my hand. It was a .25-caliber Colt automatic, nickel-plated. A short, lethal-looking weapon that packs enough punch to mildly annoy anything smaller than a house cat, and is carried mostly by people who'd only hurt themselves with real guns.

In my pants pocket was a portrait gallery of my favorite presidents, signed by great folks like Douglas Dillon and James A. Baker III. No credit cards or traveler's checks, though. Karl Malden would have hated me. But at least I had money, cigarettes with butter all over them, and a gun that would make a great cigarette lighter. And I could butter any toast I ran across.

Time to get things moving again.

The street at the far end of the next alley was brightly lit, and I stumbled in that direction. When

I reached the end of the alley, a roar deafened my ears, leaving me with a headache that could split granite. I sagged against a wall and watched as a ball of fire with a long tail moved up into the night sky until it was out of sight. I looked down and saw white and blue lights dotting the surface of a landing field of some kind. Too small for a jetport, though: those 747s have to roll forever to make it into the air.

I pushed away from the wall and looked up and down the street. There was no one in sight except an old man. He was dressed in rags and a hood, and carrying a brown paper package. He stopped in front of me. "Have you seen Leibowitz? I have something for him."

Damned winos. They're everywhere. "Beat it. I don't know any Leibowitz."

The old man nodded. "Bless you, my son. Kyrie Ellison." He wandered off. I looked at the buildings lining the street, dark windows and doorways—eyes and mouths of crumbling monsters from another age. Another roar and I clasped my palms over my ears and looked toward the white and blue lights. Another tailed ball of fire climbed into the night above. As I lowered my hands, I saw a bit of neon lighting adding some color to the otherwise drab scene, cutting through the fog like a flying saucer telling me it wanted to give back some missing pilots. The sign said:

D I S   M A L

P O R T B A R

on and off, on and off. When I got closer I saw that it really said **ALDISS MALT**, but a lot of the letters were broken. Some kind of British Beer, I figured.

But below it was another broken word. What it said was **SPACEPORT BAR**. What kind of joke was that? The only spaceport around was Cape Kennedy, and the closest thing to a bar there is the

Greyhound bus stop restaurant that serves micro-waved sandwiches.

My head ached so, I decided to stop trying to figure out the first word and concentrated on the second. Bar. If my head was telling me anything, it was that I needed a drink. I pushed open the door and found myself in a darkened vestibule staring in horror at a tall, hairy thing with lots of teeth. Another customer pushed in behind me and waved at the hairy thing. "Lookie, Wookie."

The hairy thing waved back. "How's the weather, Hal?" it asked.

The man shrugged. "Clement." Then I followed the man past the hairy thing through another door. While my ears were being assaulted by bad punk jazz, what spread before me was...well, I don't know what it was. The customer called Hal took a CO_2 extinguisher from the wall, aimed at the globby-looking thing, and gave it a short blast. The glob contracted, clearing enough space to walk by. I looked down at the mass of quivering jelly.

It shrugged and held up two tendrils. "Hey, man; I'm sorry. I just been out of work a long time. Can you spare me a couple of credits?"

I reached into my pockets, found a few bills, and pulled out a fiver—U.S. currency—and held it out.

A tendril whipped out, absorbed the bill, then nodded a glob to my left. "Thanks, buddy. I'll get this back to you as soon as I can get work." It flowed through the door; and I heard the hairy thing call after it, "Good night, and stay away from ice-skating rinks."

Beyond an orange, pinch-faced combo that was thumping out horrible music, someone in a red jersey shot to his feet and shouted something at a tableful of uniformed things with heavy eyebrows and pointy ears.

Inside, I hung up my trench coat, pushed my way through the customers milling around the entrance, and made my way to the bar. If fists started swinging, I didn't want to be within knuckle distance. I leaned an elbow against the bar and waited for the bartender. Between the noise, the smoke, and my headache, my stomach started doing the flapjack bit. At the far end of the bar, a robot was opening Beer cans, flipping each one pull-tab-end down, then deftly puncturing the tabless end. I shook my head; motion caught my eye; I found myself staring at the mirror behind the bar. I saw—I even waved my hand to make sure I was me. My face was bruised, but it was the jacket I was wearing—a loud, loud thing of black and white and red plaid. And a necktie. While I was struggling with this image, a fat man in a bloused coat came up behind me. I turned and met his eye.

He smiled ingratiatingly. "Sir, could I interest you in one of nature's most cuddly, loving creatures—"

"Scram, fatty. I got troubles of my own!"

The fat man shrugged. "Well, if you've already got one I don't suppose you need another." He faded into the haze. I closed my eyes and tried to block out the sounds of the place. The fat man had triggered —almost—a memory. I opened my eyes again to look at the mirror, but between it and me was a huge cat. It twitched its whiskers.

"Order, sir?"

"Borehole Number Three," I said, without thinking, and suddenly I was back under the old Olympica dome again, hearing the thin Martian wind blow red sand against the walls—sand that it had picked up as it swept across the Dead Sea Bottoms. And Marsdust: there was half an inch of it on the dome floor, you couldn't keep it out. And I was drinking Borehole Number Three from a quartz cup, drinking to forget Calkins and Nowlan. They'd been my drill partners, until Calkins had made one little mistake. All he'd done was to forget that gravity makes things fall *down*, but Mars doesn't forgive mistakes like that.

And now I, Erik Juan Massif, mercenary of a hundred worlds, was stuck—

On Mars?

The room jiggled like the background of a God-zilla movie. I'd ordered Martian miner's booze from the bartender, and if I couldn't think of a good explanation, I'd be sharing a padded hotel room with Napoleon and the Emperor Caligula.

Come to think of it, I wanted an explanation myself. I looked at the barkeep, but he wasn't looking at me. He was holding a ceramic bottle in tongs, pouring into a quartz cup. The bottle had a big 3 on it.

"Two Deimos in gold, sir."

I fumbled. So go ahead, tell me you wouldn't have. I got out my wad of bills, finally, and pulled off a few dollars.

The cat sorted through the bills, then licked its whiskers. "I keep telling you people: *no dollars*. The banks and I have an agreement: they don't serve drinks and I don't exchange currency. . . ."

Something flitted by and landed on the bar. The cat shook its head, took the bills, and gave me some change. The thing that landed on the bar looked at me with huge, yellow eyes. It raised its left eyebrow and said, "Bad taste." I looked closely at the creature; it was an owl. I swear it was. No, I didn't even know that owls have eyebrows. Do they? They must.

Anyway, it took off, flew across the room, and came to roost on the antlers of the mounted head of a big white deer that hung over a fireplace half-filled with broken glass. I shook my head slowly, turned back to the barkeep, whose eyes got big behind the safety goggles he'd been wearing to pour my drink.

"Oh, I'm sorry, sir. I didn't know you in those clothes." The cat leaned close. "He's in the booth over there, waiting."

I could have said "Who?" but what difference would it have made? I picked up the drink and went to the booth.

"Come in, Captain," the booth said, in a voice like oiled gravel. Captain? Why not. I went in.

Inside was a man you could have made two ordinary-sized guys out of, with a head that put me in mind of a tank turret. He evidently got his jewelry cheaper by the pound, and his coat had cost the lives of half the world's silver fox population.

On second thought, maybe he wasn't as rich as he looked. There was a girl sitting next to him, and he hadn't been able to buy her much to wear at all.

"Wolf, I'm sorry about—you know," she said, in a voice like honey and old Bourbon.

And she was looking straight at me as she said it.

"Quiet, Magda," the tank said. "Captain Lupus and I have business to discuss. Why don't you go buy yourself a drink? Hexer will keep you company."

She snorted at him and left. She had a way of leaving that inspired hot pursuit.

"Do you recognize me, Captain Lupus?"

I didn't, but then I didn't recognize myself either. "Should I?"

"No, of course not. I hide behind my wealth, much as you—heh, heh—hide behind a cutlass and a fast ship. I am Constantin L'Avectoi."

And I remembered:

Half my pirate squadron thundered down into atmosphere, half—my half—stayed in orbit to hold the Patrol at bay.

We lost ships, and men—good rogues, too: like Arcot, who once drank half the population of a water world, and Morey, who did an incredible trick with two girls, a zero-gee waterbed, and a quantum black hole, and Wade, who I knew ran a private trade in parsecs and gegenschein—but I never cared.

Kenneth "Wolf" Lupus, bold and free, master of space pi-ra-cee; that was my song—it wasn't very good, but it's in the Geneva accords you have to have a song.

There was a flash of light and a sizzling sound, and Constantin L'Avectoi slumped forward. Or he tried; he was too big to slump properly.

I moved quicker than the price counter on a gas pump, but there was no one there but an old man in brown robes showing a kid how to use a flashlight. I went to the next booth.

There were four creatures seated at the table: one looked like a huge sack with an enormous slit across its entire body. The slit opened for a moment, exposing a great, single eye. Next to that was a human: a stout fellow with closely cropped hair and beard sprinkled with grey. Next to him was another human: slender, clad in black, with a droopy blond moustache that made him look like Fu Manchu with a bad peroxide job. And beside *him* was a lively, red-haired woman with a vaguely Egyptian hairdo.

There was an empty chair at the table. I sat down in it. The eye sack staggered to its feet, tossed a few credit coins onto the table, then said, "Ah's am off."

The two men nodded as the eye sack faded into the blue haze. The one with the droopy moustache saw my confused look, then pointed into the smoke. "He talks lak dat 'cause he frum de Southern Cross."

The one with the beard looked over his shoulder at the owl on the white deer's head over the fireplace. He turned back, looking troubled, then said to the man with the droopy moustache, "I don't think he's noticed us."

I frowned. "Do you mean the owl?"

All three put their forefingers to their lips and went "*Sshhh!*"

The owl suddenly flapped its wings and swooped down from the antlers to land on the table in our midst. The owl extended its talons and put a small yellow object on the table, then flew back toward the fireplace.

I pointed at the yellow object. "What is it?"

Droopy moustache frowned. "It's a jellybean."

I reached for it, but the red-haired woman slapped my hand. "Don't! Don't ever take one of those things! If you do, you'll never get rid of it! Never!!"

I sat back in astonishment. Then memory danced by: one of the many disguises of...of...I couldn't *remember!* Droopy moustache eyed the jellybean, then looked to Egyptian hairdo for guidance. "What'll we do with it?"

The bearded man pursed his lips, then blew on the jellybean, making it roll off the edge of the table. I heard a *crunch, munch, wrrrp* sound and looked for the source. On the floor, a short, round-headed creature wearing a slick shiny uniform was licking its lips. I pointed at it, asked, "What's *that?*"

The bearded man shrugged. "An omnivore. It'll eat anything."

Drooping moustache flagged a waiter and ordered a Railroad Martini. The beard ordered a Schlitz Beer. I was still working on my Borehole Number Three, and the redhead shook her head. After a few moments, the waiter—a green, muscular humanoid—placed a glass in front of droopy moustache. Several dark pieces of wood floated in the clear drink.

The blond fellow picked out the pieces of wood and flicked them into the omnivore.

"Why did you do that?" I frowned.

He sipped the drink. "It's a *tie* composition. But you can't let them get—ah—some too saturate. Cool." He took another sip, as if that explained everything.

The waiter put a plate of dark, curly hair in front of the other man at our table. The stout man called the waiter back, saying, "You've gotten my order wrong. I want Schlitz Beer. This is Schmidt's beard."

The waiter apologized and removed the offending pelt. My mind—I felt I was closed in on *something* ...but then the old man in brown took a swipe at a black-warted creature with a glowing sword he'd gotten from somewhere or other, and the creature's severed limb landed on our table.

Drooping moustache grabbed the thing and tossed it back, yelling, "Hey, Darkness; you'll need this." The warted creature caught it. Moustache explained, "It's his left hand."

The waiter brought the Schlitz. The bearded man touched his glass to the thin man's Railroad Martini. They both said, "Dune the hatch," and finished off their drinks.

The brawl between the guys in the red shirts and the pointy-eared Mongols was getting louder—and closer. They kept yelling about the USS *Enterprise*, but they didn't look Navy to me. *Enterprise?* Maybe I was in San Fran after all. I nodded to the two men, blew a small kiss to the red-haired woman, and ducked into the next booth. If only I could *remember*...

Inside was a thin little man in a black cloak and beret. He had eyes like loaded dice, hands that looked like they'd only be at home in somebody else's pockets. With him was the girl, Magda. Her outfit was all leather, now; but they wouldn't have had to hurt the cow very bad to get that much hide off it.

"Lance, it's not what it seems like," she said, in a voice like maple syrup and cinnamon. "It's all part of the plot—"

"Hush, Lauralyn," said the sneak. "Buy yourself a drink or something."

"All right, Hexer," Mag—uh, Lauralyn said, and went. If I was lucky she'd keep going out all day long.

"How do you feel, Admiral?" Hexer said. "Is the drug wearing off? Are there many traces of the pirate illusion left?"

I didn't lose my cool. All I said was, "Huh?"

"Yes, Admiral Kildare. L'Avectoi wanted to use your incomparable piloting skills. But to do that he had to erase your true personality and overlay that of a pirate and mercenary scoundrel. He knew that Grand Admiral Lance Kildare of the Galactic Navy would never serve him free-willed."

And I remembered:

Standing on the bridge of my flagship, the *Frank R. Paul's Revenge,* in command of the vastest armada of maneuverable metal the cosmos had ever known. Across the purple void we thundered, a hundred thousand strong, dodging meteors as thick as soup and watching the starry expanse pass at half of lightspeed.

"Admiral," my First Mate was saying in his Irish tenor laced with Scotch, "it's Professor Robert, sir. He has some complaints."

A smile creased my face. "What is it this time?"

"Several things, sir. He says that there isn't any air in space so the Fleet shouldn't thunder and the void shouldn't be purple. And that meteors don't travel around and rain on ships. And that the stars outside ought to be violet-shifted in front and red-shifted in back."

"Tell Dr. Robert not to be so forward," I chuckled. Robert was a good enough man when it came to building a primary matter deinertializer or a subspace probability inverter, but his "pure" theories were wild and impractical. The Fleet not thunder *indeed!*

"Now," I said to Hexer, fixing him with an unblinking gaze, "what about this plot?"

Hexer wavered, as though a different collaborator had seized the pen. "Yeah, it is pretty thick, isn't it?" Then he snapped back. "I can't tell you that," the weasel weaseled. "I'd be killed before I got two words out!"

"Tell me," I repeated, in a voice like Helium II.

"Well, it's—"

One of the pointy-eared Mongols crashed through the side of the booth and flattened Hexer to the floor. I left my spilled drink happily eating a hole in the table and got out before one of the red shirts could come in and get pointy-ears airborne again.

After dodging another flying body and stepping over a couple more on the floor—the omnivore was getting behind in its work—I reached the bar again. Lauralyn was there, snuggled up next to a big guy in a grey jumpsuit with the biggest digital wristwatch I ever did see. I was beginning to wonder if that girl had some kind of skin allergy to clothing; everything she had on now was made of brass, and there wasn't enough of it to make a good lamp.

Near the bar a character with twice the usual quota of fingers was pounding on something that looked like a saxophone, three pianos, and a bassoon.

> It's still the same old story,
> The plot resolved in glory,
> The editors still buy;
> And much the same word rates apply,
> As time warps by.

There was a sign above the saxpinoon.

REQUESTS .... Cr 5
"RODGER YOUNG" .... Cr 10
SILENCE .... Cr 25

I found a space between the big guy and a chap in baggy tweeds, and told the robot Beer-can-opener tending bar to open one for me. Memory was coming back, but just a bit here, a flicker over there....I sipped Beer and tried to remember. That just made my headache worse, so I turned and mumbled something to baggy tweeds about the fog outside.

"That reminds me of a story," he said. "So heavy was the gloom one afternoon in the Billiards Club that I wondered why the waiters did not turn on the lights. The darkness clung to cornices and seemed to beat down from the ceiling, and it was only low near the floor that we had any light at all.

"Luckily it is this very kind of day that so often

encourages Jorkens to tell us of some adventure, and after I had ordered him a large Whiskey, this is what he told us:

"'Perhaps you would like a tale that is not entirely shrouded in darkness, and what comes to mind at this moment is what happened to me once in America, when I was visiting a well-recommended public house called Gavagan's, and a young chap was demonstrating a photographic device.

"'Mr. Jeffers aimed his camera at the stuffed owl over the bar,' Jorkens continued. 'There was a bright, noiseless flash, which caused the owl's eyes to light up yellowly for an instant. The shutter clicked, and there was a faint whirr as the film automatically wound to the next frame. "No double exposure," said Jeffers.

"'Mr. Gross looked up from his Boilermaker. "I got a cousin by marriage that got run in for that once," he said.

"'"What, making pictures of stuffed owls?" asked Mr. Keating from the library.

"'"No, taking his clothes off in the theater. He done it twicet, and the second time—"

"'Mr. Witherwax interrupted firmly, turning to another Englishman who was visiting Gavagan's that day and asking, "Weren't you about to tell us a story?"

"'"Why, yes," said the Englishman. "Have you ever noticed that, when there are twenty or thirty people talking together in a room, there are occasional moments when everyone becomes suddenly silent, so that for a second there's a sudden, vibrating emptiness that seems to swallow up all sound? It's almost as if everyone is listening for something —they don't know what.

"'"It was like that one evening when the White Hart wasn't quite as crowded as usual. The Silence came, as unexpectedly as it always does, and Harry Purvis's voice came clear across the room:

"'"'The stories that get told in bars,' Harry

Purvis said, looking thoughtfully at his Beer, 'have a great deal more truth to them than one would think. There was one in particular that I remember, from—I'd better not say just where. Anyway:

""""The spacer slammed his drink on the bar,' Harry said, 'and looked the robot bartender right in the electronic eye. "I've been from one side of this universe to the other and if I haven't learned anything else, I've learned that you can't believe everything you hear."

""""The robot swallowed the empty glass, produced a full one. He sighed deep in his gearworks, afraid that this was going to be another burned-out spacer with a tale to tell. It was.

"""""Callahan's Place was pretty lively that night," the spacer said. "Talk fought Budweiser for mouth space all over the joint, and the Beer-nuts supply was getting critical. But this guy managed to keep himself in a corner without being noticed for nearly an hour. I only spotted him myself a few minutes before someone got him started on his story, and I make a point of studying *every*body whenever I'm at Callahan's Place.

"""""This guy," the spacer went on, "owned a place himself, name of Draco Tavern, and he was talking about his place:

""""""We get astronauts in the Draco Tavern,' the guy said. 'We get workers from Mount Forel Spaceport, and some administrators, and some newsmen. We get chirpsithtra; I keep special chairs to fit their tall, spindly frames. Once in a while we get other aliens. But we don't get many Englishmen.

""""""This one,' the guy explained, 'baggy tweeds and all, had a story. Business was slow in the Draco Tavern, just then, so I sat with him and listened.

"""""""Summer had gone," the Englishman said, "and the brighter part of the autumn, and it was dark again in the Billiards Club by the time lunch was over, as though the fog had come down our little street before anyone had noticed he was about,' and had peered in at our window. But not as an autumn fog it seemed, but a spring fog.

""""""""Whanne that Aprille with his shoures soote—

[It was the flying Chaucer that broke the spell.]

""""""""""STOP!" I shouted. *I remembered!* Inside breast pocket: leather case, sharp edges; my badge. And inside...Jorkens and baggy tweeds looked at me in shocked silence. Then Jorkens—*Jorkens?* I whipped out the case, flashed the badge, flipped it open to show my Author's Guild card. The dinky-toy pistol was in my other hand. "You almost trapped me in this diabolical nest of stories within stories, frames within frames, but now ——"""""""""

—— and like farmhouses after a Kansas Twister, the close quotes came raining down, breaking the spell. The Billiards Club flickered out; so did the Draco Tavern, Callahan's Place, the White Hart, Gavagan's. The Billiards Club flared and went out again, then the Spaceport Bar, the Silver Eel, Slab's Tavern, the Aquilonian Arms...

The *Aquilonian Arms?*

I looked around wildly. The fight over in the corner was still in full swing, but now the red shirts were wearing helmets with horns and chain-mail vests, and the big guy in grey had stripped down to fur shorts and a sword and enough muscles to stock a meat market —— everything flickered again, only *backward* one flick —— heads appeared, dissolved —— backward again we went —— and the big guy was *two* guys: one a big, blond barbarian and the other a quick little guy who flicked the badge right out of my hand. I clicked off the safety and fired; the gun spat flame. One inch long, barely enough to light a cigar. It *was* a lighter. And then I was falling —— falling into a black hole, with the green, log-log grid lines spiraling up and down the sides, up and down and down and ————

* * *

The man seated in the center of the panel of seven nodded at the doctor, and the fellow in the wheelchair was rolled from the room. The door closed, leaving the room silent. The man in the center sadly nodded his head. "He was one of our best."

"Too bad," said another, wiping away a tear.

The man in the center pressed a button set into the surface of the long table. A door opened and in walked a tall, rugged man smoking a pipe and wearing a jacket, elbows covered with shooting patches. The man in the center looked at the one in shooting patches. "You heard everything?"

The man removed the pipe from his mouth and nodded. "I heard. Pitiful."

"How do you explain the gun?"

"Illustrator's fault. The lighter was the only model he had to draw from."

The man in the center shook his head, then looked up at the one with the pipe. "It looks impossible, but do you think you can do it? Can you close down the Spaceport Bar?"

The man in tweed stood erect, slightly offended. "Have I ever failed the Author's Guild Literary Cliché Squad?"

"No." The man in the center shook his head. "You've never failed us. But . . . you saw what happened to—"

"Yes, yes." The man in tweed waved a hand impatiently. "He made a mistake. They got to him first with one of their plots. That won't happen to me."

The man in the center nodded. "Will you want one of the first-run copies of this deposition?"

The man in tweed replaced the pipe in his mouth. "No. I'll wait for it to come out in paperback." He turned and left the room.

One of the board members muttered, "As soon as he does his job, then he gets the blue pencil. Wait for it to come out in paperback, indeed!"

The hearing was adjourned.

This spaceport bar tale began with Barry Long-year, who submitted it to your editors. The first version, we thought, depended on too few targets—Mr. Longyear, at the time, was new to science fiction; we sent it on to John Ford, who has somewhat more familiarity with older SF literature and who has an entirely different sense of humor (except, of course, that both have a deplorable weakness for really horrid puns). Ford rewrote Longyear's version; then Longyear rewrote Ford's. After a few rounds, we realized that this story was not (as the mathematicians put it) converging to a solution, so one of your editors—George Scithers—took the two most recent versions, patched them together, added a horrid pun or two of his own, and then purchased the result for Isaac Asimov's Science Fiction Magazine.

The framing device is pure Longyear; the trench coat, the cable cars, and the Normandie butter are all Ford's. From there, it's hard to say. Ford, Scithers, and Longyear appear in the story, as does Shawna McCarthy, who was then managing editor of Asimov's. The only part that Scithers remembers as being entirely his is the sequence of stories within stories, frames within frames, from baggy tweeds to the collapse of the close quotes. Finally, Chris Miller, our editor at Avon Books, should share some of the blame for the story's appearance here: she is the one who insisted that we include it.

Barry Longyear has remarked, "I have never been asked to autograph a copy of this story. I still don't understand it—the story, I mean; not why I haven't been asked to autograph a copy." He also still rankles "at the removal of the anal log," a comment which we refuse to expand upon.

Barry Longyear began his amazingly successful career in 1978; by 1980 he had won the Hugo, the Nebula, and the John W. Campbell awards. His story, "Enemy Mine," became the movie of the same name. At last report, Longyear was at work on some additional events in his Circus World series and on a parody of The Red Badge of Courage.

Before he started writing novels, John M. Ford was the most prolific contributor to Isaac Asimov's Science Fiction Magazine, *including one of the longest puns on record: "...how was the content of our winter's disc made a spurious summary by this scum of cork?" In 1984, he won the World Fantasy Award for his novel,* The Dragon Waiting.

George H. Scithers was the founding editor of Isaac Asimov's Science Fiction Magazine *and was the thirteenth or fifteenth (depending on who's counting) editor of* Amazing Stories. *He has won four Science Fiction Achievement Awards—Hugo Awards—for editing. He is now a literary agent, specializing in SF and fantasy.*

GEORGE ALEC EFFINGER

THE NICK OF TIME

On February 17th, 1996, Frank Mihalik became the first person to time-travel.

Intelligent, unflappable, a good friend and credit risk, virile but moral, he behaved just like a hero should.

Which was just as well, as it turned out there were still some bugs in the system. Like getting stuck in a time loop for a start. Like encountering a multitude of parallel universes where Shirley Temple, not Judy Garland, starred in *The Wizard of Oz* – or Deanna Durbin or Gertrude Stein's daughter . . .

Then there's the time when he is turned into a large green lizard with a pink tongue and a developing taste for flies. The realisation that when his girlfriend Cheryl time-travels to his rescue, she's actually a parallel Cheryl and he's nearly been unfaithful to the real Cheryl.

Such things could have upset – indeed seriously deranged – anyone less heroic, resourceful, dependable, etc. than Frank Mihalik.

Post·A·Book

A Royal Mail service in association with the Book Marketing Council & The Booksellers Association.

Post-A-Book is a Post Office trademark.

GEORGE ALEC EFFINGER

THE BIRD OF TIME

Hartstein's journey to the past was a present. A graduation gift from fond grandparents before he embarked on his chosen career in the doughnut industry.

Of course things had moved on a lot since that famous day back in 1996 when the first time-traveller, the heroic Frank Mihalik, had made his pioneering, not altogether bug-free backwards flip. Now time-tourism was pretty much routine, if pricey.

Still there were one or two things the Agency kept quiet about. Such as that 2% of their customers didn't make it back. Such as that the 'past' was acutally a patchy, not to say tacky, collection of the person-in-the-street's *idea* of the past.

In particular they never said there was a war going on.

A time war between the Agency and the Temporary Underground. A war of time shifts and ambush, of future assaults on the past and sudden destabilising mathematical coups. A war when you could get killed at any point on the space/time continuum.

Hartstein was setting out on a bigger adventure than he'd dreamed or – or paid for.

HODDER AND STOUGHTON PAPERBACKS

MORE FANTASY FROM
HODDER AND STOUGHTON PAPERBACKS

GEORGE ALEC EFFINGER

| ☐ | 41736 0 | The Nick of Time | £2.50 |
| ☐ | 42402 2 | The Bird of Time | £2.50 |

MICHAEL WEAVER

| ☐ | 42206 2 | Mercedes Nights | £2.95 |

A. E. van VOGT

| ☐ | 05904 9 | Computerworld | £2.25 |
| ☐ | 42270 4 | The Weapon Shops of Isher and The Weapon Makers | £2.50 |

DIANA L. PAXTON

| ☐ | 43054 5 | White Mare, Red Stallion | £2.95 |

All these books are available at your local bookshop or newsagent, or can be ordered direct from the publisher. Just tick the titles you want and fill in the form below.

Prices and availability subject to change without notice.

Hodder & Stoughton Paperbacks, P.O. Box 11, Falmouth, Cornwall.

Please send cheque or postal order, and allow the following for postage and packing:

U.K. – 55p for one book, plus 22p for the second book, and 14p for each additional book ordered up to a £1.75 maximum.

B.F.P.O. and EIRE – 55p for the first book, plus 22p for the second book, and 14p per copy for the next 7 books, 8p per book thereafter.

OTHER OVERSEAS CUSTOMERS – £1.00 for the first book, plus 25p per copy for each additional book.

NAME..

ADDRESS ....

....